DYING FALL

Sophie Rivers has a job she enjoys, a satisfying life and a close circle of friends. Then things go suddenly wrong; one of her students is murdered on college premises, and her best friend George meets a tragic end which everyone believes to be an accident—everyone, that is, except Sophie. Determined to find his killer, she starts asking questions, which result in someone trying to murder her. The police want her to leave the investigating to them—but she owes it to George's memory to continue. Right to the bitter end...

Please note: *This book contains a small amount of bad language, which may not be suitable to all our readers.*

DYING FALL

DYING FALL

by
Judith Cutler

Magna Large Print Books
Long Preston, North Yorkshire,
England.

British Library Cataloguing in Publication Data.

Cutler, Judith
  Dying fall.

  A catalogue record for this book is
  available from the British Library

  ISBN 0-7505-1213-X

First published in Great Britain by Judy Piatkus (Publishers)
Ltd., 1995

Copyright © 1995 by Judith Cutler

Cover photography © Last Resort Photography Library

The moral right of the author has been asserted

Published in Large Print 1998 by arrangement with Piatkus
Books Ltd.

Magna Large Print is an imprint of
Library Magna Books Ltd.
Printed and bound in Great Britain by
T.J. International Ltd., Cornwall, PL28 8RW.

Acknowledgements

I would like to thank for their help and inspiration: the students and staff of Matthew Boulton College, Birmingham, especially the A Level and Computing sections; the musicians of the City of Birmingham Symphony Orchestra; the staff of Symphony Hall, Birmingham; West Midlands Police, especially the men and women of Rose Road Police Station, Harborne. Any mistakes are mine, not theirs.

The events of this novel are fiction: if there is a passing resemblance between some of the locations in it and similar ones in Birmingham, that is purely in the interests of verisimilitude.

To my family and friends—
none of whom is pictured within

'If music be the food of love, play on;
And give me excess of it, that, surfeiting,
The appetite may sicken, and so die.
That strain again! it had a dying fall...
...Enough! No more:
'Tis not so sweet now as it was before...'

From Shakespeare's *Twelfth Night,*
Act One, Scene i.

Chapter One

Seven-thirty on a Tuesday night. The wind's slashing rain across the ill-fitting windows and rocking the whole tower block.

I have a rotten day at college. I stay late for my evening class and to finish a tedious batch of marking. And I get into a lift to escape and find I'm sharing it with a body.

I didn't notice, of course, till I'd pressed the pad for down and was plunging fifteen floors.

The boy—he looked eighteen, maybe a young nineteen—was slumped in the corner furthest from the control panel, leaning against the lift wall. His face was half turned from me. His left hand rested loosely on a ring file marked WAJID AKHTAR: INORGANIC.

I thought he'd passed out: I'd better help.

I tipped him forward—to put his head between his knees. Then I saw five inches of polished wood sticking out from the back of his leather jacket.

Round the knife there was no blood to speak of.

But an ugly splattering told me there

was blood elsewhere. It poured from his nose and mouth, flooding across the worn lino floor, lapping towards my shoes.

At last the lift doors opened. But when I opened my mouth to call for help, no sound emerged. Fortunately Winston, one of the college porters, happened to look up from his desk and see me. I pointed, trying to hold the doors open so that the lift wouldn't carry us relentlessly up and down the building.

Winston reached behind his desk.

'It's OK, Sophie,' he said, 'I've immobilised the lift. What's the trouble? Jesus!' he said, as he looked.

I forced myself to touch Wajid's neck. He was still warm but there was no pulse. Winston was stripping off his jacket, as if to wrap the boy in it.

'No,' I said. 'There's no point. Just call the police, Winston. I'll stay here with him.'

At last the police came. Just a couple of kids in a panda at first: I'd taught them both, as it happens, but they were too busy trying to be professionally insouciant to notice me. Then more cars, with men and women in plain clothes.

A middle-aged man singled me out. Detective Sergeant Dale, his ID said. But he introduced himself as Ian, and

14

mentioned other officers by their first names. The team was working like a machine, cordoning off the area and taking pictures of what lay within it. He left them to it, ushering me gently outside.

The night air smelt very good.

'Look,' I said, 'I can't just walk away. Someone's got to tell his parents. And I ought to tell my boss. And Winston's only a kid. You can't leave him in there.'

'No one's going to leave him in there. But if you could tell us who's in charge it'd help.'

I shrugged helplessly. Who'd want that sort of responsibility?

'Maybe you ought to contact the Principal,' I said eventually. 'But God knows how you'll find him. He's bound to be ex-directory.'

'If you can give us his name—'

'James Worral,' I said. 'And I think he lives somewhere in Four Oaks. But what about Wajid? Who'll tell his parents?'

'Our people are trained to do that,' he said. 'I'll just get one of my colleagues to take care of the Principal, and then we'll take you off to make a statement.'

When he got back I was being sick in the gutter. He didn't say anything—just passed me a packet of extra strong mints after I'd finished.

'D'you want one of my colleagues to

take your car back to the station?' he asked, opening his passenger door for me.

I shook my head.

'No car? That's unusual these days.'

'Used to have. They worked their way through two sets of hubcaps, then started on the wheels. Came out at nine one night to find the poor thing sitting on four neat piles of bricks. So I cycle or catch the bus, depending on the weather. And today,' I added, raising my voice against the wind, 'it was the bus.'

The college is on Birmingham's inner ring road, five minutes away from Ladywood police station. But Dale turned the car through Edgbaston and followed my daily route towards Harborne.

'I thought you said something about a statement?'

'That's right. At Rose Road nick. We've got all the facilities there. You can have a bit of a wash and brush-up, and maybe a cup of tea, and then we'll sort out your statement.'

I sat back and let myself be taken. Suddenly I couldn't stop shaking, and every time I let myself think about Wajid I wanted to vomit again.

The room they showed me into was functional but clean and not unpleasant. Ian Dale organised some coffee for me, and spooned extra sugar into it. He might have been a favourite uncle, in his worn sports jacket with archetypal leather patches. Then another man appeared, younger and altogether brisker.

'DCI Chris Groom,' he said, shaking hands with me. 'And you must be Sophie Rivers.'

Nothing seemed to be as I'd expected it. The relaxed atmosphere, for example, informal but courteous; all these first names, not an old-fashioned 'Miss' in earshot. Perhaps I'd been reading too much pulp detective fiction. At least they left some mistakes on my statement for me to correct; I certainly wasn't going to put my name to a document which accused a lift of being stationery. But they'd got everything else right: I'd been working on my own in a big, communal office. I'd heard nothing unusual—there'd been the noise of the lifts at the far end of the corridor, but that had mostly been drowned by the wind and the rain. Colleagues had popped in briefly to collect their belongings at the end of their classes or to make coffee. No one had reported seeing anything unusual. They'd all looked tired and strained, as you'd expect halfway through the winter term when flu was decimating the staff and we were all having to take on extra work. No one looked as if they'd just committed a murder. 'Most of us would like to from time to time,' I said, looking up. Everyone grinned politely.

No, I'd never taught Wajid.

'I know him by reputation, that's all,' I said. *'Knew.'*

'What sort of reputation?' asked the DCI, delicately.

'It's only hearsay. And I don't like to speak ill of the dead.'

'If speaking ill will help us find his killer—?'

I shook my head. 'It's not that easy, is it? You know what the college is like—ten thousand students use it, all from different backgrounds. Class, culture, race—I don't want to say anything that'll spark off friction.'

Perhaps I was being disingenuous. There had been an ugly incident only this afternoon, when a gang of white lads from Meat Three—trainee butchers—had hurled plates from the canteen windows at a group of Asian girls. I'd had the job of sorting out the ringleaders.

'There'll be more friction if we don't find the killer,' Dale added.

I nodded.

'Could you talk to us off the record, as it were?' asked the DCI.

'OK. But I'd like to use the loo first. All this coffee...'

The interview became a conversation. We moved to Groom's office, an unnaturally tidy room with a Monet print on the wall. What kind of policeman has a Monet, for goodness' sake? The sort that has hand-sewn Barker shoes, no doubt, and whose books include the *Shorter Oxford Dictionary*.

There was more coffee, in cups with a back-up supply in a Thermos jug, on his desk, and some film-wrapped sandwiches.

'Nice to see you're looking a bit better,' said Dale, passing me a plate.

'Thanks,' I said to both. I was beginning to feel myself again.

Groom smiled. 'I can have my colleagues swarm all over William Murdock College for the rest of the week and they'll pick up nothing. Oh, lots of facts, I don't doubt that, but I want nuances. Like the rumours you hinted at about Wajid.'

Ian Dale nodded agreement, and flicked open his notebook.

I looked at it. So did Groom. Dale flicked it shut again.

'Look, a lot of our kids are deprived. They come from rough backgrounds. Inner-city estates, inner-city schools. A lot are poor. They can't get grants, and there's no point saying they should go and get a decent job because there aren't any

19

decent jobs. So some dabble where they shouldn't.'

Groom and Dale nodded, though not necessarily in sympathy.

'There was a rumour that Wajid had—' I stopped. 'He never did anything they'd throw him out of college for. There are kids who wreck the loos or the drinks machines. Wajid wasn't one of those. Not a ringleader. When you reach the scene of crime.'

'*Macavity's not there!*' said Groom, straight-faced.

'Why couldn't you throw him out?' asked Dale, ummoved.

'Because, apart from anything else, he wasn't a monster of depravity.' I flicked an eye at Groom, whose eyes flickered back. 'He was actually a very good student. Look, we keep files on all our students—I could show you where we keep them tomorrow.'

'So I seem to have become a copper's nark,' I told George's answering machine half an hour later.

George was my friend. I was fond of him. *Fond* fond, not sexy fond. He played the bassoon in the Midshires Symphony Orchestra, and was the person I needed to confide in. George was much older than I was—fifty-six to my thirty-four.

20

We got to know each other because in my spare time I sing in the Midlands Choral Society, which works with the MSO whenever a choir is needed. I suppose we hadn't all that much in common—but we loved and trusted each other implicitly. He and the orchestra had been in Lichfield that evening. They'd probably be back already, but George hadn't been sleeping well recently and the last thing I wanted to do was ruin a night's rest for him by asking him to come over and comfort me. Wednesday would be Derby, then on Thursday it'd be Sheffield. They wouldn't be back till early Friday morning. We'd meet after Friday's concert—hence the phone message. If he woke late he'd leave one on my machine in reply. It was nearly as good as being properly in touch. But I rather hoped he'd get up early and phone me before I went into work.

Chapter Two

It was only drizzling when I set out for work the following morning, but by the time I'd got through Harborne into Edgbaston it was raining properly. Rain's bad news if you cycle. Apart from getting you thoroughly wet, it enhances your chance of being mown down by a motorist who is apparently too busy counting raindrops on his precious polished paintwork to notice other people on the road. But it was too late to go back, and no one's yet devised a way of folding a cycle small enough to take on a bus, so I toiled on.

The college buildings are dismal examples of cheap sixties architecture. There is a persistent rumour that they were intended as factories, another that they should have become low-cost flats. Perhaps both are correct: we have, after all, a low, dumpy building and a fifteen-storey tower block, neither of which is appetising. Naturally the staff based in either prefer the ambience of the other. Those who were in the tower block the day of the Birmingham earth tremor, which left cracks horribly visible in the south-facing wall, know they are right.

The buildings stand side by side but have separate entrances, and open on to a big but inadequate car park. This morning the car park was full of wet students, in large queues meandering from both entrances. As I chained the parts of my cycle I leave outside, a police car joined the others near the tower-block entrance. Ian Dale emerged and joined me. We walked towards the head of the queue, which magically parted. It must have been for him, not me.

Then I saw what was causing the delays. They were checking students IDs. Some egalitarian soul had pointed out that the staff should have IDs too, and that they should be subjected to the same scrutiny as everyone else. Quite right, except that the card tended to drift inexorably towards the bottom of my marking. I retrieved it eventually from a set of notes I thought I'd lost—an idiot's guide to the apostrophe.

There was no sign of Winston in the group of porters checking IDs; I'd ask his mother how he was when I saw her. I left a wheel and my handlebars in the caretaker's cubbyhole and rejoined the maelstrom in the foyer.

One of the lifts—*the* lift—was still taped off, and a chalk message on one of the classroom doors declared it was for the use of POLICE PERSONAL only. The handiwork of another of my ex-students, no doubt.

The grumbling which had been simmering outside was bubbling over in the foyer. None of the other lifts was working properly. I grinned at Ian and headed straight for the stairs.

'We're not going all the way up there—not fifteen floors!'

'How about stopping off at the canteen

for a coffee?' asked another voice. Groom's. I hadn't noticed him before. Presumably he'd been lurking as invisibly as six foot something of policeman can hope to lurk. 'I must say I was surprised to see you here so bright and early,' he continued, falling into step with me and leaving Ian a pace behind.

'*You* are,' I said. 'And I do have classes to teach. If the students ever get to them.'

'How much further?' came Ian's voice from behind.

'Only another couple of floors. Canteen's on the fifth.'

'Is that for everyone or just teachers?'

'Lecturers,' I said.

I pressed on up the stairs.

The high-rise part of the college is built around a core of lifts and stairs, with a band of corridors separating them from the classrooms on the outside of the building. The stairs have, of course, no natural light, and are further isolated by fire doors, which cut off both smoke and noise. The students, especially the women, dislike them intensely, preferring to wait hours for the overcrowded lifts to risking the endless series of ninety-degree bends.

Ian Dale would obviously have preferred a lift, but Groom kept pace with irritating ease. But he didn't seem inclined to talk.

It is one of my foibles that I eschew the lifts in order to keep fit—the fact that I had used one last night was attributable to a sudden realisation that I had buses to catch. Perhaps I should have engaged him in conversation to prove that I at least had enough breath to talk, but I couldn't think of anything I particularly wanted to say. And what I ought to be doing was running a mental review of the day's classes and what I should need for them. If indeed there were to be classes. A murder on the premises might well disturb the daily pattern.

'Did the Principal mention closing classes or anything?' I asked.

'I've only spoken to him over the phone. I'll be seeing him at nine-fifteen, actually.'

'How did he take the news?'

'Without enthusiasm, shall we say. But I managed to convince him that people would be more interested in the actual murder than where it was committed.'

'There was one years ago in a college,' Ian put in. 'A man cut his uncle's head off. Put it in a locker. Aston University now. And the body. An old building in Suffolk Street. Pulled down. Long since. Lift shaft. If I recall.'

'Next floor, Ian,' I said kindly.

He nodded. Groom paused between landings and looked about him.

25

'There don't seem to be many other people using these stairs,' he said. 'Any particular reason? Laziness apart, that is?'

I looked round, guiding his eyes.

'You can see the only rooms on the landings are loos. There's been a series of petty little—incidents, I suppose you people would call them. The last flasher who tried waving his silly little prick at me ended up in tears. And I got him thrown out of college. If not from a fifteenth-floor window.'

'Never thought of calling in your friendly neighbourhood constable?'

'Loads of times. But the college has its reputation to think of. Which makes me wonder how they'll deal with this business.'

It was fortunate that they wanted refreshment this week, not next. Soon the canteen would be commandeered to house a new suite for the administrators, and we would have either to share with the students—who emphatically did not want us—or to eat sandwiches in our offices. But management had statistics on their side: few people ever patronised the canteen anyway.

'Bit of a hole, isn't it?' said Ian, on cue, surveying through heavy breaths the cracked Rexine benches and cigarette-pitted floor.

I nodded, but then concentrated on cajoling water out of Vesuvius, the ancient urn, into the thick green cups that Noah had used in the Ark. I threw some money into the empty honesty box, carried two of the cups to the table they'd chosen and went back to collect the third. A pallid sun had emerged and lit the men's faces side on. Ian Dale, with his long, lined face, reminded me of Eyore, but Groom had little in common with Pooh apart from the colour of his hair. Even that was thinning. His complexion was a delicate pinky white that probably burnt to brick red in summer. Unlike Dale, who still wore that sports jacket, he looked very sleek in a suit, remarkably like one my last boyfriend paid an indecent amount for in the Aquascutum sale. It looked better on Groom, possibly because Kenji never made it above five foot six.

'Right,' I said purposefully. 'How can I help you? I only ask because I'm teaching GCSE English in thirteen minutes, and I have to make it to the fifteenth floor to collect the register and then get back to the eighth. I think I can deduce that you don't need to be shown the scene of the crime—'

Groom permitted himself a wispy smile. Dale jumped in. 'Been reading too much Agatha Christie, eh? There was a whole

27

team of people here overnight, dear, going over the place with a fine-tooth comb. SOCOS.'

'Scene of crime officers,' said Groom quietly. 'If you're in a hurry, why don't we get hold of Wajid's file? We'll come back to you if there's anything we need to ask.'

Presumably most of my colleagues were still stuck either in the queue to get in or in the foyer waiting for a lift. But Shahida was in the fifteenth-floor office, looking very much as though she shouldn't be. When I introduced Groom and Dale, and explained why they were there, she forced a smile, then put her hand to her mouth and bolted.

I stopped the men following her. Ian already had his mints at the ready, and Chris clutched something that looked incredibly like a bottle of smelling salts.

'The first time I went into a morgue,' he said, 'was to attend a postmortem. It's part of everyone's training. I fainted. Occasionally I still do. I must be the only serving officer to carry these.'

'I don't think they'll help Shahida. And she prefers people to ignore it. Morning sickness.'

'If she's that bad, why doesn't she take a sickie?' asked Ian, still holding the mints.

'Because people don't,' I said, 'take sickies. Not unless they have to. Can't let the students down. Or your friends, who get lumbered with extra work. Esprit de corps, or something.'

'Sounds familiar,' said Groom, as if awarding Brownie points.

When she returned, Shahida accepted a mint. She explained our record-keeping system: one on computers, which might one day be networked, if ever the funds ran to it, and a paper-based one for computer-illiterates like me. She fished a manila folder from the cabinet next to the computer. 'This is easier,' she said.

The folder held a copy of Wajid's timetable—he should have been in Computer Science this morning. Someone would have to break it to the class. I pointed and looked at Groom. He nodded. His job, or one of his colleagues. I reached for one of Dale's mints.

There was a list of Wajid's qualifications: seven good GCSEs. A set of comments on his Christmas exams—As in all of them. And his punctuality and attendance were exemplary. Then there was a note in ill-formed handwriting asking if he might have leave of absence because his father had died. A college reference—he'd applied for a local-authority grant and his tutor, Shahida, had written a glowing report supporting him very strongly.

'That's odd,' I said.

'Odd?' repeated Groom.

'Yes. Applying for a grant on the grounds of extreme financial hardship.'

'He was absolutely broke,' said Shahida.

'Broke students don't wear designer jeans or a Rolex.'

'They'd be cheap copies, Sophie,' said Dale.

They hadn't looked like that to me, but he'd no doubt taken a closer look than I had. There wasn't time to argue, anyway. I had a class to go to, and the phones had started to ring. I took the nearest. It was a parent. He wasn't letting his daughter come to college till they'd caught the murderer. Just to make sure, he was sending her back to Pakistan for a holiday.

I reported back to Shahida.

'Shit! The bastard!' she said, slamming her hand on a desk.

'Seems reasonable enough to me,' said Dale. 'Can't help worrying when you're a parent. Wouldn't want my girls taking any risks.'

'But you wouldn't marry her off just to make sure. A holiday in Pakistan is all too often a euphemism for an arranged marriage, officer. These poor girls end up with country cousins, real hicks some of them.'

30

Groom's eyes flickered to her wedding ring.

'I was lucky. We fell in love: our parents got on and arranged it,' she said.

I gathered up my folder and the register and headed for the corridor. Groom followed. I stopped.

'Can I ask you something, Chief Inspector?'

'Chris. Of course.'

Dale coughed gently. To urge discretion, perhaps.

'Fire away,' said Chris.

'Why didn't you suspect me?'

A couple of my colleagues, late and anxious, pushed by. We exchanged terse greetings.

'Would you rather we had? We wouldn't have had the coffee and cakes in my room, for sure.'

'Sandwiches. But why should you and all your colleagues assume I was telling the truth?'

Dale fidgeted his feet. I looked at Groom, wishing I was taller so I could stare him in the eye. As it was, I must have looked like a supplicant.

He looked down at me, crow's feet of amusement spreading from his eyes.

'Let's see: you must be about five foot tall?'

'Five foot one,' I bridled.

'And weigh not much above eight stone? And though you're fit—very fit!' He glanced across at Dale—'you don't break any records weight-training. Nor are you an ex-medical student.'

'You saw my file before you saw Wajid's,' I said evenly.

He nodded, almost apologetically, and then regained the initiative. 'So it was most unlikely that you killed that lad. You'd have to be an expert or extremely strong. Both, for preference. Whoever did it managed to get at the right angle between the ribs, the right distance from the spine. And he—let's assume it was a he—had to be strong enough to cut through that jacket. Leather, remember.'

'A lot of...of blood,' I said.

'Not from the point of entry, though. The blade severed the aorta. He bled to death very quickly. It's just that all the blood collected in his chest cavity.'

'So that when I—' I gestured.

Ian Dale offered another mint. I took it.

'Quite,' said Groom.

There was a little silence.

'Can I just clear one thing, so we know where to find you? We've seen the canteen, such as it was, and we've seen your office. Where's the common room?'

'There isn't one. They had that last year

32

for the Computer Suite. We use our offices for everything.'

'Everything?' echoed Dale. 'You mean you eat and work and relax and everything there?'

'Not much relaxation,' I said, 'as you'll see if you hang around. But now we're losing the canteen, yes, everything. There are offices—we call them staff rooms—like that scattered at intervals throughout the building, housing staff doing different types of teaching. Engineering. Beauty. Languages.'

'Must make communications a bit tricky,' said Groom, making a note.

'Phone, rumour or carrier pigeon,' I said. 'And now I really must dash.'

The ideal is to get a whole class together and attentive before you start teaching. Today, my GCSE group fell far short of that. I was a couple of minutes late myself, but it was a further five minutes before anyone else turned up. This was Karen, a girl whose classroom silence was always catatonic, and she retired to her regular corner to chew her hair and look morose. I tried asking about queues and lifts and she looked as if for once she might utter. As she opened her mouth, however, the door was thrown open and a green-uniformed young man strode in.

'You,' he said, pointing his radio at her. 'ID.'

The college management had evidently decided to tighten security. To be honest, I'd expected little more than a flurry of memos and a succession of protracted meetings to which the lower echelons, of which I was one, would not be invited. This sudden overreaction was as startling as it was unpleasant. I ached for the gentle but firm Winston and his long suffering colleagues, who endured constant abuse from the students but managed to keep a tenuous control over the incipient drug dealing, gambling and general nastiness which constantly threatened.

'Good morning,' I said.

He contrived to ignore me.

'I said, good morning. You are in my classroom, young man, and I expect you to behave as I expect anyone else in the room to behave.'

His radio spluttered. He started to reply. I caught his eye. He left the room. Karen started to weep, silently.

By eleven, there were still only six out of a possible twenty-four students. I gave them some work to prepare for the next week, and toiled back up to my office.

There was sufficient uproar to divert attention from my minor role in last night's affair. Where you have two lecturers gathered together, there are generally at least three opinions. Since I shared a room with thirteen colleagues and three hyperactive telephones, the noise level was unbelievable. I herded out into the corridor three or four students who'd strayed into the room and shut the door. In general they have more or less free access, but today would have to be an exception. For good measure, I locked the door.

I joined the seethe and made what I could of the arguments.

The basis of it all was shock and distress, there was no doubt about that. We valued our students, all of us, and were outraged that a young life had been wasted. But our outrage took different forms. Clearly one or two had been weeping. Another couple were scapegoating the porters, and were engaged in a loud argument with several others whose students had been subjected to the treatment I'd just witnessed. A couple of the older inhabitants were trying in vain to find cover for classes so they could go to a meeting to discuss the new security arrangements. A latecomer erupted into the room brandishing copies of a memo instructing us not to talk to the press, and warning us to be careful what we said to the police. I slipped a copy into my pocket to show to Chris.

Another phone call, from the Principal's

secretary this time: I was bidden to see the Principal at lunchtime.

I turned and caught Shahida's eye. She nodded imperceptibly. Yes, she would back me.

'I'm sorry,' I said, 'but I've arranged to see poor Wajid's family this lunchtime. Shahida and I are going to take them some flowers.'

I said the same thing to Ian Dale when he saw us leaving the foyer, and he nodded with apparent approval.

'Keep an eye open, eh, Sophie,' he said.

'I wonder what he was going to say,' said Shahida, opening her Fiesta's passenger door for me.

'Ian?'

'H'm. And why all this first-name business? I expected them all to refer to me as Miss. And to patronise me by being too considerate, just because I'm pregnant.'

'You don't show enough.' I grinned.

Shahida had had the foresight to order a spray from a florist in Handsworth, which was where we were heading. She parked on a double yellow line while I dashed in to pay for it.

I read the *A to Z* while she picked her way through increasingly depressing streets. Then there was a pleasant surprise.

Although the houses in the street we wanted were tiny two-up, two-down terraced villas, the street itself had obviously been on the receiving end of urban renewal money. All the houses had been reroofed and parking areas had been indented into the pavement, which was also new. Different road textures reminded motorists that they were not on the Super Prix circuit.

Wajid's house hadn't been repainted, as some of the neighbours' had, but someone had cleaned the old paint, and the minute paved front garden had recently been swept. Someone was trying very hard.

The voices inside the house stopped as soon as Shahida knocked.

She knocked again.

At last it was opened, slowly, by someone I knew. Iqbal. Another William Murdock student. Ex-student. Not one of our successes. One or two of us suspected the videos he dealt in were not necessarily legitimate.

'Is Wajid's mother there?' asked Shahida.

He muttered something and shut the door.

'And the same to you,' said Shahida, taking my arm to steer me away.

'You wouldn't care to translate?' To my shame, I didn't even know which language he was insulting us in.

' "Fuck off", more or less. But he's speaking Mirpuri, so I may have lost some of the finer nuances.'

Angry but helpless, we headed back to the car.

'Mirpuri?' I repeated.

'A variant of Punjabi. And his was more of a variant than most.'

'Miss! Miss!'

We turned.

The door had opened again, and a slight figure was hurtling towards us. Yet another William Murdock face. Aftab, the star of my twilight GCSE-English class and one of the best students of the year.

'I'm sorry. My cousin. He's very upset. Wajid was his cousin, see.'

Aftab was upset, too. He was ashen pale, with green smudges of grief below his eyes.

'He shouldn't have spoken like that. My aunt is very angry. She appreciates what you were trying to do. Please, come in.'

I demurred. I didn't want to intrude. Neither did I want to cause offence. I glanced at Shahida.

'Just for a moment, Aftab. We have to get back to college.'

The front door opened straight into the living room. We were aware of people melting into the kitchen. An Asian woman grey with grief hitched her dupatta across her face. Aftab muttered something. This must be Wajid's mother.

Shahida passed over the flowers.

With great dignity she took them and placed them on a hard chair. She took my hand between both of hers, then Shahida's. She spoke slowly to Shahida. I looked covertly around the room. Like the outside of the house it was shabby but clean. There were pale patches on the wall as if someone had taken down pictures.

Aftab saw me looking.

'A custom. After a death in the family, some people cover mirrors. Others take down family photos. We don't like to have photos where people are praying.'

I touched his arm lightly. He nodded, and blinked hard.

'The funeral?' I said hesitantly. 'Should the college...?'

He shook his head. 'It'll be a very small family funeral. Islam teaches that we should bury our dead at once. As soon as the police give permission, we go ahead. Maybe tomorrow, they said.'

'At the big mosque in Highgate?'

'You wouldn't even know it's a mosque, miss—just a house in the next street. Very small. Just family. Then there's the burial.'

'Would it be OK if—'

'The women mostly don't go to the

cemetery. It's not very nice. Not for women. They have the coffin open, you see.'

'What about one of the male staff from college?'

'My aunt thinks you have brought the flowers from the whole college. You've done all you should. More would be...' He gestured, hunting for the word.

'Intrusive?'

He nodded. I caught Shahida's eye and we turned to the front door. Aftab opened it.

'See you at college, miss.'

'Take however long you need, Aftab. You'll soon catch up,' I said.

He shook his head. 'Can't miss college. Got to get those A levels. They're asking two As and a B for Law. If we can't have the funeral, I shall be in tomorrow. Without fail.'

The rest of the day was unnervingly quiet. The green-uniformed security men were still around, but had evidently been instructed to show more sensitivity. At the end of my last class, I sought out Winston, the porter.

He was sitting in the cleaners' rest room, what looked like a physiology textbook open on his lap.

He got up when he saw me, but I

perched on a large drum of cleaning liquid, and he settled again.

'Fascinating stuff,' he said, tapping the book. 'When I've qualified maybe I should look into it. Pathology. The stuff those guys could tell from one wound. Amazing.'

'How did you get on with them?'

'I just a porter, man. I don't know nothing, man,' he said, his Afro-Caribbean lilt much exaggerated.

'Don't give me that, Winston, or I'll set your mum on you.'

'She does it better than me!' he said, his accent returning to normal.

' 'Course she does. More practice. They obviously didn't suspect you, anyway. Not if you're here.'

Winston was, after all, the right size. As tall as Groom, at least, and very powerfully built. He bowled a wicked inswinger, very fast indeed. He'd had trials with several county sides, and had received a couple of offers. But he'd also been given a place at St Mary's to read Medicine, and would be leaving for London next September. Meanwhile he earned enough to live on and save, and enjoyed playing the sleepy dim giant. And the students respected him.

'Gave me a tough time, Sophie. And I reckon they'll want to hassle me again. All they need is a motive.'

'Have you got one?'

He shook his head.

'I told them, I reckon it's some Muslim Mafia business. And maybe they believe me.'

I touched the textbook.

'Do they know about this?'

He shook his head again. 'No, man.'

'I'd tell them, Winston. Before someone else does.'

On my way back up the building, I stopped off at the Departmental Office, ostensibly to check my pigeonhole for mail but in reality to catch my breath and rest my leg muscles. Straight into the bin went a load of brochures for books the college couldn't afford—God knows why they'd found their way to someone as lowly as me anyway. A fistful of memos; I'd check those later. Some telephone messages. One was from the Principal cancelling the lunchtime meeting and asking me to phone his secretary. One from a friend I was supposed to be meeting for a drink: he'd got flu. And one from George—what the hell was going on at William Murdock? He'd see me on Friday, after the choir's rehearsal and the MSO's concert.

When I reached the fifteenth floor, I found the office unlocked and apparently deserted. So much for our new enthusiasm for security. Then I realised I wasn't alone. Shahida had her head down on her desk and was fast asleep. I'd meant to invite myself round to fill the gap in the evening left by Carl, the man who'd invited me for a drink. Shahida's mother cooks the meanest samosas I've ever eaten, and keeps her daughter supplied. If I gave the smallest hint I was lonely, she'd offer at once. But clearly she needed rest more than I needed company. I gathered my marking up quietly, found my coat, and padded out. I locked the door behind me.

I must have some nasty masochistic streak which refuses to let me leave my bike at work and take a taxi, even when it's dark and dirty on the roads. I got wet through just reassembling it, and found I had to battle the long haul up to Five Ways against the wind. By sticking to the gutter I overtook the cars forming a solid jam. At Five Ways itself, a monster traffic island controlled at peak times by lights, I simply took illegally to the pavement. I'd seen enough blood recently to convince me that I didn't want any of mine to be shed.

And I didn't want to go home. It didn't make sense, but I didn't want to be alone. I promised myself I could stop off in Harborne and spoil myself with a bag of goodies from Safeway. Whiskey—I'd finished the last of the Jameson's last night in an attempt to sleep; a packet of mixed salad; chicken tikka; a small baguette; continental butter. And then I dithered by the check-out. Wouldn't it be nicer to take myself out for a curry? But I would still have to come back home and it would be even later, even lonelier. I told myself that I was being stupid, added a box of Belgian chocolates to my basket and paid.

My postal address is Harborne, what the classier Sundays refer to as the Chelsea of Birmingham. Balden Road, however, is almost in Quinton, a bastion of suburban respectability, full of identical semis. Mine is joined to its neighbour by the hall, rather than the living-room wall. It is mine purely because of the failure of one of my relatives to make a will. To the rear are the extensive and expensive gardens of FitzRoy Avenue. The neighbours to whom I am not attached aspire to move, and meanwhile subject their house to an endless succession of improvements and extensions. Since their drive is more often than not occupied by a skip, their cars spread across my frontage and that of my other neighbour, Aggie, whose carless state and uneven distribution of aitches enable them to patronise her or, better still, ignore her. I get on very well with her, however: she is a sternly fit septuagenarian, who guards my house as fiercely as she guards her own. I thought I would pop round to see if I could borrow some sugar later in the evening—not for the sugar, of which I had two bags in the pantry, but for her company.

But Aggie had put a note through my door: her granddaughter, the one who was expecting her first child, Aggie's first great-grandchild, had flu, and Aggie had gone down to Tewkesbury to nurse her. Would I keep an eye open for the binmen and make sure they didn't leave the black sack to blow away? If she wasn't back by the weekend, could I water her plants?

I stuck the note on my kitchen cork-board.

The house was too quiet. I seemed to rattle round in it. I went round switching on lights, drawing curtains, checking doors.

I must have been suffering from PMT or delayed reaction or something. My home is usually a positive refuge and yet now it seemed hostile. Even the cars outside seemed threatening: surely I hadn't seen that big white van before? It was the sort that was ubiquitous round college, generating the rumours of the Muslim Mafia that Winston had half-joked about. But they were not usually found round here. Even as I looked, however, someone got in, and drove it away. I wished they had remembered to put the headlights on.

George always looks anxious if I drink spirits before a meal, not because he's afraid I shall become an alcoholic but because he says it'll destroy the sensitivity of my palate. Bother George! I reached for the Jameson's.

Helen, I could phone Helen. She was always happy to share a glass of wine and a moan about teaching. I could phone and invite myself over.

Except she had a migraine. The GNVQ group always gives her a migraine. Her husband was just taking the kids to McDonald's.

Nothing for it, Sophie, but another finger of whiskey, and an assault on your marking.

In the end it wasn't so bad. The food perked me up. I found a good concert on Radio Three, and the essays were better than I had dared hope. And George phoned. God knows how much the call cost him. He wanted to hear all about the goings-on at college, and to moan about their conductor.

'But I thought Ottaka was good? All those recordings?'

'As I've said before, it's one thing to

sound good in a recording studio, another to bring everything together on stage. If we knew what was good for us we'd play it like he's conducting it. That'd show him. And d'you know what the bugger wanted? Only to rewrite Beethoven's Fifth!'

Beethoven was George's passion.

'How?'

'You know that bit at the start? Po-pop-pop-poooom? For the horns? Well, Mr Ottaka thought it might be better with a couple of bassoons.'

'Don't tell me: you and Jools decided to show him it wasn't!'

He'd spent the whole morning working on new reeds. Some musicians bought them ready-made. Jools did; George didn't. The reed affects the sound a woodwind instrument makes, and George considered it too important to leave to anyone else. On this occasion he'd persuaded Jools to be his partner in crime. So when at afternoon rehearsal Ottaka put his new orchestration into practice, the hall echoed with what sounded like a massive fart. Ottaka changed his mind, and in five minutes the MSO would be playing Beethoven as Beethoven intended.

'Thank God we've only got one more gig with him,' George said. 'Then Mayou rejoins us. At least he's a musician, which is more than you can say for this guy. He's

47

on Radio Three tonight, with the LSO. Go and listen and see what you think. See you Friday.'

I obeyed. Schumann's *Spring Symphony*. So good I ended up singing along with it, forgot I needed extra whiskey, and fell asleep like a baby.

Chapter Three

Thursday. If I skipped lunch there'd just be time to nip down to collect my watch. The road from college to the Jewellery Quarter is so steep it was hardly worth putting the cycle back together. In any case, there's an island that motorists prefer to shave rather than circumnavigate, and on more than one occasion my bike and I have ended up on the island itself. So I decided to go on foot. The wind had dropped to no more than a brisk breeze, and the sun had emerged from hibernation. Like Pooh, I hummed, but my choice was a bit of *Carmina Burana*. Probably a fairly vulgar bit.

The watch was ready; the repair was cheap and guaranteed; and I remembered in time that I needed a pillar box. I had a red gas bill to post.

I thought at first someone had stuck some of those children's stickers all over the postbox. Then I looked more closely. There was a poor photocopy of the newspaper headline announcing Wajid's death, and a red scrawled message.

ONE DOWN, HOW MANY TO GO?

I managed to get the worst of it off; then I turned my attention to the rest of the decoration—nasty little caricatures suggesting that the only criminals were Asian. British National Party. I forced myself to be calm. If I was to get the vile stuff off in one piece I had to be calm. I worked with fingernails and the nailfile. The police would see this.

My anger carried me all the way back up the hill, past the security guards and into the foyer. I toyed briefly with the idea of correcting POLICE PERSONAL with my red pen. But I saw the face I wanted and gave it up, for the time being at least.

Ian invited me courteously into the room. I expected it to be packed with computers and other useful equipment, but found little more than a couple of coats and a plan of the building.

'Doesn't seem to be much activity,' I remarked, perching on a desk.

'Time you got up to date, Sophie,' he said, smiling with avuncular indulgence. 'I suppose you were expecting us to be

49

running the show from here.'

'Well, I did expect what you get on TV: an incident room, do you call it?'

'No need, these days. Telecommunication links and everything. We'd use a room at Ladywood nick if we needed, but really everything's directed from Rose Road. Regional centre. Now, I don't suppose you came to talk about policing in the West Midlands—'

'No. I came to show you this. Found it on a pillar box down the road.'

I dragged the unlovely collection from my bag and dropped it on a desk. He poked it with a biro.

'Vile. Not much we can do, not unless we catch them at it. And we can't watch every pillar box, much as we'd like to.'

I took a deep breath and said nothing.

He reached a large hand to crumple it up.

'Don't you have to report it to anyone?'

'Who to?'

'Anyone!'

He stared at me: he'd never seen me angry before.

'Can't people be prosecuted for printing stuff like that?' I pursued.

'Who? Didn't see anyone sticking it there, did you?'

'They've left their address, Ian.'

He shook his head. 'Not my territory,

Sophie. And I'm trying to find out who murdered young Wajid, remember.'

'You don't suppose there could be a connection?' I asked dryly.

He sighed. After a moment, he dug in a pocket and fished out a polythene bag.

'There you are then,' he said, shoving the papers into it. 'Evidence,' he added, with great irony.

Someone had bought a kettle, and people who'd remembered to bring in mugs were drinking their first non-Vesuvius tea. The person who unwisely remarked it tasted better free was reminded tartly that we all had to contribute to the kettle and the milk fund. We'd already agreed to go independent in the matter of tea and coffee. There was supposed to be a washing-up rota but, having been in other places where cups grew green and furry, I suspected it would be more breached than observed.

The students were beginning to drift back: that was the general consensus. Most people had classes at least 80 per cent full, and some of the absences could in any case be caused by flu. Two more of the staff had succumbed, and Shahida was looking ominously pale, but she claimed she had no more than a headache and insisted on returning to her class when break ended.

'How's young Aftab?' I asked, as she

gathered up her papers.

'Not in. Funny, I thought he said he wasn't going to miss classes on any account.'

'The funeral?'

She nodded. 'Maybe I'll phone him after class,' she said. 'He's a good kid; be nice to offer him a bit of support.'

We grinned at each other and went our ways, she to her Law A level, me to yet more GCSE English.

If I stopped off at the supermarket without a list, I should forget three-quarters of what I needed. I sat at my desk and tapped my teeth with a pencil. Teabags, coffee and a mug. And kitchen towel, a bottle of washing-up liquid and a scourer. All for work, naturally. I had also better apply my mind to food. The freezer was depressingly empty—I'd cleaned it out at the weekend—and my fridge ditto, since I had been threatening myself with the direst of punishments if I didn't defrost it soon. I braced my shoulders; I would do it straight away and reward myself with a steak; it was ages since I'd eaten red meat. Steak in a pizzaiola sauce. Yes and—

The expression on Shahida's face brought me back to William Murdock with a bump.

'I just phoned Aftab,' she said slowly,

52

'and he's not at home. They say he's at college. Has been all day.'

'Wagging,' said someone.

'Not like him,' said his Sociology lecturer.

'Not at all,' I agreed.

'Could be he needed some time to himself, I suppose,' said Shahida thoughtfully. 'But I said to call me if he didn't get back soon.'

I was feeling unpleasantly smug. I'd bought all the items on my list, to which I'd added a bottle of Valdepenas. I'd emptied the fridge, defrosted it, wiped it down and refilled it. And I'd managed to prepare some work for my Eng. Lit. group the following morning—Joyce's *Dubliners*. Now for my steak.

The garlic was just browning in the olive oil when the phone rang. Perhaps it would be George: it must be about the time for the concert interval.

It was also the right time for the break in Shahida's evening class, and more than time for Aftab to be home. But there was no sign of him, she said, her voice tight with anxiety.

There was no point in telling her not to worry.

'Listen,' I said, 'the only thing I can think of is that they should tell the police.'

'I've suggested that. But they say it'll make it look as if he's involved in the murder.'

'It does,' I agreed. 'But not if you know Aftab.'

'So what shall I do?'

'Call the police?' I said.

The garlic was charred, and with it the pan. I put the latter to soak. Somehow steak wasn't such an attractive prospect after all. Wrapping and all, it went into the freezer. Tomorrow, perhaps. Or the next day. Meanwhile I'd content myself with bread and cheese. If I could face the cheese.

There'd be no call from George now: the orchestra would be on the way home. I wanted to leave a message on his machine, but had to be careful: if he thought I needed him, I wouldn't put it past him to come straight over, no matter what time the coaches got back to Birmingham. In the end I just confirmed the arrangement for the following evening—that we'd meet in the pub at about ten.

I'm terribly priggish about drinking and cycling, so on Fridays I always take the bus. I go straight from college to the choir rehearsal, and then to the pub. This Friday wouldn't have been a good day for cycling anyway. It was blowing a gale already, and storm force winds were threatened for later.

If I go down the road, there is a choice of two buses, neither of which follows the main Hagley Road into town. The Hagley Road is thick with traffic whatever time you use it; at rush hours it is solid. So I prefer either the 10 or the 103. On the bus I'd reread the Joyce short stories. Friday morning was the highlight of my week, a couple of hours with really interested students.

The walk down the hill from Five Ways cheered me even further—I like March days, with the sun battling it out with the wind. To hell with the havoc to my hairdo: my only real extravagance is a regular visit to a classy stylist on Harborne's High Street. All I have to do is shake my mop and it falls into place. I was in mid-shake, waiting in the queue to show my ID, when I saw Ian Dale, shoving his way into the building with none of his usual courtesy. With him was a young woman, whom I dimly recognised. I caught Dale's eye; he gestured me over, and into the POLICE PERSONAL room.

'You'll remember Tina,' he said.

'Of course: YTS police, wasn't it?'

'Ah. And I got me a job in the end, too. DC Reed at your service, miss.'

'Sophie,' I said. 'What's up?'

'You haven't seen this then?' Ian threw on to a desk a copy of the local paper.

' "Missing student kidnap fear"? Jesus, not Aftab!'

'The same. Bloody hell, who do these people think they are?' He pointed to a photograph of a smiling city councillor. 'The kid may lose his life because of this.'

'I'm sorry?'

'You can't just go messing around with kidnap cases. There's a procedure laid down by the Home Office. We're quiet, we listen. We want to find the victim alive, not in a black sack somewhere. But it seems his cousin went and told his councillor we were refusing to act.'

'Hang on. When did he go missing? I know he didn't come in yesterday, but surely you don't assume every kid on the skive has been abducted—you'd need a whole force just for our college.' I grinned at Tina, who blushed.

'Wednesday night, according to his cousin. Apparently they were on their way to some do at their mosque when a car pulls up beside them. They think it's someone who's lost his way, go over all friendly-like, and get bin liners pulled over their heads. By the time this cousin's free, there's no sign of Aftab and the car's speeding off, no lights.'

'And the cousin's Iqbal Ahmed.'

Dale nodded.

'Wonder why he didn't tell the family: they thought he was in college yesterday.'

'You're sure about that?'

My turn to nod this time. 'And what's all this about a councillor? You'd think he'd act in the kid's best interests.'

'I'm sure he thinks he is. Got the idea we're racists. Don't bother about crimes committed against Asians.'

I did not speak. There was no point in trying to score points. Maybe he was overcasual yesterday but there was no doubting Dale's anger and concern today.

'Look,' he said, 'that nice girl Shahida's off today. Doctor's appointment or something. You couldn't do the honours, could you? Show us his files, tell us about his mates, that sort of thing. It's the inside stuff we need, like the Guv'nor said the other day.'

I shook my head. 'I don't recall telling you anything you couldn't have found out for yourselves.'

'No, but you introduced us to Shahida, and she did. It's not the big things, Sophie. Just little things.'

'I'll show you his file with pleasure,' I said. 'I take it that's been OK'd by the Principal? But honestly, Ian, I can't think of a nicer kid in the college than young

Aftab. He's decent, honest, hard-working. Very bright. Could be the first Asian Lord Chancellor. I'd like him to be.' The words came into my mind unbidden—'If he lives'. 'OK, Ian. Anything—just ask. Anything that'll help bring him back alive.'

After the melodrama of what I'd said, my actions were very prosaic. All they wanted of me was a list of his contacts at college, and information where they'd find them. I pointed them in the right direction, and that was it. I felt there was something distasteful about delivering sixteen-year-olds up to Dale, avuncular or not, and reminded them—in front of him and Tina—that they should tell their parents. And then I went into class. Without any tea, free or otherwise.

It is an unwritten rule that no one ever interrupts your class, not for anything short of a nuclear disaster. There is a strong rumour that one of my colleagues emerged from a three-hour session to find a note on his desk telling him his mother had died. So I was furious when a student erupted right into the middle of 'Eveline'. Then I saw the panic on her face. Manjit Kaur.

'They'll kill me, miss. They'll kill me!'

I scooped her out of the room; thank goodness this was one class I could afford to leave unattended. They'd get on without me, quietly reading.

The only place I could find to talk to Manjit was the nearest women's loo. I couldn't imagine anywhere less ideal—who knew what ears were lurking in the occupied cubicles?—but all the classrooms were full, and you might as well try to be private on New Street Station as in our staff room. But as if she were safe, she started to sob openly. For several minutes all I could do was hold her shoulders. Then I thought it was time to try to calm her.

'Manjit? Manjit? Try to tell me.'

And at last she did. Garbled and disorganised, her story came out. Manjit was afraid someone would tell her parents about being friends with Aftab.

'I thought they were quite enlightened,' I said. Certainly they were keen for Manjit to go to university, didn't mind her leaving Birmingham if that was necessary. Surely they wouldn't mind an inter-community friendship, provided it was no more than that?

'They are. They are. They've been so good. All that money they've spent on me. I don't want to let them down.'

I held her as she started to cry again.

So what was all this about killing? She was certainly frightened of something. But there was nothing I could say except that I was sure the police would be absolutely discreet unless she was actually involved.

She assured me that she wasn't. I promised to talk to Ian. And I resolved to do a little investigating on my own account to see what was so upsetting Manjit.

But not immediately. We had a long meeting over our lunch hour to plan a new course, and seemed to spend most of it griping about IT provision. So far I'd missed all the computer courses I wanted to go on, and my prowess in the area was zero. I still found it easier to burrow in our filing cabinets than to summon a file on the student database. One of these days I'd get round to it. In fact, there and then I filled in an application for a course designed to make anyone proficient in a week. Even me. And then—late—I hurtled off to engage in my weekly battle with Beauty Two.

I had returned, exhausted, to the staff room, to find all three phones demanding my attention. I picked up the nearest. The others continued to shrill.

I had chosen the right one. George. But he was trying to lure me from the paths of righteousness with a free ticket for tonight's concert.

'George, you know the only thing I can't resist is temptation. But I've got to. If I miss any more rehearsals I'll be drummed out of the choir before the Royal Concert.'

'But it's going to be a little cracker. Schumann—Mayou's hot on Schumann. And that kid who won Leeds doing the Brahms D minor. Come on. And I'll buy you a drink in the interval.'

But I resisted, nobly. Ten, in the Duke of Clarence—and not a moment before.

Chapter Four

The rehearsal had been exhilarating but exhausting. Our chorus master had extracted more effort than most of us were capable of after a day's work. It was, after all, the last rehearsal before we started work with the MSO.

Birmingham's city fathers had at last decided to build a prestige concert hall, the Music Centre. There were some who said it sounded more like something on a shelf in your living room, and others who insisted it looked like it. But it was a huge improvement technically on the dear old Town Hall, and there were vastly improved facilities for musicians and audience alike. In April there would be an official, royal opening, with a concert by the MSO and the MSO Choir. It was for this that we were preparing. The first joint rehearsal would be tomorrow, in the auditorium of the Music Centre itself. Never mind that the Music Centre was unfinished, that we'd have to pick our way through unfinished piazzas and walkways; we'd got to get it right for royalty. In any case, the general public were faced with the same hazards: tonight's concert had been moved there from the Town Hall.

I joined the exodus from the thirties church hall we use for our rehearsals and headed not for the car park but back towards the city-centre pub where I'd arranged to meet George. The wind was still vicious—lazy, we call it where I come from, in the Black Country, lazy because it goes through, not round you. My eyes were streaming; I'd have to go and fix my mascara as soon as I'd greeted George.

The bar of the Duke of Clarence was full of streamlined coffins. They were guarding thousands of pounds' worth of valuable wood. But George's heavy, rectangular case was not among them. Nor was George at our usual table, sipping his Old Peculiar. He was no doubt still chewing the fat back in the band room, probably picking someone's brains about his van conversion: he wanted to turn it into a motor caravan so he could tour the world on the cheap when he retired. We aimed to celebrate his sixty-fifth birthday with lunch in Lima.

I was thoroughly tidy when I returned to the bar, but there was still no sign of George.

'Luigi says you found a body,' said a voice. Aberlene's.

Aberlene van der Poele is just turned thirty and five foot eleven inches tall. She has a figure any woman would covet and walks like a goddess. She is also black. She has the most difficult job in the whole orchestra—she is the leader—and does it well. Even the men in the heavy brass agree about that.

'Come on: tell us all about it.'

I grinned. It didn't seem quite so terrible now I was back with my friends, and I was still on a high after the rehearsal.

'Not till I've had a drink—Luigi, could I have some of your Lambrusco, please? Your special?'

He nodded and disappeared.

Luigi's special was nothing like the pink pop you get in litre bottles at supermarkets. It came from his family's vineyards back home, and fizzed with light and life.

If I was going to drink, I'd better eat too. I groped in a plastic-covered dish for something film-wrapped.

Luigi smacked my hand. 'If you drink my Lambrusco, you don't eat that. Maria!'

'I've had nothing since breakfast, Luigi.'

'You don't look after yourself.'

'Another meeting.'

'You should eat lunch. Everyone should eat lunch. Maria!' He bustled off again.

'There!' He plonked a plate in front of me. On it was a crusty roll which overlapped by an inch each end. It was still not large enough to hold with any dignity all Maria had crammed inside it—antipasti for four at least. As I picked up the plate, an olive rolled free. Hands swooped like gulls on a herring. I smacked a finger looping towards the salami and headed for the group clustered round our usual table. It was in the corner furthest from the jukebox. We'd chosen it before we realised Luigi had intended the jukebox purely for decoration. As if by magic, a label-less bottle and four glasses appeared on the table. I had a suspicion that this was illicit, to put it mildly, and that we ought to buy individual, British standard glassfuls. But this was how Luigi did it. And no one was ever going to be churlish enough to complain.

He still wasn't there. 'Where's George got to?'

Aberlene, satisfying at my expense her passion for red rollo lettuce, shrugged. 'George? Probably fiddling with his reeds. You know what these woodwind types are like.'

String players, of course, think wind players are neurotic. I suppose they might have something.

'I have to admit that he and Jools saved our bacon last night,' she said. 'I suppose you heard about that cretin Ottaka rewriting Beethoven?'

I nodded.

Aberlene stood up to check the bar. She sat down again so no one could grab her stool. 'No sign of him. And Jools is late too. Or should I say "again"? She's been last on the platform every night this week. I even had to wait for her tonight.'

A hand reached for an olive that hadn't so much strayed as been lured away. Pam.

'George left before I did. I held the Band Room door for him. It'll be great when everything's working properly—automatic doors, lifts, everything.'

Pam had a vested interest in such technology. She was one of the few people not to have brought her instrument. Since she was four foot ten in her socks, and weighed about six and a half stone, this was hardly surprising: she played the double bass.

Talk turned not to the murder or even Aftab's abduction, but to the Centre itself. I was happy to let it. George would

65

certainly want to hear my news properly, and repeating it wouldn't make it any better. Aftab: the last person I'd ever have suspected of doing anything wrong enough to get kidnapped for.

Aberlene topped up my glass and caught my eye. I made an effort to smile, and she patted my hand kindly.

And then Jools appeared. Jools was second bassoon. Her real name was Julia, but no one seeing her would doubt that her nickname was more appropriate than her given one. We'd known each other since university days, and until recently we'd seen quite a lot of each other. Then she went and took up a new hobby, and became totally obsessed with it.

I waved the bottle at her and she pushed her way over.

I knew she wouldn't drink; she didn't when she was training. And of course, she was training all the time. She was into body building. By the week, she was turning what was once quite a respectable body, not one you'd give a second thought to, really, into a perambulating anatomy lesson. Each set of muscles was so well defined as to be grotesque.

To think it was all my fault because I'd nagged her into going to an aerobics session with me.

She started to fillet out the remaining

66

slices of cucumber.

'Where's George?' I asked.

'Isn't he here?'

'No,' I said flatly.

'Said he was coming. Said, "see you in a bitter". You know, his usual memorable quip.'

So they'd had another row.

'Perhaps it was his domino,' said Aberlene. 'Right in the middle of the Brahms B flat instead of B natural. Damn it, you'd think he could play it in his sleep. Not like George.'

'So why isn't he here, drowning his sorrows?'

'He said it was his reed,' said Jools. Then she added something I didn't catch, because some uncouth person had decided to liberate some musically illiterate pop group from the decent silence of the jukebox.

Luigi stopped pouring in mid-glass. 'Time!' he yelled.

I joined the little group fumbling with change to telephone for taxis. Jools had already slipped out when I returned.

And where was George?

Chapter Five

I left an irate message on his answering machine, of course, and retired to the bath with *Persuasion*. Half an hour of Jane Austen is an excellent way of cleansing a week of William Murdock from the system. On the other hand, I was glad I hadn't a Captain Wentworth lurking in my past. At the moment I didn't want another relationship—I'd only just got rid of the rabbit hairs from my most recent partner's house-trained angora. Kenji had got so sick of my nightly marking sessions he'd gone back to Japan to research the dietary habits of sumo wrestlers. In any case, even Anne Elliot would have regarded me as well past my sell-by date—wasn't thirty-four middle aged in those days?

When George didn't phone back, I left another message. And another.

I was sparking with anger by the time I got to the Music Centre. The bastard still hadn't called me, and trying to phone him had left me too little time to get a bus without running, and I'd celebrated the arrival of the 103 with an asthma attack. I don't get many these days, and they respond to a quick puff from a Ventolin spray, but I'd rather not have them anyway. And I blamed George for this one.

But I soon got caught up in the general buzz of anticipation. No one had bothered to tell us how to get into the choir area behind the orchestra, and the air spluttered with references to the British Empire and its spirit of exploration. Even the orchestral players weren't as insouciant as they pretended—although they'd taken their places on the platform briskly enough, they were spending more time looking round at their new home than tuning up. If Stobbard Mayou, the previous night's conductor, had inveigled a good performance, he must be worth his salt. Mayou was an American, brought in to replace the resident conductor, currently flat on his back with what the *Guardian* had described as an athletic performance of Beethoven's Seventh.

The omens were good. There was an immediate silence as Mayou strode on to the platform. Several of the string players went so far as to rattle their bows against their music stands—a sure sign of approval, which has to be earned. There was a frisson among some of the women in the choir: Mayou was a very handsome young man. Not that I was going to get a close look at this Chippendale look-alike—back-row sopranos are quite a distance from the centre of power.

But his smile sizzled even me.

Some conductors get straight into the music; others prefer a more sociable approach. It seemed Mayou might be one of these. He settled himself on a high stool on the podium. 'Good morning, ladies and gentlemen. And ladies and gentlemen of the choir. May I say how honoured I was to be asked to assist you while Maestro Rollinson is—what d'you call it over here?—indisposed. Yeah, well, I guess I'd call it sick. I've already met some of you—in the women's chorus—in the States, of course, when we did *The Planets* together. And of course, the orchestra and I got acquainted again last week. And yesterday.' He paused to smile at Aberlene and the other front-desk players. It must have been a good gig last night. 'Now, to work. I believe Maestro Rollinson is unlikely to be available for the Royal Concert, and I guess we all want to make it a right royal occasion. Let's start, then.'

So far, so good. He had the entire choir ready to eat out of his hand. Aberlene was ready to start. But the perfect Music Centre acoustics let us in on a little exchange between two of the heavy brass.

'How long does it take to get over a sodding bad back?'

'Hope to God it's not very long.'

Aberlene's head jerked up; orchestral bad manners put her in an awkward spot.

But Mayou merely raised an ironic eyebrow and picked up his baton. I suspected, however, he might not be generous if they dropped any dominoes.

Someone had chosen *Carmina Burana* for the royal delectation. Quite what they'd make of its vulgar earthiness I didn't know; but they'd like the tunes, anyway. And here we were, about to start the opening number, 'O Fortuna'. Lovely.

Mayou picked up his baton and raised his arms. Then he put them down again.

'Why, if I might make so bold, do we have no principal bassoon?'

I hadn't even noticed George wasn't there. My God, where could he be?

If the orchestra had any idea, no one was letting on, any more than my students would have snitched on a colleague for playing hooky.

'Traffic's very bad today.'

'Nowhere to park.'

But the principal horn forgot the rules. 'No, he's here somewhere. His bassoon case was on the bench next to mine.'

'He'll be on the bog,' said Bass Trombone.

'Must have bloody diarrhoea, then.'

'Fags: he could have slipped out to buy some fags.'

Everyone knew this was a joke. If you could buy personal fire extinguishers, George would have had one. And used it.

Stobbard Mayou did not find it amusing.

He swung off the stool and stalked off the stage. He rather spoiled the effect by stopping to pick up the collection of paper tissues that had fallen from his lap.

I'd seen conductors have screaming, yelling tantrums before, but never one make a theatrical exit. Like everyone else, I suppose, I felt uneasy, embarrassed.

And I was worried about George.

'Well,' said the woman sitting next to me, a dentist when she's not singing, called Mo. 'How irresponsible!'

I wouldn't have put it as strongly as that.

'Fancy missing such an important rehearsal!' she continued. 'I hope they can fine him, or something.'

I bit my lip.

'Mayou's so attractive, isn't he? He must have had a wonderful orthodontist.'

I nodded.

'When you think about it,' she pursued,

'there aren't many attractive classical musicians about.'

I considered. Apart from the thinking woman's Mick Jagger, Peter Cropper of the Lindsay Quartet, music doesn't seem to generate sexy men.

'How about Michael Tilson Thomas?' I said at last. I ought to make some effort.

'Yes! And he's got exactly the same smile. So warm, so friendly.'

So absent from the auditorium.

Meanwhile there was activity on the platform. After a whispered consultation with her desk partner, a wizened gnome of a man old enough to be her grandfather, Aberlene had slipped off the platform too. We all knew what she'd be trying to do—to smooth the ruffled Mayou ego. Backstage Tony Rossiter, the orchestral manager, would be tapping away at his portable phone trying to raise a substitute. You can't keep two hundred and fifty assorted musicians and singers waiting. Not to mention Stobbard Mayou.

Aberlene strode back: we could take a fifteen-minute break.

'So where do we get coffee?' Mo demanded.

'No idea. But you can share my flask.'

'Thanks. But first I'd better find the ladies'.'

Perhaps some coffee would make me

feel better, even if it was too strong after an hour in the flask. I sipped it, looking round. No sign of Mo. And then I too went in search of a loo.

Some of the complex still relied on scaffolding. Outsize yellow Sellotape held down cables thicker than your thumb. Orange twine secured doors. For no apparent reason, orange plastic netting enclosed areas of marble floor.

It didn't take long to discover a sin of omission in this cultural heaven: lavatories. Those set aside for the women in the orchestra might just have been sufficient. But they certainly couldn't cater for the additional forces of the choir. So, rather than queue dismally, several braver souls set off through the unknown corridors.

Despite the soundproofing and the buzz of conversation, we all heard the scream.

It felt like half a minute before anyone moved. Then everyone did.

I had not been teaching ten years for nothing: everyone miraculously gave way to what sounded like the voice of authority.

I found Mo crouching on the landing by the Grand Circle—roughly halfway up the building. She was gibbering with hysteria, pointing wildly.

'The doors to the loo?' I prompted.

She nodded, then shook her head frantically. I approached with caution.

Mo must be the sort of person who peers round doors before going through them. It's fortunate for her she is: behind the door marked LADIES CLOAKROOM there was nothing but a forty-foot drop to the floor of the auditorium.

It was almost an anticlimax to have to return to our seats. But by now Aberlene would have soothed Mayou back into working order, and there was nothing anyone could do except register loud complaints. My niggling worry about George developed into a painful ache. I tried to tell myself that there was no reason for him to have gone wandering round in search of nonexistent loos. But I thought of Mo, now being taxied home at the MSO's expense, and felt sick with fear.

It was Tony Rossiter, not Mayou, who came on to the expectant stage. His smile tried to convey both distress at what had happened and confidence that all was now well.

'I do assure you that Ms Morgan is now absolutely fine, and that on Monday I'll complain,' he was saying, 'to the Building Inspectorate, the Health and Safety Executive and, of course, to the contractors in charge of the site. I did warn you—yes, I did specifically ask you all not to stray off limits,' he added. 'We

75

must all use our common sense. Please. Oh, and I've found—'

George. Please let him have found George.

'—a bassoon player. He was heading for Manchester for a gig. He'll be here as soon as he's escaped from the roadworks on the M6. Shame about the Halle.'

'Surely he can't just do that? Just cut a contract like that? This is only a rehearsal, after all. Jools could have taken over, just for now?'

Tony hesitated. We were standing side by side in the covered piazza outside the auditorium, watching the up escalator chugging smoothly downwards. So, as it happens, was the down one.

'Don't worry: he'll be up in Manchester in time for the concert.'

'With no rehearsal,' I expostulated.

'It used to be like that all the time. And Mayou's important. It was quite a coup getting him for so much of the season at such short notice. Don't want to lose him.'

Tony's coup, of course. A rising managerial star, our Tony. A far cry now from the Black Country council estate where we'd both been reared. We'd been friends on and off for thirty years, from our first weepy days at infants' school together.

We'd always competed for prizes—I guess we used to score about even, but in recent years he'd far outstripped me. Sometimes I minded more than others, especially when he paraded his trappings—the cell phone, the yearly new car, the new flat, the superb holidays. Mostly when he used the sort of tone he'd used to dismiss the claims of the Halle.

'Tony, is there any news of George?' Management Tony might even have heard bad news but suppressed it to prevent another Mayou exit.

'You're not worried about him, are you? He's always rambling off when we go on tour. Talking to people. Phoning you. Damn it, when we were in Sheffield, we found him at the Crucible, watching the bloody snooker. He'd forgotten we'd changed the concerto and needed him.'

'But I bet you found him clutching his bassoon case.'

'Yes, as a matter of fact I did.' His tone was getting offhand: I was becoming an irritant to be dismissed.

'Are you sure it was his instrument in the band room?'

'I checked when I locked it in my office. It's still got the transit stickers from the US tour.' Decidedly cool now.

'In that case, Tony,' I said, 'I'm worried. Very worried.'

Aberlene joined me for the quickest of sandwich lunches at the Duke of Clarence, and then dropped me off at home. Before I took my jacket off, I had jabbed the replay pad on the answering machine. All I got was the library telling me a book had come through.

I told myself firmly that there was simply no point in sitting by the phone like the HMV dog. The weather was fine and dry, if cold, and I should go for a run. When I got back I could reward myself with another try at George's number. I took myself the long way round the Beech Lanes estate, dodging dogs and their deposits, round Queen's Park, and back up the road. I forced myself to shower and dry my hair. Then I looked at the phone. A message.

Ian Dale's voice.

I could have been sick with disappointment.

I had to listen to it twice to take it in. And it was good news, too. Aftab had been found, safe and well. Dale would tell me all about it on Monday.

That was all.

I sat on the stairs. Now what?

In practical terms there was only one answer. Safeway's. If I didn't shop now I wouldn't eat this weekend.

I was just going to bed when I remembered Aggie's plants. It wouldn't do any harm to go round closing a few curtains, switching lights on and off. Anything to deter burglars. I suppose that was what gave me the idea. First thing tomorrow I would burgle George's house.

I did it the easy way, of course. I waited till it was light, and cycled round. I knew he kept a key somewhere in his garden. He was always afraid of coming home at one in the morning only to find he'd dropped his keys in a band room somewhere in the sticks.

I tried his rockery. I must have heaved aside every single piece. I cleared out a great deal of dead convolvulus and an incipient crop of enchanter's nightshade. But I didn't find the key. And then I sensed that I was being watched.

I turned. George's neighbour, in a bathrobe so short that at any other time I should have found him amusing, was staring at me from his front doorstep. It was simplest to tell the truth. I wanted to check that George hadn't been taken ill. He hesitated, but I persisted: we'd met, hadn't we, at George's Guy Fawkes barbecue? Hadn't he been the one letting off the rockets?

He had. But plainly he didn't remember me.

At last he produced the key, and paused to watch me. He gathered up a pile of Sunday papers from his porch, quite forgetting that in all modesty he ought to bend at the knees, and eventually grunted that I should push the key through the letter box when I'd finished.

George's house was appallingly empty. I knew as soon as I stepped into the hall. His kitchen: there was no washing-up left in the sink, nothing on the draining board—but then, there wouldn't be. His living room was equally immaculate. He'd left a couple of scores open on the piano in his music room, and a pencil had dropped on the floor. I tutted and picked it up.

There was no point in going upstairs.

I went.

The bathroom. The toothpaste squeezed from the end of the tube, not the middle. Towels hung neatly to dry.

Two spare bedrooms, one with the ironing board folded against the wall. In a wicker basket a pile of neatly folded washing waited to be pressed.

His own bedroom. The smell of George which was not quite the right smell because it was stale, not newly showered. If he'd been here, he'd have thrown open the window to air the duvet he'd pulled back.

It seemed easier to cycle round to the police station and tell them what I feared than to try and explain over the phone. I was just locking my cycle to the railing when a Cavalier pulled up beside me. The driver wound down his window, smiling pleasantly. DCI Groom—Chris.

'You've come about your body, have you?'

'No,' I said. 'Another one.'

All the time he was escorting me through the corridors to his room I was wondering why I'd made such an inane quip. From time to time, I could catch him glancing sideways at me.

We sat down on opposite sides of his tidy desk. He wrote down the facts as I gave them. He was taking me seriously.

I wonder how much he'd have told me about Aftab's return if he hadn't been filling in time while his colleagues busied themselves with the inquiries he'd set in train. He plied me with coffee while he talked—he'd just acquired a percolator, which bubbled irritatingly on the windowsill. Biscuits or cake? All this talk. Then at least the hard facts about Aftab. A PC in Bradford had found him sicking his guts up outside the Photography Museum.

I shook my head; I wanted to laugh in

disbelief, and I fancy that Groom might, in other circumstances.

'Why Bradford?'

'He's got family up there. And the museum because he'd always wanted to go. That giant cinema screen, with all those special effects. He'd stayed in so long he'd got something like travel sickness.'

'Not kidnapped?'

'Doesn't seem like it.'

'So why did his cousin—'

'We'll find out. But Iqbal's in Amsterdam at the moment.'

'Amsterdam!'

'Amsterdam. Flew out yesterday, as soon as they'd had the funeral. Oh, he cleared it with us first. Said it was essential, even with the family in mourning. And since he had an unbeatable alibi for the time, we couldn't argue.'

'Alibi?'

'In Erdington nick. He'd cheeked a constable who booked him for playing silly buggers in that XR3 of his. So we pulled him in for a couple of hours.'

'When you talk to him,' I said, 'I suppose you couldn't ask him why he told you people Aftab had been kidnapped before he even told the family.'

I went through the motions of living for the rest of the day—I ate because I knew

I ought, pushed on through my pile of marking because it had to be done. When I saw Chris Groom's Cavalier pull up outside my house at about five, I knew why he had come, even before I saw his face.

I made coffee automatically. Made my mouth open to ask the right questions.

'Where?'

'At the back of the Music Centre, Sophie. Where they're still working.'

'How?'

'A blow to the head. A scaffolding pole, probably.'

'Do I—will I have—' I made an effort: I'd known since Friday evening, after all. 'Do you need me to identify him?'

Groom shook his head.

'Then who?'

'Mr Rossiter, is it? The manager?'

Poor Tony.

'Death was instantaneous. He wouldn't have felt anything. Though why he should want to wander round a building site, in the dark, in a force-ten gale, entirely defeats me. Asking for trouble, I'm afraid.'

'But George wouldn't do anything like that. He was an orderly man. He always used to tidy my kitchen when he came here. Books, records. Couldn't stop himself putting them in order.'

He shook his head. 'The evidence we

have so far points to his having tried to take a short cut. "No Access" signs everywhere. Just ignored them. Going to meet someone, perhaps.'

'I told you. He was going to meet me.'

I thought he'd never leave. He found cake for me to eat, then the whiskey bottle. He offered to phone friends or relatives. What about a neighbour? Finally, in desperation, almost, he mentioned a counselling scheme staffed by trained police officers. But I shook my head to that, too. I didn't want anyone, not yet. I had lost someone I loved more than I'd ever loved anyone. I thought of him on that slab, peered at by Tony and gently covered. I felt guilty. It was I who should have done him that last service.

Chapter Six

When you've been at it for ten years, you can teach on a sort of automatic pilot, so my classes went as normal. One or two of my colleagues remarked how pale I looked, but attributed it to incipient flu. It wasn't until I started getting a little stream of sympathetic phone calls from people in the orchestra that someone realised there might be something wrong, and Shahida cornered me in the staff loo.

'Why on earth did you come in?' she asked.

'The students—'

'—could have taken care of themselves, for once. You're allowed time off for a bereavement, for goodness' sake.'

I shook my head.

She looked at me shrewdly. 'You'd rather be here? Company? But you'll have to mourn some time, Sophie. Have you had a good cry yet?'

I shook my head. I'd sat at the piano playing Schubert till about three when the whiskey and I had fallen asleep on the sofa. I'd woken at six, and made sense of my aching head and body with a long shower.

'Is Aftab back?' I asked, retiring to the cubicle.

'Talking to the police, I gather. They mentioned charging him with wasting police time. But I had a long talk with the nice sergeant—Mr Dale, is it?'

'And?'

'He said they were still thinking about it. The point is, they think he's hiding something, Sophie, and no one knows how to persuade him to say anything. I've tried. Nothing.' She paused.

I flushed the loo and emerged to wash

my hands. The water was cold and brown. So was the water from the cold tap. Preferring not to use the towel, I shook my hands dry and waited. I sensed there was something else she wanted to say.

'He—Mr Dale—says he wants to talk to you. He said he'd be here about six if you could wait that long.'

Six! But I had nothing to go home for, nothing but an empty house and the knowledge that George would not be phoning.

Dale met me in the foyer, full of students coming in for evening classes. Two lifts were now out of order. He passed me an expensive-looking white envelope addressed in an elegant italic script.

He turned aside to scan the noticeboard while I read the letter. If I glanced up, I could see him making the occasional note.

Groom wondered if I might want to lay a few flowers where they had found George's body. Would I care to meet him at the Music Centre? He'd already spoken to the Music Centre's security service.

I was touched. The human face of the police once again. I found myself grinning: all those preconceptions I was having to revise. And perhaps Groom was right.

Seeing the place the accident happened might help.

'I'll drop you off, shall I, Sophie?' asked Dale, appearing at my elbow. 'You know,' he continued as we left the building, 'I'd have expected the college to be making more fuss about this poor kid. A collection or something.'

I nodded. ' "Panic but emptiness",' I misquoted.

He laughed. 'Better try that on Chris. Great reader is Chris. But as it happens I know that one. Forster. One of my girls did him for A level.'

We talked about his family as he drove the two or three hundred yards to Tesco's so I could buy some flowers. White roses. Sentimental white bloody roses.

'Did you know,' I said, as I slipped back into the car, purring away on double yellow lines, 'that one of your rear lights has failed? The nearside one.'

'Blast! We're supposed to check them, you know, every time we take one from the pool. Have to get it fixed. No bike today?'

I shook my head. 'In this weather?'

'Probably best not to anyway, in the circumstances,' he said.

'Why on earth—'

'I was just thinking, Wajid's death, George's death—'

'Things happen in threes? I'm not superstitious, Ian.'

'Neither am I. I was just wondering if you might not be a bit—vulnerable, shall we say?—on a bike.'

Groom, his shoulders hunched against the rain, appeared from the shelter of the building to open the car door. He made no attempt to help me out. He was about to shut the door again when I remembered my marking, in a plastic carrier in the front foot space. He looked at it with distaste: perhaps he'd expected an executive briefcase, but briefcases aren't cyclist friendly—they're hard to clip into place and don't have enough room for sandwiches, a spare pair of shoes (I cycle in trainers) and wads of marking.

The security officer, a kid in her teens, picked over the contents.

'What about the band's instrument cases?' I asked. 'It must take ages to check all of them.' I opened my handbag obediently.

'They have passes issued by the security people,' she said. 'And come in through the Artistes' Entrance.'

'The side door, you mean?' I'd come in that way on Saturday. I didn't realise I was an Artiste.

Groom picked up the roses and tucked

them stem first into the crook of his arm, letting them hang like a rifle. 'This way.'

We passed through the central plaza. Two men were still working on its centrepiece, a futuristic fountain involving, according to the press, a system of balances and valves which would form the visible mechanism of a huge water clock. Obviously they wouldn't want a huge, ticking affair so close to the concert arena. But I suspected that somewhere hidden away was a neat little electronic chip that really ran it. A haze of dust covered everything: you couldn't imagine it being clean enough for the Visit. One of the men started a power drill; without speaking, we speeded up, heading for the far doors.

I could feel the silence as they closed behind us.

'You've been here before?' asked Groom.

'That's right. We did a joint rehearsal, the choir and the MSO. The band room is down there, and the changing rooms and loos. Typical, isn't it, that they didn't provide enough: goodness knows what'll happen when everyone has to get through in a concert interval.'

'Enough what? Sorry.'

'Enough women's lavatories.' I meant to embark on some heavy joke, but stopped short. Suddenly a door slammed.

It shouldn't have alarmed me. There were people working all over the site, after all. But Chris had tensed as well. Then came another noise, more homely, infinitely less menacing. A sneeze.

The tension dropped swiftly: we started to laugh.

'That's probably Stobbard Mayou,' I said. 'The conductor. He suffers from chronic hay fever, they say. And dust is likely to make it worse.'

As if on cue, Mayou appeared from the shadows of the far corridor, slinging an enormous sports bag, the sort favoured by our students, over his right shoulder. He was wearing a blouson jacket and snug-fitting jeans. Chris Groom's eye fixed on what he carried in his left hand. I suspected he would dislike on sight what was indisputably a handbag.

I was right.

'Chief Inspector Groom, West Midlands CID,' he said formally, flicking out his ID.

Mayou shifted his sports bag to the other shoulder and put out an easy hand. 'Good evening, Chief Inspector.'

Even during the stress of Saturday's rehearsal, I'd liked his smile, and now I realised how pleasant his voice was—a very warm baritone. Beneath his blond, curly hair his face glowed with clean-shaven health under an unobtrusive tan. His eyes, cold and dominating during the altercation on the platform, were now merely alert and interested and very blue. Obviously all that arm-waving did great things for the pectorals. And he had the most beautiful hands—long-fingered and elegantly boned.

I thought Groom's handshake looked a bit perfunctory.

'Any problems, Chief Inspector?'

'None. But I'm surprised to see you here, sir. I understood the building would be empty.'

'Far from it, alas. It sounds like they're pile-driving out there. And I'm told some of the guys will be working all night, they're so behind schedule. Tell me,' said Mayou, turning his immaculate smile on me, 'don't I...haven't I—?'

'Yes. Sophie Rivers. The back row of the sopranos.'

'Sophie,' he repeated slowly. 'Sophie Rivers. Funny thing, names, they're a closed book to me. But faces—they're all here.' He touched his forehead. 'Particularly pretty ones—Sophie.'

A short silence. I could hardly respond to that sort of line. And both men were waiting for the other to leave. A matter of not losing face.

I relieved Groom of the roses. 'I've come to lay these on the spot where George died,' I said. 'The bassoonist.'

'Ah yes,' said Mayou. 'A real tragic loss. I admired and respected that man.'

'It was mutual,' I said, smiling, but suddenly shy.

'I expect you'll be wanting to go on your way, Mr Mayou,' said Groom suddenly. Although, like Mayou's, his voice was warm and pleasant, with no hint of a Brummie whine, he could also pitch it two or three notes higher and make it very cold.

I expected Mayou to bridle, but he didn't. He smiled equally on us both, showing just enough of his teeth. 'Sure. I guess it's a kind of private occasion. Tell me, how did he come to have this accident?' He swung his sports bag on to the other shoulder. He intended to stay, whatever he said.

'That's still under investigation.'

'But surely not by the police? Tony Rossiter said it was a matter for—what did he call it now?—those safety people?'

'The Health and Safety Executive. I'm just here to accompany Sophie,' he added, his voice dropping rather too possessively on the last two syllables.

'Ah,' said Mayou, altogether too mean-ingfully. 'See you around then—Sophie. Inspector.'

We watched him walk towards the

automatic doors. When he rehearsed us, he wore an enormous sloppy T-shirt, so this was the first time I could observe the perfection of his buttocks. Halfway down the corridor he turned, and gave us a deprecating wave—you could imagine him using the same gesture to raise audiences to even greater levels of rapturous applause.

I can only describe the noise Groom made as 'Tcha'.

'You don't like musicians then?' I prompted him as we followed the corridor through another set of automatic doors.

'We are into generalisations, aren't we?'

'Sorry. But you don't like Mayou?'

'No.' There was the slightest pause. 'Do you?'

'George did. And George was the best judge of character I ever knew.'

Groom said nothing, but turned abruptly towards another security desk. This time he had to sign us in, and a sad-faced Irishman handed over a couple of hard hats. He nodded at the flowers. 'Nice gesture, like. I like a nice rose myself.'

I touched the tip of one of the roses. I wished they smelt. But roses like that never seem to.

Why George should ever have ventured out there simply defeated me. All the things he loathed most were there: diesel fumes, arc lamps, brutal machinery ('Plant!' he would exclaim. 'Haven't they ever seen a plant?'). Labourers were still busy, their voices overloud across the occasional sudden silence.

I put the roses down quickly and turned back into the building. There was no sense of George in all that mud.

Chapter Seven

Tuesday passed. That is the best I can say about it. I got home weary after my evening class to find on the doorstep a spray of flowers and a note from Aberlene. Inside on the mat, with several bills, lay a note from Aggie, who now had the flu herself. Had I remembered the binmen and her plants? I did the weekend's curtains and lights routine again. Then I forced myself to eat—I do a truly reprehensible cheese on toast, oozing with Worcester sauce and raw garlic—and reached for the day's *Guardian*. The education section. And a possible job in Huddersfield! A promotion. A nice part of the world to live. The Choral Society and infinite numbers of *Messiahs!* George used to regale us with the story of the violinist who dreamt he was playing *Messiah* in Yorkshire and woke up to find he was.

There was a phone number, so I used it, and started to draft my CV.

I have taught students, every year for the last ten, how to draw up a CV. We discuss what's relevant and what order to put it in. I remind them always to keep a copy, preferably on disk, so they can constantly update it. Obvious. Easy.

Except I'd not applied for a job for some time, and didn't have a disk to my name. That would be a question I could ask at interview, if I got that far. Would they allow me IT training? I wrote it down. And then started messing with CV headings.

The front doorbell rang.

Crazy: my hair stood on end. And I could hardly walk.

Whoever it was rang again.

I forced myself to the window, to peer through a gap in the curtains. I couldn't see much—although I'd got one of those intruder lights, I kept it switched off because our local foxes activated it all night long. So all I could make out was a dark, bulky shape. Perhaps the car would give me a clue. No car except my neighbours' collection.

The movement of the curtains must have given me away, because the figure stepped back, looking round.

And then I laughed. No one to be afraid of. Jools.

As I let her in, I gabbled with embarrassment and relief.

We hugged, but without enthusiasm, it seemed to me, on her side. It was patently a duty call. I'd have felt awkward myself, trying to console someone for the loss of a person I hadn't liked. They'd had to get on when they worked together—there's no room for prima-donna-ism in an orchestra. And George spent a great deal of time helping her with her technique—she'd never quite lived up to the promise she'd shown at her audition and at her subsequent trial. Not that he ever complained about her, because he was sensitive to my loyalties: Jools might not be a close friend but she was an old one.

Without saying anything she pushed a couple of tapes at me. *The Firebird,* with a particularly lovely solo from George, and a couple of Haydn symphonies. I was very touched.

She accepted my offer of coffee but was scathing when I produced my last drop of the summer's duty-free brandy.

'I don't drink, remember. Not when I'm training.'

'But there's only an eyeful—'

She pushed the bottle away. Her sleeve caught in the glass, sending it spinning across the table. I caught it.

'I'm taking this seriously. So no alcohol. And you'd be a lot fitter if you cut down.'

This was not the conversation I'd expected. And I resented any suggestion that I wasn't fit. I cycled everywhere, jogged regularly, and when I was bored—which I suppose was not all that often, really—I worked out with weights at a fitness centre.

'Jools, please—'

'Tea. Coffee. All that tannin and caffeine,' she continued. 'Look at your teeth.'

'What have my teeth got to do with George's death? Or even, to stretch a point, the murder of Wajid? Because those are the only things I can spare time to worry about at the moment.'

'Worry about? But they were accidents. At least George's was. And the kid died in a family feud, they say. You keep out.'

' "They"?' My turn for an ironic repetition.

'Everyone. The papers.'

'Since when have the papers been interested in the truth?' I admit to having a problem with the British press. But I refused to get on my soapbox. I merely smiled, grimly.

It's difficult to describe Jools's movement

as a flounce, but no other word comes near. It took her from the table to the chair where she'd slung her jacket. I could smell the leather, it was so new. She shrugged herself into it: 'I might as well go. I only came because I thought you'd be upset.'

'I am. Aren't you?'

'Of course. I mean, I never liked him the way you did. I always thought he was a bit of a bore. Always had his nose in other people's business. Those stupid jokes. All that fuss about making his own reeds.'

Expecting George to buy ready-scraped reeds would have been like expecting me to buy TV dinners.

'And he used to rabbit on about the government. All the time.'

Our views were very similar.

'And another thing—'

'He was my friend, Jools.'

She looked at me, an expression on her face I couldn't identify. Anger? Grief? I couldn't be sure.

'I'm sorry. You know, I'm really miserable. Don't know why. Like PMT, only it isn't.'

Any other time I'd have given her a quick hug, but tonight she'd hurt me too much.

'You're sure it isn't that weird diet of yours?' I asked eventually.

'Nothing weird about it. All the supplements are pure and natural. You just have this bee in your bonnet. I've had enough. I'm going home.'

I stood up politely, suppressing an almost overwhelming desire to throw her out physically. Not that I could have done, anyway. Not the new-look Jools. 'We'll meet up another night, shall we? When we're both feeling a bit better?' I suggested.

'If you like. But I dare say I'll be pretty busy. They'll be wanting me to sit up.'

'Sitting up' has nothing to do with posture. It means moving up in the pecking order. And I didn't think they would want her to do anything of the sort.

Accidental death, my arse.

I'd managed to wangle some time off on Wednesday morning to go to the coroner's court for the inquest on George. Some time, no doubt, I'd have to give evidence in the Wajid affair, but there'd been a perfunctory adjournment since the cause of death was so palpably unnatural.

If I was fizzing with a volatile mixture of anger and pain, Tony Rossiter's face showed scarcely disguised relief. There are times when I wonder if being a manager ought to carry a government health warning, it does so much harm to your moral judgement. He'd phrased his replies so carefully that the impression of George the coroner must have got was of a man on the verge of senile dementia. I didn't wish to speak to him and rapidly put as much space between us as I could.

I was staring into the street, seeing nothing, when I smelt an aftershave approaching.

'Sophie?'

'Mr Mayou?'

'Stobbard. I was thinking all this might be a bit upsetting for you.' He leaned forward, his head slightly to one side.

I smiled, grateful for the sympathy in his voice. Before I could speak, however, another aftershave arrived.

'I'd like to talk to you, Ms Rivers, if you've a moment,' came Chris's voice.

I assumed from his tone he meant officially. Stobbard Mayou lifted an ironic eyebrow. 'Ms Rivers?' he repeated, sotto voce.

As Chris shouldered forwards, Stobbard took my hand lightly between his, and brushed a kiss on to it. Then he backed away and was gone.

There didn't seem to be any special reason for Groom's interruption. He made a few bland comments, and then, almost as an afterthought, asked me if I fancied a sandwich. Which is how we came to be sitting in a miserably loud wine bar, drinking an exceedingly quiet mineral water apiece. Chris was officially on duty, after all, and I had to battle later with a stroppy group of GCSE repeats. Aftab's group, as it happened.

We had started to bicker.

'Of course we make mistakes. Very highly publicised mistakes they are, too. But we get it right most of the time.'

'So I should bloody hope. But you haven't got it right this time.'

'So you're suggesting someone lured this absent-minded old geezer out into the mud and whacked him?'

'Take out those derogatory adjectives and yes, you have it to a T.'

William Murdock has the sort of minimalist sartorial philosophy that means if you turn up in a suit people will ask how you got on in your interview. So I preferred to dash home to change before I tackled the GCSE group.

I was just putting the key into my front door when a car sighed to a halt. Another status symbol for my neighbour, no doubt. Should I even bother to look round? They'd expect me to admire the bloody thing and I wasn't in the mood for giving fulsome praise.

'Sophie?'

The big Renault wasn't a new toy for the neighbours, then. It was a new toy for Tony Rossiter. He smiled, perhaps a little shamefaced.

'OK, so you wanted to show off to someone,' I said. Then I grinned. 'Tell me all about it.'

He opened his mouth, then closed it. We both understood that all those years behind us made apology difficult but forgiveness essential. And in a way, showing me this car—only 459 miles on the clock!—was his apology.

The car sat sleek and opulent among the beat-up Fiestas and Allegros (most of them *non troppo* by now), and asked to be stroked or vandalised, depending on your persuasion.

'Five-speed gearbox—'

'So I should hope,' I said seriously.

He looked at me sideways. 'And air conditioning—'

'For this climate!'

'Well...' He looked sheepish. Perhaps I should give up baiting him and try to be simply nice. He joggled his keys at me. 'Try it?'

I knew better than to think he meant me to drive it. What he wanted me to do was savour the leather upholstery.

A couple of neighbouring curtains twitched. Him in his executive suit, me in my serious-occasions one. A posh car. The man waving phallic symbols around. I felt as if I'd stepped into a TV advertisement. At least I could do something about my clothes.

'Give me two minutes to change and you can run me in to college if you like.'

'Want to see what'll be pulling you?'

Another man, another relationship, I might have suspected him of an awful pun. But the bonnet was already up. The engine was very clean. I peered at the front wheels.

'They'll have those off in two minutes. They used to collect mine.'

'Ah, but yours were only wheel trims. These are integral. Alloy wheels,' he said clearly, as if to a child.

'You're sure you won't wake up one day to find the whole thing sitting on little piles of bricks?'

'I should hear them at it. A very efficient theft alarm—shall I—'

I shook my head. Almost as an afterthought, he went back and opened the boot. I thought for an unworthy moment that he merely wanted to show off a bit more, but no: as he straightened I saw in his right hand an instrument case.

'Tony, that's George's.'

'Of course it is.' He pressed a finger to the side of his nose. 'Look, I shouldn't be doing this, and I really don't know why I am. But it seemed to me—well, he'd have wanted you to have it.' Seeing I couldn't speak, he looked away. 'He's left it to you anyway. I witnessed his will. Go on. No one'll know. I'll tell the executors when they get round to asking.'

'Bless you, you're crazy. You know you're taking a big risk.'

But I took it from him anyway and carried it gently into the house.

Which is how, six hours after we'd made it quite clear that we despised each other, I came to invite Chris Groom into my bedroom.

But not, of course, until after my GCSE class. And Aftab was there, back in his usual place, looking tired and subdued, but ready to hand in work none of the others had even got round to starting. He lingered when the others had surged out. At first we talked about a short story he'd produced for his folder. But I knew there was something else he wanted to say.

At last I asked mildly, 'You had to miss the funeral?'

He nodded miserably.

'You want to talk about it, Aftab?'

He shook his head. 'There's others involved, see, miss. But I've been thinking. About Wajid. All that money.'

'Money? I thought he was as hard up as the rest of you.'

'All that time I was with the police, I was trying to think who might have wanted to hurt him. He was a bit flash, miss, but he didn't have any enemies. He didn't make a great fuss about his religion, but he was a really good Muslim. No problems about him trying to date a Hindu or a Sikh.'

'So what do you think?' I prompted.

'Miss, it's got to be his money. Did you ever see that watch of his? That Rolex?'

'Surely—' I echoed the police line—'that was just a junk copy?'

'That's what his mother would have thought, if she ever noticed it. And his jeans.'

'Is there a student in the college who doesn't wear jeans?'

'Not designer jeans, they don't. And I reckon his were real, not some copy from down the rag market. I know he applied for a grant and everything when his dad snuffed it, but that was because Shahida said he should. He couldn't tell her he was flush, could he?'

'How flush?'

He shrugged expressively. 'I shall miss my bus, miss, and I promised our dad I'd give him a hand stocktaking. He's opening a new branch down Smethwick, really big, and we shall have a film-processing and a photocopying franchise. Tell you what, I'll do copies of all your handouts when your college photocopy card runs out.'

'I'll take you up on that,' I said, wondering how much of this he intended me to pass on to the police.

After supper I phoned Chris and told him curtly that there was something he ought to see, and that Aftab had let drop an interesting idea. He was hammering at my door within five minutes. I made him wait until I'd put the kettle on and drawn a few curtains before I said anything useful. Then I told him about Aftab. He sighed rather extravagantly as he took my last biscuit. 'For goodness' sake, Sophie, you shouldn't do that sort of thing. It's police work. Work for professionals. If you start talking to dangerous people you could be exposing yourself to great danger. Or you could be clogging up the works for us.' He started on the biscuit. 'What did you get out of him, anyway?' He had the grace to look sheepish.

At last he closed his notebook very delicately, as if he did not want to interrupt his own thoughts. I waited.

'I'll check out the watch,' he said. 'I should have done earlier. And the jeans, of course. But there was no sign of money in his home. We did search, very discreetly, before you ask. Nowhere much to hide anything, of course. Jesus, imagine fitting eight kids in there!'

'I gather the father didn't make much before he died?'

'Apparently back home he was in the force. A sergeant. And when he came here he had to take a job in a foundry. A labourer. Poor bastard. I wonder what he'd have thought about his son being knifed. I gather you took some flowers to the mother? Nice woman, I thought.'

We smiled at each other. Any moment he could become Chris again.

'So where did Wajid keep all his money, then,' I prompted him, 'if not in a sock under the bed?'

'He had a TSB account—'

'Ah!'

'—with twenty-five pounds forty-seven pence in it.'

'My God, don't tell me he had an offshore account!'

'That may not be a joke, Sophie.'

So he did indeed progress from Groom to Chris, but it wasn't this increased intimacy that led me to invite him into my bedroom. I wanted to show him George's bassoon case, and the bassoon case was on the bed. Unfortunately this was one room where Kenji had insisted on particularly low levels of lighting, and I hadn't yet got round to reinstating hundred-watt bulbs.

'I wore rubber gloves,' I said, perhaps a little defensively. 'Best yellow. The sort I wash up in. But I daresay they did, too. If not yellow.'

'They?'

'Whoever did this to it.' I opened the case.

'Did what?'

I pointed. 'Tore out all the padding. See, this plush-covered stuff should be glued to the wood, to make a nice secure nest for the instrument.' I went to remove the sections of bassoon, but he put out a quick hand.

'Better not. Just in case.' His voice became quite brisk again. 'Why bring it up here anyway?'

'The bedspread, Chris.'

'The bedspread?'

'Exactly. My last partner didn't like duvets any more than he liked adequate lighting, so I'm probably the last person in Harborne to own such an outmoded item. And I put the case on it.'

At last he smiled, and scooped all the corners to the middle, so the case was completely wrapped. 'And I'll bet you even have a bin liner handy so I can take it off to Forensic.'

I'd soon scotch that note of patronage. ' "Forensic" means "of the forum"—or in this case "of the court". It's bad enough when the BBC talk about forensic experts. Forensic experts are—'

'OK, OK. I will take it to the Forensic Science Laboratory. But tell me, Sophie, what are you expecting them to find? Drugs?'

The thought of George being involved with anything like that!

'No,' I said. 'Mud.'

Chapter Eight

There are some days you know it would be much simpler to leave teaching altogether and become a Trappist monk. Or nun. Thursday was one such.

The trouble is that teachers are used to taking responsibility—like doctors and police officers, I suppose. And when you see a situation that obviously warrants some interference, the instinct is to get in there and interfere.

At first, when I saw a bunch of students milling round a flash car in what is supposed to be the staff car park, I assumed that someone had had a wonderful eighteenth birthday present and was showing it off. Shades of Tony.

But I hadn't screamed when Tony had invited me in, and someone was now screaming. From the corner of my eye I could see Winston drifting out of the foyer—something he's not supposed to do—and nibbling the aerial on his radio. I'm not required to stay put anywhere, so I moved nearer. The screams had subsided but there was a great deal of pushing and shoving. It would be sensible to see who was at the centre of it all.

I caught Winston's eye and waved to him. He waved back. This time he seemed to be speaking into his radio. OK, I would move in. Not security, not a police officer. Just an unaccompanied woman. No one should feel threatened by that. Except perhaps the lone woman herself, surrounded by big, strapping lads. These were Sikhs, not Muslims. Many of the girls wore more gold than I possessed. Perhaps I'd been wrong—it was just a very expensive present, a brand-new Toyota to be precise, and a daytime party was proposed for later. Most of our kids aren't allowed to evening do's so they hold dayers. Their term. But if they were all getting into party mood, why should Manjit be in tears, and why should there be a big, handshaped red patch across the side of her face? And why should a young man have her in what seemed to be a painful grip and be forcing her down into the passenger seat? She started to scream again. I pushed my way through to her. Someone shouted. The young man let her go with a final thrust. He ran round to the driver's side and tried to start the engine. Another youth tried to shut the passenger door. But I got there first.

I suppose I expected Manjit to reach out to me with relief. Instead her eyes and mouth became O's of horror.

'What's going on?'

'Family business,' said the youth by the door.

'Yes? Nice family.' I pointed to Manjit's face. 'Who did this?'

'Told you. Family business. So why don't you piss off out of it?'

By now, Winston was by the driver's door. I could see why the young man hadn't tried to gun the engine again. Winston's right hand, blessedly huge and impregnable, held the ignition keys.

'You tell the lady, nice and polite now, what she wants to know,' he said.

'Manjit?' I prompted.

She looked at me with despair, and with a loathing that hurt me like a blow in the face. 'Just do as he says, can't you? Just piss off. Just fucking well piss off.'

I straightened, but still kept the door open. 'I will go away, if that is what you want me to do,' I said, very formal in my anger. 'But before you come to any more classes, you will report to me and make a proper apology. And you—' I bent back into the car to speak to the driver—'you will ensure that Manjit isn't hit again. My colleague over there has your registration number. The police can easily trace you. And if Manjit doesn't come into college tomorrow, I shall assume it's because someone has further assaulted her and I shall put the matter in the hands of the authorities. Do you both understand?'

'Just fuck off out of it,' said the driver. 'And give me my sodding keys.'

I glared quickly at Winston, who clearly had no intention of returning them but wanted to protect me again.

'Mr Rhodes will return your keys when you and Manjit show me that you understand what I've said. You'll be in my office at nine tomorrow, Manjit, and if you have any further injuries I shall call the police. And if you're not there I shall call the police.'

'That's blackmail,' said the youth at my side.

'Quite. So you'd rather Mr Rhodes called the police now?'

'OK, miss, OK. Now just fuck off, will you?'

There seemed nothing more I could do

112

without losing my dignity or escalating it further. I looked at Winston. He nodded minutely, and tossed the keys back into the driver's lap. Painfully, I hoped.

We stood side by side to watch them drive away. The others seemed in no hurry to disperse.

'OK. Fun over. Time you were all in class,' I said.

One girl turned back to me as they drifted towards the entrance. 'You shouldn't have done that, miss. Not interfere with the family.'

'Nor you shouldn't,' said Winston, as we followed them. 'Took a bit of a risk there, man.'

'And you.'

He grinned. 'All the same, some of that lot are in the Posse. Not very nice people, Sophie. Are you going to tell the police?'

'I'll talk to Manjit first. I did sort of promise.'

'Well, I didn't. Next time I see young Rob Williams, I'll have a word.'

'Williams?'

'Community cop. He pops in for a bit of a natter when he passes. Keeps his ear to the ground. OK guy, considering he's Old Bill.'

'What about the rest of them? Groom and Dale?'

'No more grief from them, man. I s'all

set my mum on them if they start hassling me again. Ol' Philomena, she tell 'em what for.'

'You treat your mother right, Winston.'

'Wouldn't dare do anything else, man.'

We grinned at each other, and then—he'd never done it before, always remembering that I had been his English teacher and he my student—then he put up his hand to give me a comradely five.

'I was watching from my window, of course,' said Richard, more drawn than ever after his flu. 'But I reckoned you could handle most things and Winston could have done some damage.'

'And unless you'd put your underpants on over your trousers you could scarcely have flown down to my rescue,' I agreed, earning a tired chuckle.

Richard is my boss: line manager, I suppose I ought to call him. King of A Level and GCSE Studies. ('Why the "Studies"?' I'd once asked him. 'Because the Chief says so,' was his reply. And we all obeyed the Chief. Even me. Up to a point.) He's a decent man, who sought promotion because he was the obvious man for the job and then, when it was too late, found he'd always liked teaching. He's banking on premature retirement and the end of the recession so he can retire to a country town and open a bookshop.

'I'm sorry I was away for all the panics last week. Are you coping all right? The body, the kidnap? And now this?'

I nodded.

'You're OK coming into college? Don't need to take any time off?'

'And how would you cover my classes?'

I knew the answer to that. He'd teach them himself if he had to. He flapped a hand, acknowledging the hit.

'But the death of your friend—how did the inquest go yesterday, by the way?'

'It looks as if it may have to be reopened,' I said.

'You'd be better if you had a good cry, you know. I know there's no privacy up there. Just come and turf me out of here if ever you want to. Need to.'

I smiled at him. Even bosses could sometimes surprise me. 'Thanks. Now, about these changes to my timetable...'

I staggered back up from Richard's eighth-floor office to find two notes on my desk: one announced that my lunch break had been appropriated by the head of English who wanted a meeting to discuss standardisation procedures for marking GCSE coursework; the other, in a sealed white envelope, a request from Chris Groom to call him—he wanted me to help the police with their inquiries. Since the term was in inverted commas and was followed by an exclamation mark, I assumed he was referring to my complaints about the misuse of the word 'forensic'. When I phoned, he was out, but he'd left a message asking me to meet him at the Music Centre at seven that evening. How he'd managed to whistle up tickets, I'd no idea. All concerts were sold out for the next six months. The Royal Concert was to be an invitation only affair: it was a good job I'd get in as one of the choir.

'Is this what you call undercover work?' I asked when we met by the box office. My glance appreciated another well-cut suit, with more blue in the fabric, this time.

He glared.

It was not because I was wearing jeans. I too can dress up, even if not quite to the standard of the other concert-goers who'd decided to celebrate the removal of the MSO to its permanent new home with a fashion parade of shoulder pads and glitz that made me feel dowdy. Nor was it because I was late. He'd been at fault there, hurtling in just as a disembodied voice was making a final call. I'd passed the time getting outside an extravagant ice cream purchased at disproportionate expense from a man with a cute little machine, more fitted, with its wheels and parasol, to the front at Brighton than to the central plaza of a major concert hall.

He waited till we were moving towards the auditorium before he put his ear surprisingly close to mine, and muttered, 'Yes, as a matter of fact, it is. Undercover work.' He grinned, irresponsibly. 'I just wanted to get the feel of the place, as it were.'

Oh, God, perhaps he had misinterpreted the bedroom business last night. And I'd been chatty with relief that I had at last found something to challenge the verdict on George's death: perhaps he'd thought I was flirting. I'd have to watch out.

Mayou had taken over Peter Rollinson's programmes with hardly any changes. But tonight we'd started with a brisk performance of the overture to *Ruslan and Ludmilla,* which he'd chosen in preference to Webern's *Five Pieces* for orchestra. Purists had tutted—but I thought it fitted better with the piano concerto, which happened to be Rachmaninov's Second. It was an extremely lush account.

'My God,' said Chris, as soon as the applause had died down and we were fighting our way to the bar, 'what was Mayou doing to his body? I thought he was going to have an orgasm right there on stage.'

I laughed, of course; but I felt vaguely uneasy.

No one seemed to be lingering over their drinks, not just because there were no seats in the bar but because there was so much to see and explore. In the summer there would be even more. The Centre had been built alongside a canal basin which was in the process of being tarted up, and there were rumours that there would be waterside terraces and even floating restaurants. Meanwhile, a great deal of tidying-up had been done since Monday, even, and the corridors along which we drifted had been laid with immensely thick carpets.

Suddenly Chris grabbed my forearm and squeezed it lightly. But when I glanced at his face he was failing to suppress a grin. 'How many meanings can you work out for that?' he asked, pointing to a label on a door.

COMPLEX MANAGER, it said.

'I wonder if they've relabelled that door yet,' I said.

'Which door?'

'The one we nearly lost a soprano through.'

'What?' Then he remembered we were supposed to be music-loving yuppies, and he lowered his voice. 'What are you on about?'

'The doors that opened on to nothing. That near-miss we had on Saturday.'

I explained about Mo's incident.

'Show me.'

The speed with which we retraced our steps and hammered up the nearest staircase was far from fashionable. At first I stared hopelessly around me.

'There it is!' I pointed. 'The one that says "Strictly No Admittance—Acoustic Equipment". It said "Ladies Cloakroom". And there was no apostrophe.'

'You're joking!'

'I'm not. I meant to write and complain—'

'About the signs being confused.'

'Look.'

We peered at a ghostly rectangle: the dust had settled on the adhesive left by the first nameplate. The new one was a different shape.

'Go and see that loo's what it claims to be.'

I obeyed. It was. I came back to find Chris opening the EQUIPMENT door. He shoved a bunch of keys quickly back into his pocket. Through vertical slabs of wood we could see an ornamental balcony like all the others round the auditorium. He closed the door and locked it, tapping the side of his nose with his index finger. I saluted in acknowledgement, and, as we made our way back for the second half, gave him a detailed account of the previous Saturday's events.

'What I can't understand is why no one reported it,' he said, as if we hadn't paused in our conversation for the forty minutes or so it took for Stobbard Mayou to get through Sibelius' Second Symphony.

George had loved Sibelius. He used to take especial pride in making reeds to produce a particularly dark, elemental timbre to match the musical landscape. None of the bassoon-clown-of-the-orchestra syndrome for him.

Jools was acting principal bassoon tonight. I suppose the most damning thing I could say was that she'd done her best. And I could see from the expression on the face of the *Birmingham Post* music critic that it was simply not good enough. Her reed hadn't got that dark sound, but that wasn't the only problem. She couldn't deliver the nuances of tone and pace that Mayou was trying for. And there were several dominoes. She'd have to practise longer and harder if she wanted to sit up on a regular basis. That would mean limiting her work on the weights.

Why had she got away with it so long? Everyone else practised: muscles have to be kept fit as athletes'. And Jools had never pushed herself hard. She ought by rights to have been eased out years ago. Why had Tony never grasped the nettle? He'd shifted other players around, got rid of some altogether. He was getting quite offensively pleased with his reputation for being a hard manager.

But he'd let Jools get away with murder. Her hair, for one thing. No, it was all right this season, although it looked as if it might have been cut with a knife and fork. But last year she'd had it shaved round the sides and back, leaving a Mohican tuft down the middle. Then she'd dyed it orange. Then it went black, with a treble clef sculpted into the shaven area at the back. I rather liked that look. With jeans and Docs, anyway. Perhaps it was less successful with the long black dress that forms a woman musician's uniform.

These days, of course, the long black itself was a disaster. Aberlene had adopted a heavy silk trouser suit, with a neat little mess jacket instead of tails. Jools could never aspire to such chic, but at least she'd look less like an unsuccessful drag artist.

Mayou was calling all the principals to their feet, one by one. Rollinson had been known to ignore one who'd performed badly, but here was Mayou smiling at her as if she'd played perfectly. What was it George had said about them? George rarely gossiped about orchestral liaisons. But I wondered—no: I refused to buy that theory.

'I said, who did Tony Rossiter say he'd reported the door incident to?'

I jumped. 'Everyone. Why not ask him yourself? He'll be backstage, being nice to Stobbard Mayou.'

'Maybe it can wait till tomorrow,' he said.

The architects had decided that the musicians were to be not merely performers but performing animals: the Band Room might have been soundproofed but, like the penguin pool at Dudley Zoo, it was glass-walled. Anyone interested could watch them eating and drinking, playing cards, doing OU assignments or—in the case of the heavy brass—reading girlie magazines. If they wanted to quarrel or weep they no doubt had to book a practice room in those gloss-painted backstage corridors horribly like those at William Murdock. Haydn or Mozart would have recognised the distinction immediately—the front-of-house luxury and the spartan performers' territory. There was an insidious rumour that the management of the Music Centre were trying to insist that no performer should be allowed anywhere except back-stage, and that the MSO felt that Tony wasn't backing them strongly enough in their opposition.

We were about to turn into the underground passage leading to the car parks when we heard running feet, and someone calling. Tony Rossiter.

I stopped, and smiled to Chris. 'You can ask him now after all.'

Chris did not show much delight. He showed still less when Tony kissed me, as he sometimes does in public.

Tony was off for a drink with Mayou. They'd both be delighted if we would join them. Caste, of course, must be maintained, so the Duke of Clarence was out of the question. We must go to the Mondiale, the hotel where Mayou had a suite, a hotel I'd never done more than cycle past.

But how? The hotel, one of a clutch of new ones on Broad Street, is all of three hundred yards from the Music Centre, very near the Five Ways island. One of the men would take us in a car. Which man? Which car? Poor Tony and Chris were falling over each other in their efforts not to insist.

Mayou was looking as if he regretted the whole affair. My feet were getting bored too. I'd persuaded them into my only pair of high heels in honour of the evening. I don't wear ugly flatties all the time, don't think that. Very stylish flatties, à la Princess Di. A fall from my bike long ago left me with a tiny weakness in my back. Walking, running, training—it copes with all of these. But heels above an inch high and it soon screams. Mayou caught my eye. He made a minute gesture with the first two fingers of his left hand, his right being occupied by the controversial handbag. He repeated it. His fingers were walking. He smiled: we were to walk too. That was how we reached the Mondiale. The champagne was already on ice when the others arrived.

Mayou fell silent almost immediately. Completely silent. I got no help from Tony or Chris, who were busy condoling with each other on the fortunes of West Bromwich Albion. I'd have been happy to join in—I'd cheered them from the terraces in my younger and their more successful days—but could scarcely talk across the silent host.

Abruptly Mayou excused himself.

I sat staring at the champagne bucket, feeling thirsty and angry in unequal measures.

He returned quite swiftly, charmingly apologetic, and signalled for the champagne to be served. His first glass made him sneeze repeatedly.

'That goddamn dust,' he said, mopping his eyes. 'Half the time I can't see, my eyes water so much, I'm sneezing like I had hay fever, and now my physician's talking about my getting asthma, for Christ's sake. Asthma! Isn't that what old men get?'

Quietly I produced my Ventolin. 'Not just old men.'

During the subsequent discussion of symptoms and treatments he became elated, as if he were really interested in how I dealt with the problem. Say, why didn't we jog together? Could I really teach him to ride a goddamn bicycle? As for leaving Birmingham for somewhere less allergenic, he had a job here. He was a professional. 'Goddamn it, Sophie, I bet you don't stay off school just because you've got hay fever. I just wish I could do justice to this marvellous group of musicians here. I feel like I'm letting them down when I'm like this.'

'Well?' asked Chris, fastening his seat belt.

'Well what?'

'Well, what did you get out of him?'

'Get out of him? I wasn't aware I was supposed to be getting anything out of him. He was telling me all about his studies in Finland and the outsize mosquitoes they grow there.' I didn't want to discuss Stobbard with anyone.

'Great. That'll be a terrific help.'

'And what did you get from Tony, apart form an intimate review of his new car? All that black leather. A real seductionmobile, isn't it?'

We did not speak again until we reached my front door. Chris was busy demonstrating that he'd passed the police driving course with all available honours. I was trying not to pee secondhand champagne. He braked sharply, but pulled on the handbrake as slowly as if he were trying to reach a decision while he did it.

'That friend of yours is hiding something,' he said at last.

'Tony? Never!'

'Bloody cagey.'

'His mother was an oyster, his father a clam. And being a manager's made him worse.'

'Shouldn't stop him reporting incidents like that.'

' 'Course it shouldn't. Look, I must go in. I'm desperate for a loo.'

'OK. I'll phone you.'

He let me get out and only then got out himself. He followed me slowly.

There was a dull thud. His hand shot out, as if to pull me back. Then he pointed. Aggie's bin. A fox had knocked it over and was worrying the lid.

We started to laugh.

He touched my arm. 'Good night, then,

Sophie. You will be careful, won't you?'

I couldn't understand why he sounded so earnest. 'Don't worry. I can take care of myself.'

But he was still watching and waiting when I shut my front door.

Chapter Nine

Friday is the day of my favourite class, that Access group, but today I had the business of Manjit to attend to before I could start teaching. She presented herself outside the staff room at nine sharp, wan, a bruise on her face where the red mark had been. She was far from apologetic, however. True, she presented me with a note, torn off her lined A4 notepad, apologising for using bad language, but when I tried to ask her about the circumstances she repeated that it was none of my business and I ought to back off.

I unlocked a classroom and gestured her inside.

'Sit down and listen,' I said.

She did as she was told. But every line of her body expressed resentment and something else—fear? I returned to the door and locked it, so we wouldn't be interrupted.

'Manjit, I'm trying to help you. You were very upset last Friday, upset enough to interrupt my class, and I know you're too responsible to do that without good reason. I haven't told a single soul about our conversation. OK?'

She nodded. Her face was still sullen but she glanced up briefly.

'There's something wrong. We both know that. When you said it was none of my business you weren't quite right. Anything that makes a student as unhappy as you were—and still seem to be—is the business of people who care about her. And I care about you. Right?'

She nodded, and she tried to smile. But her eyes were filling with tears.

'Maybe you don't want to talk about what's upset you. Maybe you're afraid to.'

She flinched.

'If you can't talk to me, couldn't you talk to one of the college counsellors?'

She shook her head. 'And I don't want you to, either, miss. Things get around.'

'Not from our counsellors. Everything you tell them is confidential. You know that.'

She shook her head stubbornly.

'How about I talk to them in general

terms? Find out—'

'I don't want you to find out nothing. Oh, miss—'

'OK. Manjit. I won't do anything without your say-so. I want you to know I'll always listen if you want to talk to me. Right? And I want you to write down this—it's my home telephone number.'

She looked me straight in the eyes. 'Thanks, miss. Miss, promise me you won't tell anyone—anyone. Please.'

I hesitated.

'Miss, I daren't be late in case anyone—you know—'

But although I nodded kindly, I wasn't quite sure that I did.

I was out of my depth. I knew I ought to be doing something but I'd promised to do nothing, in particular not to talk to those very colleagues whom I'd have trusted with my life. I worried my way round the situation for the rest of the day. There was a meeting across the lunch hour I had to go to, but I might not have been there for all the contribution I made to the new College Development Plan. Shahida and Richard kept eyeing me with concern. As we split up to go to our classes, Shahida gave me a quick hug.

Richard hung back. 'You're sure you

don't need some time off?'

I smiled at him sadly: he'd want to know about Manjit, might be able to help her, but I could no more confide in him than she in me.

'Remember, all you have to do is ask. Call me at home if you need me: I'm always ready to help.'

I nodded my thanks. I didn't expect to have to take him up on his offer before the weekend was over.

Saturday morning's rehearsal with the MSO started off as a fairly flat affair. Stobbard Mayou's rhinitis was better, but he was much more dour than I'd seen him. Aberlene and Jools had come on to the platform together, obviously in mid-row. But they'd settled in their places, and provided no entertainment for the onlookers. When the break came, I opened my coffee and Mo went to the loo. I sat there gloomily. Normally I'd have sought out George. And there was something more trivial to worry about too. I kept getting the feeling that Mayou was looking at me. With no great affection, either. Very odd, since we'd parted on the best of terms on Thursday, and I wasn't singing out of tune. Then there was a movement beside me: Aberlene. She sat down and accepted the remains of the coffee.

'This must be very hard for you,' she said. 'The first rehearsal without George. Bad enough for us playing on Monday. You know we played something in his memory. Not *Nimrod*. Mayou and the soloist got it together and decided to do the *Adagio* from Mozart's D minor concerto. John Murray. Nice man, as well as being a great pianist.'

I nodded. One day I'd turned up at George's to find John Murray flat on his back under George's sink.

'Are you all right, by the way?' It was crude but I didn't feel very subtle today.

'Fine. Apart from bloody Jools, that is. Sophie, she's really pissing me off at the moment. I know she's a friend of yours, but I've got to sound off at someone. You know she's always had a bit of a reputation for hobnobbing with guest soloists and conductors?'

I nodded. 'George used to loathe it. Used to make awful jokes about officers and other ranks.'

'I mean, she was all over that violinist, Jacques Whatshisname—the one that had the accident.'

The young man in question had fallen from his hotel room in Rome a week after he'd played in Birmingham. There was a strong rumour he'd been trying to fly, but it had been discreetly hushed up.

131

'And now she's in and out of Mayou's room as if they were best buddies. Which I'm sure they're not. They have the most awful rows.'

'She seems to have the most awful rows with everyone,' I said. 'Including me. What was she having a go at you for?'

But Mayou was already coming on to the stage, and Aberlene had to scuttle to her place.

The second half of the rehearsal was much more impressive. Apart from an awful bout of sneezing, Mayou was altogether more alert, and he contrived to wake us up too. He sang all the choir parts—simultaneously, it seemed. He pushed aside the stool and reached and dipped, scooping music from the air. Five minutes in, he pulled off his sweatshirt to reveal an Oxfam T-shirt, a textbook set of muscles and, when the T-shirt lifted with his arms, a golden torso that simply demanded to be touched.

We allowed ourselves to be seduced.

And then it was all over. A smile and a wave and he was gone.

Mo sighed, reached into her handbag, produced a spray and covered herself with Opium.

And she covered me.

My sneezes rivalled Mayou's. My eyes flooded. Any moment now I'd succumb

132

to an attack of asthma. Thank God for Ventolin. But I was still wheezing and crying when Tony Rossiter ran into me—almost literally—on the stairs.

He peered at me with what seemed like genuine sympathy. 'Are you sure you're all right? I suppose you've got this flu bug.'

I didn't have enough breath to deny it.

'I don't think you should get close to Stobbard. Not like this.'

'Stobbard?'

'He sent me to find out how you are. He's in his room. No, don't go down. I'll tell him you've gone straight home to bed.'

I ran down the stairs beside him.

'Tony, why was Stobbard asking for me?'

Before he could reply, Stobbard's door burst open and Jools shot out, thrusting her way between us. Stobbard had followed her to the doorway and now stood looking at us. He shook his head gently and strolled towards us. 'My, my. All that just because I asked her to produce a more authentic sound. Hey, Sophie, you don't look so good.'

'Flu, Stobbard,' said Tony, stepping between us.

A sneeze cut off my denial.

'Sounds like you've got it real bad.' His hair was still wet with sweat—it curled, irrepressibly.

A phone rang. Tony ran to answer it. Aberlene emerged from the band room.

'Stobbard,' she began, 'I really must—'

Tony came back at a gallop. 'Stobbard, it's Munich! Can you take over from Muti? He's got the flu. Any Beethoven Symphony you like and some Japanese doing the Brahms D minor concerto.'

'What is it you say over here? No peace for the wicked? Tell them Beethoven Four and fix a flight. Sophie, why don't you—no, I guess you'd best take care of that flu.' He smiled and was gone.

Back in Harborne, the allergy a thing of the past, I glowered at my marking and wondered what Stobbard would have asked had it not been for my sneezes.

Then the phone rang. But it was only Jools. Jools? Apologising?

'I said some things that were out of order. Can I cook you a "sorry" dinner some time? Like tonight? I've been let down by my date, see, and there's all this food.'

I presented myself at eight, at Jools's very pleasant flat in a modern block just off Augustus Road. I'd have thought any accommodation attached to anyone else's was inappropriate for a musician. But Jools claimed never to have had any complaints from her neighbours, and they always greeted her pleasantly enough if we encountered them on the stairs.

I'd caught a bus. I don't like Saturday evenings full of boy racers who don't see cyclists till they've knocked them over and maybe not even then. I'd treat myself to a taxi home. I took a bottle, of course. There wasn't any reason for me to follow Jools's abstinence. It wasn't as if she'd just become a strict Baptist.

Her flat didn't look as if she was a strict anything. She was the only person I knew who had her pad done up by interior decorators. None of your MFI furniture. Maples or Lee Longlands for her, upmarket stores not far from the Music Centre. In the far corner of her living room were a neatish pile of music, her music stand and her bassoon case. Unlike George's, it was the light-weight, cylindrical type, the sort musicians with cycles or motorbikes prefer. It was as pristine as the rest of her flat. She actually greeted me with a gin and tonic. She stuck to tonic herself, but I took her offer as a tacit peace offering. I followed her into her fitted-everything kitchen to gossip while she cooked.

Gossip! We hardly spoke to each other. I knew she hated being interrupted while she was cooking, so I got on with dressing the salad while she poked baked potatoes and

135

showed the steaks the grill. I had to ask her to let mine linger there a little. Rare I like but not *bleu*.

I did learn that she'd had a fight with Tony over coach travel, and if what she said was true I couldn't blame her. Apparently she'd asked if she could use her car for the recent trip to the North, and he'd vetoed the idea. Then he'd gone and taken his own. 'Whoever heard of a grown man getting coachsick?'

I tried to remember school outings. Had Tony been one of those who had to sit at the front/by a window/next to teacher lest he be sick?

'New girlfriend?' I asked idly. 'New car, of course.'

'No. He's been doing it for weeks. Long before Stobbard came.'

Stobbard. Not Mayou. Stobbard.

'How do you get on with—Stobbard?' I asked in a carefully neutral voice.

'All right.' The way she said it, she might have added, 'And what is it to you?'

While she brewed coffee I went to use the loo. If the rest of her flat was luxurious, the bathroom was truly opulent. I pondered on some weird Perspex lining to the bath, and envied her bathrobe which would have taken me a week to dry. So, for that

136

matter, would her towels. I knew we earned roughly the same: no doubt her parents had paid for this lot. There were times when I rather wished I'd chosen my ancestors a little more carefully.

I peered at myself at the beautifully lit and angled mirror. Whoever had bequeathed me my genes had ensured that I would be small and wiry, with mousy hair and an undistinguished face. All that activity outdoors was wearing my skin: I ought to take as much care of it as Jools apparently did. I picked up a bottle at random: 'Capture. Anti-aging complex'. At thirty-five? But Jools had always had a lovely complexion. I'd ask.

'Jools,' I began, stirring sugar into the coffee, 'I was looking at some of your cosmetics and—'

'How dare you touch my stuff! How dare you go poking round my things?'

'Hang on, Jools. I only wanted to ask—'

I thought for a moment she was going to strike me. Then she sat down.

'What did you want to ask?'

'Only how you keep you skin so nice.'

She condescended to talk cosmetics for a bit. The conversation became beautifully normal and trivial. When the phone rang, however, she carried the receiver into the hall. I might have had a prowl round and inspected her latest acquisition, a small bronze. But I didn't want to provoke another outburst, so I stayed where I was, letting my eyes rest with great pleasure on the elegant room. George had always admired it. I suppose it was that which made me say, when she came back into the room, 'Tell me about George. His last concert.'

I don't know what response I expected. Another flounce. A moan that she'd been over it time and time again with the police. A bored reiteration of what she'd said in the pub.

I didn't expect her to turn chalk white. Nor could I work out why she did.

After a moment's consideration she said, quite calmly, 'He played OK. Until that domino in the slow movement. Afterwards, he said he was going to meet you. But he stopped on the platform to talk to Aubrey. Aubrey'd managed to get his hands on some pheasant feathers from somewhere and was drying out his oboe. You know how seriously he takes the whole business.'

I nodded. Aubrey takes his oboe very seriously indeed.

'So I went down to the Band Room. With Chloe. Then I came to the pub.'

'So you didn't see him after that?'

This time when she went white I'm sure it was with anger. 'I've already been interrogated, thank you. I'm sure your policeman friend would give you a transcript.'

'I'm not trying to interrogate you. I just need to know about George. To lay him to rest. Goodness knows when the funeral will be. I tried laying flowers at the Centre.' I stopped at the memory of all that mud.

'So I heard. Why don't you ask Tony? When I left, Tony was threatening to kill him. As I hoped he told your policeman friend.'

To have phoned for a taxi would have meant asking a favour of Jools and waiting till the taxi came. I preferred to do neither.

It wasn't a bad night. The clouds were still high, and when I saw the back of the number 10 bus pulling away from the stop I decided to make the best of it and walk. I'd simply follow the bus route: there weren't any short cuts to tempt me.

Of course, walking's a wonderful way to mull over an evening. There was Jools's moodiness to think about. She'd always been abrupt; tonight she was abrasive. Steroids—weren't they supposed to cause aggression? Not that she'd ever admitted to taking anything. There was her flat to reflect on, too. There was something different about it. In my mind I paced round that living room of hers. The full-length curtains. The subtle lighting. The leather chairs. All those were familiar. So what was it?

At this point I realised I was not alone.

I'd reached the end of Woodbourne Road, where it turns left into Gillhurst Road. Practically the home straight.

A car pulled up beside me. And stopped. I ignored it. Walked faster.

As I turned the corner, the car turned it with me. Pulled ahead of me. Stopped.

If there's one thing I hate it's kerb crawlers. I don't care whether they're prominent men in posh cars or young idiots in elderly Datsuns like this one. Hate them all. My usual trick is to embarrass them. Stop. Stare as if memorising a face. Peer ostentatiously at the number plates. Write down the number.

That's what I meant to do this time.

But the man didn't accelerate sharply away. He got out of the car.

A woolly cap pulled well down. A scarf over the face and heavy-rimmed glasses. A slit, then, of dark skin. A tracksuit suggesting heavy muscles. Gloves.

He started to walk towards me.

At this point I did a really stupid thing. For years I've taught elementary self-protection to groups of vulnerable women students. Don't run, I tell them, unless you can run somewhere safe. A well-lit house; a group of people; even a

140

car with an alarm to activate.

And what did I do? I ran. I zapped off into a piece of waste land which labours under the name of Chadbrook Walkway. Stupid, stupid, stupid. As I realised when he followed me.

The thought of being raped on a March night with the rain just starting concentrates the mind wonderfully. I could just lead him round in a circle. I could head for one of the other exits—one would take me to a playing field, the other to a couth housing estate. And in one of those elegant houses lived Richard. No contest.

Now I knew where I was heading, my breathing cleared. I realised I was grinning. I was going to make my pursuer regret this. He'd have to follow me through the prickliest thickets and back again. All the time I was edging closer to where I wanted to be. Now for the little stream, and the delightfully boggy surround. I knew where to jump. He didn't.

I made the last couple of hundred yards without company.

If Richard and his wife were irritated by my eruption into their quiet Saturday evening, they were too kind to show it. They found dry slippers, whisky, a towel for my hair. And left Schubert on the CD while we waited for the police. Sheila offered to come with me to the police station, and urged me to return after I'd made my statement. But I thought I might be gone some time, and it was late enough already.

I had a terrible sense of *déjà vu*. It was all done with efficiency and professionalism. The woman interviewing me made the connections I hoped she'd make—no, I didn't think it was coincidence that I should be attacked so soon after finding that Asian student's body. She ran me back herself, saw me safely into my house, and left a contact number.

Weird, it was only when I was in the bath that I realised that the dark skin of the Datsun driver was feigned. I would swear that he was neither Asian nor Afro-Caribbean.

And even weirder, as I hauled myself out to phone Inspector Hathersage, that I should quite suddenly realise what was different about Jools's living room. Hanging on the wall was what looked very like an original David Cox.

Chapter Ten

Ian Dale's Sundays must begin earlier than mine. But then, I suppose that my Saturday evening had been unnaturally long. He'd come about the attack, of course.

'Give me a minute to get dressed,' I said. 'I can't think in a nightie.'

The poor man sighed almost visibly with relief. I can't think why. My dressing gown was impregnably decorous—I'd never got round to buying anything more erotic, even when my relationship with Kenji was at its most interesting. And looked at dispassionately, the tracksuit I chose must have revealed far more of the Rivers anatomy. I made tea—it seemed we both liked Earl Grey with lemon—and waited for him to begin. Nice avuncular inquiries about my health. But something was worrying him. I let him drift round to it. Yes: this suggestion that my assailant had been in some sort of disguise. Why did I think that? Brown eyes? Dark skin? Had I seen his hands? Had he spoken?

Eventually I shook my head. 'I'm sorry,

Ian. You'll just have to trust me. I know, that's all.'

He sighed and shut his notebook. We talked about the rest of the day, and whether it was too early to risk pruning roses. What did I propose to do?

'Keep out of harm's way.' I smiled glibly.

He'd be happier not knowing what I had planned.

I'd never expected burglary to be so easy.

I'd never quite got round to returning George's key, of course, and it struck me that Short Dressing Gown should still be in bed with—at very least—the Sunday papers. But as I stepped into George's hall I found I was shaking uncontrollably.

I wanted to say goodbye. That was one reason for coming. I could only do it in his home—Oxfam's now. He'd willed it to all those millions of children whose brothers and sisters had died for want of vaccination or rehydration. I didn't know about the rest of his will—except for the bassoon, of course. The other reason I'd come was to check through his papers to see why anyone should wish to kill him.

His diary? The diary he'd have patted back into place in his inner pocket after our phone call. A meeting confirmed. Duke of Clarence, 10.00, Sophie. No sign of it.

144

Then I realised it must be locked in some official file. He'd have had it on him when he was killed.

I forced myself into the kitchen. His calendar, the one by the phone. A bird for each month—he supported the RSPB too. But he hadn't filled in the spaces usefully. There was a pencilled S, and a faint R for the same day. R? The cork board listed telephone numbers for his dentist, doctor and bank, a need for coriander (fresh), and a couple of charity appeals he might respond to. The herbs on his windowsill needed water; I put them in a carrierbag to take home.

Back to the living room and the bureau. A slot for bills pending, another for bills paid. Photos from the American tour. They were all blurred. Unlike George, that. He was always most punctilious in his composition and focusing. Then I realised: it was my eyes that were blurred. I wiped the tear splodges from the top print and shoved the wallets—some three or four into my cagoule pouch.

I tried his bedroom, of course, as I'd done before. Now a smell of emptiness to go with the stale bedclothes. I put my head on the pillow that still smelt of his aftershave and wept.

I could smell Sunday lunches cooking as

I cycled back. Comforting roasts, milky puddings. Safe as childhood. I ought to eat. There was that steak. I could eat that steak.

I reached for the Jameson's. A good slug. Then I saw George's eyes, reproachful across my kitchen table.

'Damn you, George! Damn you. You leave me but you won't go away!' I think I said it out loud. I tipped what I'd poured down the sink. 'There! Is that good enough for you?' But it wasn't, and I smashed the tumbler at the floor.

The bathos of scrabbling round picking up splinters of glass calmed me a little. Enough to work out that a cup of very strong, sweet drinking chocolate might be just as good, and that I might then be able to think about food. As I sipped, I looked at George's photos.

Mostly they were of his colleagues, singly or in groups, usually with a landmark in the background. There was a lovely study of Aberlene, proud as an African princess. Jools arm-wrestling with a horn player—by his expression he was losing. Pam under her double bass's travelling case. Stobbard Mayou—he'd conducted the band for the first time on the tour in a huge sombrero. Had George realised how beautiful the man's body was? But of course he had: he'd waited for exactly the right moment to press the shutter. Tony with the woman violinist who'd toured with them. Perhaps she might be the reason why Tony preferred to travel by car; perhaps he was snatching time with her on the way.

But I ought to ask him. And I ought to ask about his threat to kill George.

It had occurred to me that cross-questioning an old friend was something better done on a full stomach, so I filled mine with the promised steak. I permitted myself a glass—one glass—of Valdepenas, gesturing, before I drank, at the photographs.

I cycled to Tony's flat near Edgbaston Cricket Ground. I wish he'd chosen it because he shared my passion for the game—my father bowled leg breaks for Durham—but Tony can't tell an off-drive from an over, despite my years of patient nagging. The development cowers behind a decorative but very high wall, and I found to my horror—imagine it, living under someone's surveillance the whole time—that I was required to tell my business to a security guard before I was allowed in. He was from the same green-coated firm as the guards at college and just as aggressive, though perhaps if I'd come in a Rolls he'd have discovered courtesy.

Tony was standing at his open door. That was for some time the only indication that my visit might be welcome. He was cool to the point of frostiness, but showed me into his living room.

'Well?'

I hesitated to pollute his cream leather armchairs with my jeans and cagoule. I pulled the latter over my head before sitting. Reminded of his manners, he took it from me and left the room, presumably to hang it up. I looked around me—at a room as elegant as Jools's. Tony's interior designer had conceived what he probably described as a more masculine ambience, but it was one I wouldn't have minded living in. That built-in hi-fi, for instance, with its concealed speakers, would have suited me down to the ground.

Tony came and sat opposite me, barely troubling to conceal a glance at his watch.

'I thought you might want this,' I said, producing the US tour photo.

His face flooded with colour. 'Where did you get this?'

'Why d'you ask?'

'Because—Jesus, because I'd like a copy of it!'

His emotion seemed genuine enough.

'Enough to kill for one?'

He looked bewildered. 'Sophie, I get the feeling you're not joking. Jesus, you're

148

not, are you? What the hell are you suggesting?'

'George took this. Someone overheard you threatening to kill him. Tony, please, please tell me you didn't kill him.' Damn it, my voice had broken, and I could feel tears coming.

'Of course I didn't bloody well kill him! For Christ's sake, Sophie, he—I—Look, let's have a coffee and sort all this out. OK?'

I followed him into his kitchen, to remind us both, perhaps, that we were friends. He filled the kettle, allowing me a view of a still forbidding profile. Then he reached out china mugs, and, in an odd touch of domesticity, loaded a plate with biscuits. And he made tea, not coffee. I started to laugh.

'Well?' Then his face softened slightly. 'Incongruous, I suppose. But George always liked biscuits with his tea, didn't he? Why the hell should I want to kill him, Sophie? I loved that man. He was my friend, too, remember. And remember the verdict.'

'Why should anyone want to kill him? And I think they're likely to reopen the inquest. Thanks to you bringing me George's bassoon,' I explained.

'So why accuse me of killing him?'

'Because you met him the day he died.

There was an R on his calendar that must have been you. And—like I told you someone overheard you threatening to kill him.'

'Jools. Yes, it was. And she told Groom as well. What a good job I'd already talked to Groom and told him all about it. I didn't realise I was supposed to tell you too.'

'You weren't. But I had to ask. Because it was about George.'

He poured the tea and pushed my cup over to me. 'OK, OK. I know. But I hate all this questioning, all these people trying to prove me guilty—you, of all people.' He stopped and looked at me. He sighed. 'Sorry. I can guess what you're going through. There's trouble at work, see. A lot of unrest in the orchestra. Guess who's at the bottom of it? Punctuality. Missing rehearsals. Not the greatest of musicians even on a good day. People resent it, you know, someone letting them down all the time. They want people to remember a concert because they've played well, not because someone else has been scattering dominoes everywhere. So there have been moves to...get rid of her, to be honest. And that takes years. Bloody Musicians' Union poking its nose in.'

'Not if you follow the agreed procedure, surely?'

150

'Still takes years. And every time she makes a mistake it's another crack in the band's reputation. We're living in harsh times, Sophie, in case you hadn't noticed. Too many orchestras fighting for too few gigs and too little money. So if the Liverpool Phil sound better than the MSO, who gets the next contract? Anyway, I had a deputation the other day. Had to respond somehow. And Peter Rollinson's been pressing me to act for years.'

'Any reason why you only act now he's off sick?'

'Only that the players brought it to a head.'

'Mayou been complaining?'

'Oh, how casual! Come off it, Sophie. Don't come the innocent with me. I know you've got the hots for him. And I reckon if it hadn't been for your flu you'd have had yourself a weekend in Munich. No, he's not been complaining officially. He said it was a domestic dispute and it would be inappropriate for him to get involved. But he's certainly criticised her. Not in public but he's had her back to his room on a number of occasions. And you could hear that it wasn't to discuss the weather.'

'I thought the rooms were soundproofed.'

'They're still yelling when they come out.'

151

'Ah.'

'Anyway, to get back to George. He promised to try and do something. Make it clear she had to improve. Offer to help her. Anything. Because he loved the band, Sophie. The whole band. The man was so loyal. So although I'd had the official warning letter typed—I'd even signed it—I put it back in my pocket till the next day. And I told him if he didn't manage it, I'd bloody kill him. So there you have it. And before you ask, Groom has a copy of the letter. And a duplicate with a new date will go out as soon as the hoo-ha's died down a bit.'

'Any idea what's the matter with her? She used to be my friend, Tony, but she's weird at the moment.'

'Got to be anabolic steroids, hasn't it? But she's always been up one minute, down the next. Long as I've known her.'

'Artistic temperament.' I laughed. 'Tony, love, I don't envy you your job.'

He launched into a list of the week's rows: smoking on coaches, not smoking on coaches; how long is a long dress; what happens if the principal cello forgets his black socks and comes on stage in yellow ones; how do you reconcile Mayou's demands for afternoon rehearsals with the orchestra's long-agreed system of morning sessions; when is an injury wear and tear?

'Bloody hell, Sophie, I'm a manager, not a bloody nursemaid. Never mind: tell me how your job hunt's going.'

But I couldn't because I'd forgotten I wanted to leave Birmingham.

Chapter Eleven

There is nothing like a migraine for losing a day. Monday vanished as completely as if it had never been there. So here I was at home on Tuesday after my evening class, toiling through piles of marking accumulated on my day off sick, and wishing I wasn't. Even a quiet drink with one of my colleagues would have been nice, but Carl's wife had now caught his flu and he was keeping an eye on her. I didn't dare reach for the whiskey, not on top of the stuff I'd been taking for my head.

Chris Groom, then, was a welcome interruption, but he was being singularly obtuse. He'd come to tell me the results of the forensic tests. If he was as busy as I was, I was surprised he didn't simply phone. But he'd brought a bottle of wine and seemed disposed to stay.

'So what did the lab report say?' I

prompted him.

'That it was mud on the outside of the case, and that there was no sign of anything untoward in the lining. But where does that get us? Apart from your living room, at nine p.m. on Tuesday the...' Chris's voice dwindled to a halt.

Covering my face with my hands and sighing with exasperation were not entirely theatrical gestures. I had, after all, been teaching since nine o'clock that morning with only a fifteen-minute coffee break in which Manjit had wept again, but still refused to talk. I'd lost my lunch hour, too, for a meeting which would have been acrimonious had not Richard sacrificed his Saturday night for me: it's impossible to yell thoroughly at a man who sports cerise paisley pyjamas. And here was Chris, who I suspected was a very intelligent young man, displaying less intellectual acumen than one of my students.

'Can't you see? No, you can't, can you? Look, Chris, it gets us to the fact that George wasn't, of course, smuggling drugs OK?'

'You never thought he was. But someone else might have used his case.'

'His case never left his sight.'

'Sophie, don't exaggerate. I've had a rough day.'

'You too? Has one of your students got

154

bruises all over her face and sits there crying and you're sure one of her relatives is sexually abusing her?'

'And you haven't called us in?'

'She'd deny it. I have to persuade her to tell me first. Then we'll think about the police and social services. And anyone else I can think of. Then. And I spent my lunchtime listening to my boss explaining why I can't go on an IT course. He says it's not likely to benefit my teaching.'

'True?'

'Not entirely. I'm sure it must have its uses in the classroom. And I could certainly produce less amateurish teaching materials. But I suspect they think that if I got computer-literate I'd be off like the clappers.' I overrode his protest. 'Hell, I've put in ten years' hard labour up there on the fifteenth floor. I've worked my socks off for them. And it'd be great to be able to make my CV look professional.'

'DTP it.'

'Pardon?'

'Desk-top publish it. You need a 486 IBM-compatible PC and a laser printer, for preference—come on, Sophie, you're winding me up!'

'No. Honestly.'

'Are they still into quill pens at your place?'

'Only me. I always seem to have missed

155

out. And now they say there's no money left for staff development.' I set down the wineglass sharply, a full stop to my disappointment. 'So: over to you. Any news on George's murder?'

'Can't you get it into your head it was an accident? According to the Health and Safety Executive report. Experts. The inquest verdict.'

'He took his bassoon case with him.'

'According to about eighty independent witnesses, your Tony Rossiter among them, his bassoon case was in the Band Room—' He stopped. 'His bassoon case had mud on it. Mud. Which means, Sophie, that—'

'—that he took it out, but someone brought it back in. And I'd bet my boots that whoever did that was a musician,' I finished, triumphantly.

He grabbed his anorak. 'What are you waiting for? Come on!'

'Where?'

'To the Music Centre, of course: I presume you want to come with me?'

No Cavalier today, but a new—brand-new—Peugeot. I'd noticed it, of course, when I'd opened the door for him, but I'd omitted to say anything. Pure malice, if that isn't an oxymoron. And a lurking embarrassment. Surely Chris couldn't be indulging in some weird competition with Tony? I'd thought more highly of him than that. But he was certainly showing off now, fiddling with the hi-fi and taking us on a route that certainly avoided the Hagley Road traffic—if there was any at nearly ten—and also clearly demonstrated his new toy's cornering capacity. How fortunate I'd had the foresight to use the loo before we set out.

The MSO were playing in Bristol so a London orchestra had been trying out the Music Centre's acoustics. Their coaches were just pulling away as Chris swung into the restricted parking area. If he wasn't even pretending to be a member of the public, I'd no idea how he could justify my presence. He signed us in, as before, and got us hard hats, as before. No one asked any questions. And almost at once we found what we were looking for: two properly labelled doors. One was an exit to the canal towpath and a short cut to the Duke of Clarence. The other was the one I'd used the night I'd laid my flowers in the mud where George had died. Been murdered. It was official. Chris had used the word.

The notice read: HARD HAT AREA. AUTHORISED PERSONNEL ONLY. The adhesive plastic covered completely anything that might once have been there. But the other notice was a simple EXIT.

It could not conceal that other words had been there instead. Ghostly outlines, like those we'd found on the doors upstairs, were still just visible.

'So who would go to the trouble of changing notices?' I asked, rhetorically.

'Someone, perhaps, who wanted your poor George to wander out here on a nasty, stormy night with loose scaffolding flying around?'

'Did it fall or was it pushed?'

He grinned. 'You heard the verdict—accidental death. But in view of this—' he nodded at the door '—we'll get the inquest reopened. You see, the pathologist would be looking to see if the blow was obviously struck by an assailant. It wasn't. Damn it, scaffolding poles are a bit heavy to wallop someone with. It's logical to suppose that a pole just fell. I don't suppose the best medic in the world could tell if it fell or if it was really dropped. But I think the evidence of the doors suggests the latter, don't you?'

'What about the ones upstairs? Were they changed to lure someone to his—or her—death? Or was it just to fog the issue?'

'Could be either. Only the killer would know.'

'Killer?'

'Killer. Murderer. I'm sure now you

were right all along.'

I was so pleased I could have kissed him. But on the whole I thought I wouldn't.

There wasn't any point in my hanging around after that. Chris had to set in motion the efficient machine that would cordon off the area and set investigations belatedly in train. I would only get in the way if I stayed. He was embarrassed enough as it was: he clearly wanted to get on with his job, but was adamant that I shouldn't travel home on the bus. A taxi seemed a sensible compromise. But as he saw me into it, he seemed to be hunting for something to say. And when I simply smiled and thanked him it seemed the wrong thing.

I was glad when the driver put the taxi into gear and trundled me off home.

Chapter Twelve

I'd set the alarm clock for the unimaginable hour of six o'clock, and cycled in to college along blessedly deserted roads. Winston was alone in the foyer, without the backup of the green guards: no doubt it had been decided that the college's security would be threatened by people turning up during normal working hours only. He greeted me with disbelief and a cheery grin, rapidly transformed into a yawn.

So here I was, outside the Computer Suite, ready to teach myself about IT. If the college wouldn't fund a proper course for me, like the Little Red Hen, I'd do it myself. Or die in the process.

The first problem was to get into the Suite. Naively I'd supposed the staff key would open it. It did not. It seemed I'd have to approach Richard for a special one, and although he was conscientious to the point of mania about his timekeeping, I couldn't expect him to be in college for another hour yet. I was about to retreat to the staff room to finish the marking Chris had interrupted last night when Philomena, Winston's mother, rounded the corner.

'Good grief, Sophie, what you doing at this hour?'

'I'm going to master computing,' I said grimly.

'Oh, and which system do you propose to master first? We got all sorts, Sophie. There's the Amstrads and the IBMs, posh people only need apply, and there's those Elonexes, and I do believe we got a little collection of dear old BBCs, them steam-driven ones, tucked away. And then you've got to decide which word-processing package—WordPerfect, WordStar, Word for—'

I held up my hands in surrender.

'And of course you need your own floppy, dear. All them kids ask me where they keep the floppies, as if Old Philomena knew anything about it. All she know is the pile of paper they all waste.' She settled on her mop, to all intents and purposes the archetypal cleaning lady. She winked at me as a student appeared. 'Hello, Jagdish, lovie, come your ways in. Old Philomena got a key.'

I grinned. Then kicked myself for not thinking of something earlier.

'Tell me, Phil, did that kid who died spend much time in here? Young Wajid?'

'More hours than he put on that time sheet they're supposed to sign,' she said, at last abandoning patois for received pronunciation. She was at least as highly qualified as most of the staff, a theatre sister in a specialised neurological unit which had been absorbed into a bigger hospital. 'You know, Sophie, that kid really changed. To start with he was a real sweet little lad. Then he gets the idea he runs the place—"Philomena, do this, Philomena, do that." He says he's head of the house now his father's dead. And then he starts to use the phones, Sophie. I know he can't dial long distance now they've put that block on the switchboard, but goodness knows what he did to poor old William Murdock's phone bill. I mentioned it a couple of times to poor Greg, before his breakdown, but I suppose he was too ill to do anything about it. Any idea when he'll be back? I know the computer people are sharing out his work, but there has to be one person to take responsibility for a big enterprise like this, with members of the public using it and all. Lordy, lordy, look at that old clock. Philly, she spend all her time gossiping, she get nothing done.' She winked at me ironically as the caretaker, newly rechristened 'Estate Manager', limped into view. Gathering her dusters and the vacuum cleaner, she strode off. Then she remembered, and resumed her bottom-rolling shuffle.

Jagdish, the student, was too busy on a project to do more than switch on the machine for me. As Phil had prophesied, I was quickly stumped. As I packed up, I spoke to him again, asking about Wajid, but clearly my street cred was too low for him to give me any serious answers.

There was no way I could find the open sesame to the magic cave of computers without some help, it seemed. Then I remembered Samuel Smiles's dictum of self-help. The library—there'd be some computer manuals there. But it wouldn't open till nine, and in any case I'd have to return some books before I was allowed any more. Nothing for it but to get on with my working day.

My living-room floor was almost covered in photocopies of information about computers and computing when the doorbell rang. Chris. He stepped in blithely, a man sure of his welcome, and moved aside a couple of computer manuals so he could sit on the sofa.

'It's no good,' he said. 'You can read about computers until the cows come home, but you need hands-on experience to understand. It's like music: no point in reading about it, you need to listen to it. Or love—'

'I'll bet I find something useful,' I said, stubbornly. 'I spent more than ten pounds copying it all, so I better had! What can I do for you, anyway? Or have you come to bring me news?' Suddenly the world seemed a brighter place.

But he shook his head. 'No news about nothing. That's one reason I came round. Just to go over things we've talked about before. See if anything new occurs to you. Or me. We could start with that attack on you last Saturday. Let's see—you were just coming back from Jools's?'

I nodded. I didn't want to talk too

much about Jools herself, not till I'd had a chance to talk to her again. Her behaviour had been so weird recently, I wondered if there might not be another problem apart from her body building. And I didn't want to speculate, even about the David Cox, not if my musings might be taken down and used as hearsay.

'I've spoken to Jean Hathersage,' he was saying. 'And we agree that the oddest point, probably the most important point, is this assertion of yours that your assailant was in disguise. Are you positive?'

I went over it all again, wondering aloud why I hadn't noted the car number and cursing myself for running. He was easy to talk to—he didn't try to interrupt, and his posture was that of a concerned friend rather than an interested professional. But I couldn't come up with anything new for him. Except, at last, a question I'd been trying to suppress: 'Why me, Chris? Why me, and why then?'

'Coincidence?'

'I suppose it has to be. Has this guy attacked anyone else?'

'We've records of the odd Afro-Caribbean male assailant, the odd Asian one. But no one else reckons she was attacked by someone in disguise.'

'You have to be grateful,' I said sternly, 'that I wasn't chased by someone in drag.'

164

At last we sighed, pretty well simultaneously, and I got up to make some coffee.
He followed me.

'I thought you said George used to tidy
your kitchen,' he said, passing me a couple
of mugs from the draining board. 'Looks
neat enough to me.'

I suppose it did. It was as if I didn't want
to let George down. I'd always matched
my standards against his while he was
alive, but I could tease him about his
excesses then. When this summer came,
I'd wonder if my lawn was as weed-free
as his, the path as cleanly swept. But he
wouldn't be there to seize the secateurs
and finish the roses for me with the excuse
that he'd had a light week and I looked
done in.

I slopped some of the coffee. I stared
blindly at the little puddle. Chris reached
for the J-cloth and mopped it. Then he
picked up the tray.

This time he sat on the floor, his legs
stretched out in front of him, crossed at
the ankles. Occasionally he would draw a
circle in the air with one foot or the other,
his shoes creaking softly.

'George and Jools must have worked
very closely together,' he said at last.
'But from what you've said of George,
and what I've gathered myself of Jools,
they don't seem to have been very similar.

Chalk and cheese. Did they get on?'

'Ask Jools.'

'Sophie, I know she's a friend of yours, but don't be quixotic about trying to defend her. As far as I know she doesn't have to be defended. I just need to know about her. About anyone. But I thought I upset you in there when I mentioned George.'

'It's just that I need to brace myself. If someone mentions him without warning, I—But I can talk about him all evening if you want me to. Where shall I start? His worn cartilage? Buying his evening clothes from the Oxfam shop? His addiction to Spender? Loved a bit of anarchy, did George. But he was rock solid. Ask Tony Rossiter. He used to get George to sit in on auditions and interview panels far more regularly than anyone else because he was such a good judge of character. And Tony's probably told you that he sometimes asked George to have an avuncular word.'

Chris responded with not so much as a flicker of an eyelid.

'With Jools, for instance,' I prompted. 'You see, Tony's my friend too. It's an incestuous little world, isn't it?'

He scrambled to his feet and ostentatiously rubbed cramp in his left calf. Whether it was genuine was impossible to say. But he started to prowl round the room, peering at my china, my pictures, my books. He straightened a frame. I rescued piles of photocopies as he headed towards them, but I didn't try to interrupt. I'd have done the same in his home, perhaps. It struck me how very little I knew of him. To have reached such a senior position while he was still in his thirties suggested he might have been on one of those accelerated-promotion schemes so resented by my less well-qualified police YTS students. If he was a graduate, what might his specialism be? Or did the police take over your life and soul to the exclusion of all your interests?

At last he pounced on a book. A Penguin, *The Canadian Air Force Exercises*. Pity: I'd hoped he'd reveal a sudden passion for Greek philosophy. But at least it gave him an excuse to start talking again.

'The trouble is that they're so boring.' he said, flicking the pages. 'Wouldn't you find a fitness centre more inspiring?'

I opened my mouth to reply, and closed it. Then I started to laugh. 'Any fitness centre? Or the one Jools just happens to use?'

He shrugged, but not very convincingly. Then, as I held his eye, he started to laugh too. 'OK. A hit. But the one I used to use has gone bust, and I'm looking for another.'

'I don't see you as a weights man.'

'I'm into weights like you're into computers. But I liked the rolling road and the rowing machine. And the sauna. Do you use a centre?'

'I do. And it's the one I introduced Jools to. Are you planning to join? Or do you merely want to case the joint?'

'Perhaps we could go along together one day,' he said. 'I'd enjoy poseur-watching with someone. Tell me, do you wear a snazzy leotard?'

His crow's feet were much in evidence; damn it, the man was flirting with me.

'Strictly a battered tracksuit. Lycra should be banned once you reach thirty.'

The phone rang. I rather expected him to leap for it, saying, 'That'll be for me.' But he sat down almost sombrely while I picked my way across the photocopies. He might as well have answered it. It was Ian Dale. They had a short, terse conversation. Chris terminated it and picked up his anorak.

'Missing child,' he said briefly as he opened the front door. Then he turned. 'If you like,' he said hesitantly, 'I could DTP your CV for you. If you let me know what you want where and so on.'

'Thanks,' I said.

I watched his car out of sight. Perhaps I had some notion of expressing sympathy and solidarity. As he headed down Balden Road, a taxi came up. It stopped opposite me, then did a trundling U-turn to wheeze to a halt beside me. I stepped back as it disgorged Stobbard Mayou.

'Sophie! I came to see you.'

'Come along in, then. Bit of a mess, I'm afraid.'

Not great conversation; but I for one was wondering if he meant to step our relationship up a gear. Maybe more than one gear, from that smile. But he didn't pay off the taxi.

He surveyed the chaos in the living room with bewilderment. Suddenly he asked, 'You don't have any tissues, do you, Sophie?'

I ran upstairs. He should have the new box from beside my bed even if I had to take off my make-up with toilet paper.

He refused a drink: it might react with the antihistamines his physician had prescribed. He turned down tea and coffee, too, even decaffeinated coffee. I stood helpless, irritated. What on earth had happened to his savoir-faire? And why was he here? It seemed a pretty extreme way to cadge a box of tissues when he could have found a late-night chemist just as easily.

At last he smiled. He unzipped his handbag.

'I got hold of these. For the ballet. Week after next. I'd be honoured if you'd accompany me. As my guest.'

'I'd love to, I—'

'I'll call for you—say, six-thirty? Maybe a drink before the performance. And the reception afterwards. The fifteenth.'

I went to write it in my diary.

'God, it's a Tuesday. That's my evening-class night.'

'Cut it.'

'I'm the teacher.'

'Cut it anyway.'

'I'll try to swap it—I'd better let you know.'

I followed him out to the taxi.

'Six-thirty, remember,' he said. Suddenly he stuck his head out of the taxi window. Then he pushed it down further and thrust a small box at me. Inside was an orchid.

This time George didn't tell me off when I poured a finger or two of Jameson's. But I could feel him eyeing me with concern when I started to worry about buying a dress for the ballet. Could I really be planning so much effort for a man who'd been not so much casual as offhand about our date? Why didn't I phone him and tell him where to put his gilt-edged invitation?

And his orchid.

And I might give Chris much the same advice about his leotard.

In the end I stomped off to the bath with *Persuasion*. The chapter where Captain Wentworth, noticing Mr Elliot's admiration for Anne, begins to admire her himself.

Chapter Thirteen

I'd almost forgotten that I was to spend Thursday not at William Murdock but at a conference centre in Bournville. It was the sort of day I always approached with mixed feelings. At the moment the dominant one was pleasure. The surroundings were almost rural and the centre itself was clean and quiet. But there was guilt, too, and on any event like this colleagues could be found totting up how much the day must have cost and trying to equate it with decorating just one of our college rooms to a civilised standard. And there was frustration: we were supposed to be sharing ideas with other further-education colleagues, not about the subject we all held most dear—teaching—but about a new government initiative called Records of Achievement. Students were to record all the positive things they'd learned during their education, and the suggestions of my more cynical colleagues were pleasantly ribald.

To look at the name badges across the table was to see the history of Birmingham in the history of great men. Cadbury College. Joseph Chamberlain. Josiah Mason. William Murdock. Matthew Boulton. No James Watt—he was commemorated by a school in Sandwell. What about the future? The Sophie Rivers survival school?

I suggested it to Shahida when we shared the mirror in the carpeted loo. She did not overwhelm me with her enthusiasm. But she sparked when I mentioned Stobbard and the ballet. 'Of course you must go! And wear something good, too.'

'I haven't got anything good.'

'Well, buy something good. Just because we live our lives in a scruffy, dirty building, where we daren't wear nice clothes for fear of wrecking them, doesn't mean we're not allowed best bibs and tuckers!'

'And I don't even know if I like the guy. He's so bloody moody.'

'Treat it as just a posh night out, then. How many times have you gone to a posh reception? Well, remember there's a first time for everything. And what was it you were saying the other day—the older you get, the more you ought to experience? Experience this. In a really posh dress.'

'I can't afford a posh dress.'

'Hire one, then. There's a shop in Harborne my sister went to. Don't you dare make any more excuses. Just go.'

'You couldn't spare the time to come with me? On the way home, perhaps?'

'Do you want my opinion or just a lift? Come on, cheer up. Cinders will go to the ball.'

But it was Shahida who needed cheering at the end of the afternoon. She came back from coffee looking strangely subdued, and made a hash of her presentation. While she was unlocking her car, I said, 'You'll have to tell me what it is, Shas. Who's been upsetting you?'

'I don't want to talk about it.'

'Yes, you do.'

She had let me in and fastened her belt before she said, to the windscreen rather than me, 'There was this guy in the coffee lounge. Very well dressed, very suave. About fifty, I suppose. With some other group—not one of us, thank goodness. He just turned to me and looked at me and said, "Breed like fucking rabbits, that's the trouble with your sort." And he just walked away.'

I took her hand: what could I have said? There was the logical objection that she didn't even look pregnant yet, but that wasn't worth making.

She drove so carefully I knew she was forcing herself to concentrate. She botched her parking—eventually I had to see her into the space. And then she laughed. 'Good job that bastard didn't see that. "Can't park a fucking Fiesta, that's the trouble with your sort!" ' And she tucked her arm into mine and steered me towards the dress shop.

All through my Friday classes, I told myself the letter didn't matter. But it did. Every time I didn't have to think about anything else, it pushed back into my consciousness again. But I didn't have any time to do the obvious thing, which was to phone Chris or Ian and ask them to handle it; perhaps I was afraid their reaction would prove the letter did matter.

There was nothing intrinsically offensive about it: no abusive language, no overt threats.

My dear young lady,
  It is safer not to interfere with that which does not concern you.

But Chris and Ian, now sitting with me in

the quietest corner of an increasingly noisy city-centre pub, stared at it grim-faced.

'You should have told us about this straight away,' said Ian reproachfully, tapping it with a heavy forefinger, 'not wait till this hour of the evening.'

Chris, who looked if anything even wearier than Ian, was less restrained. 'Why the bloody hell didn't you ring us earlier? This arrived at eight this morning, did you say? And now it's ten at night. So whoever wrote this has had another fourteen hours to perfect his plans to fix you.'

'Fix me? You mean—Chris, this isn't serious, surely!'

'You know bloody well it's serious, don't you?'

Ian put in more gently, 'In a murder case, everything's potentially serious, Sophie. And you're involved with two, don't forget—we don't even know which one this is connected to. There!' He slipped the letter into one polythene bag, the envelope into another. They had become Evidence. 'Whoever wrote it doesn't give us much to go on,' he added.

'I thought you could identify which typewriter was used from the shape of the letters or something.'

Chris sighed ostentatiously. 'First we have to find the typewriter, Sophie. But in any case this is not a typewriter. It's been produced by a word-processor or a computer, then printed.'

'Don't computer printers have identifiable characteristics?'

'Daisywheels might. Even dot-matrix printers may have, I suppose. But whoever wrote this has done something else to confuse us—photocopied it.'

Ian reached for it and pointed. 'I reckon they've done it several times, reducing it, enlarging it. You can see how blurred the print is.'

'They'd never use it on that advert for photocopiers,' I said. 'Tell me, do photocopiers have fingerprints? I mean, can you tell which machine copies come from?' I touched a zigzag mark half an inch long which appeared at the bottom of the letter.

I might as well not have spoken.

'For God's sake, Sophie, can't you get it into your thick head that we can't identify anything until we have something to compare it with? And to do that we have to have some idea who sent it. And this particular "who" knows who you are, knows where you live, thinks you know who he is. And wants to shut you up? We don't yet know what lengths he'll go to either.'

He. Or she. But I shut my mind firmly against that suspicion and turned my attention to the envelope. Recycled paper by the look of it. A self-adhesive label. It looked as it it had been printed several times in a mixture of faces, roman and sans serif. The print was so blurred I was surprised the postman could read the postcode.

'What's the matter, Sophie?' Chris asked sharply.

I shook my head.

'Come on. Do you recognise something?' He leaned towards me, his voice no longer harshly official.

'It just seems...so cold and professional. A house number, yes, even a street—you can get those easily enough. But the postcode! He must have had to look it up.'

Ian pushed gently from the table, taking our empty glasses with him. Chris waited, then said, 'You're very vulnerable, Sophie. What if I were to offer you protection? Would you be sensible?'

'Protection?'

'To make sure the cold and professional author of that cold and professional note doesn't get too close to you. At very least, go and stay with a friend.'

'Might that put the friend at risk?'

'I can't deny it might. What about having a WPC to stay with you? Tina, for instance. You know her.'

'What? All the time?' I didn't yet have a love life but being chaperoned would seriously damage my chances of getting one. 'For the time being, couldn't I just fit a few more locks? A burglar alarm? My back garden's enclosed with a Berlin Wall and there's one of those rottweiler hedges at the bottom—'

'Berberis,' put in Ian, plonking malt whiskies on the table.

'And I've got one of those automatic lights. I've switched it off—the foxes...'

'Switch it back on the minute you get back in,' said Ian. 'What about the front? Open plan?'

'No, they are in the Beech Lanes Estate, but I've got a fence. And another automatic light.'

'Also switched off because it might scare the foxes?' asked Chris.

'No. Just because they keep activating it.'

He swirled his whisky thoughtfully. When I looked up I found him staring at me. He dropped his eyes swiftly to the whisky.

'Tell you what,' he said at last, 'I'll have a word with an old friend. He'll send in a team looking like gas men or decorators or something and upgrade your security. You'll have to give up that bloody bike, too. I take it you're more than capable of putting it back together if I have to dismember it to get it in my car.'

'You wouldn't pollute your nice new Peugeot with a tatty old push-bike? My God, that's concern above and beyond the call of duty! But as a matter of fact I shan't call on you to make the ultimate sacrifice—it's Friday, remember. And Friday night is drinking night. Came on the bus today.'

He didn't laugh. 'OK. So you're safe for tonight. I'd like you to take taxis—get the drivers to take different routes. I may even be able to organise a driver for you. I suppose you couldn't deign to take a few days off work?'

'I don't know how the Principal would like that. And I'm not sure how I would. I like teaching and I like the company. And surely to goodness I'll be safe at college?'

'I'll bet Wajid thought that too.'

The scream came louder and louder. I dragged myself from my nightmare to find the noise got worse as I woke up. I was shaking, my heart pounding so much that it hurt. And the screams went on.

Someone had to help.

I forced myself to the window.

No sign of anyone.

I dragged on my dressing gown and hurtled downstairs.

There it was again. A choking gurgle. The sort Wajid might have made if he'd had time. Desperate. Inhuman.

Which is, of course, precisely what it was. Through the glass of my front door I could see the shape slinking away. A fox.

But although the vixen did not call again, the sound echoed on and on in my head, and I did not want to fall asleep lest I heard it again for real.

Chapter Fourteen

Saturday's rehearsal was completely un-remarkable. Stobbard Mayou worked us hard, but without drama. He did not attempt much eye-contact with me, and he concluded the rehearsal early because he had to dash off to Bournemouth for a gig with the Sinfonietta. Tony ran him to New Street Station, so I saw nothing of him, either. On Chris's instructions I took a taxi home. The house was full of workmen ready for tea and coffee, and the house rang with Radio One. One of the men—who introduced himself as Gavin, a friend, he said, of Chris's—casually slipped off his overalls and accompanied me to Safeway, making interesting suggestions about cheese and selecting a Hungarian white wine which he swore would be fruity. An instinct to stay away as long as possible made me insist on buying my meat from a local family store. Gavin stayed in his awkwardly parked pick-up truck while I exchanged badinage with Roger, the butcher, and his team. As an afterthought I bought a home-made pizza and a variety of pâtés and exotic sausage. Yes, I agreed, I was stocking up for a siege, and yes—with what emphasis I said it they were of course unaware—yes, I'd welcome a relieving army.

The rest of Saturday I spent cleaning up after the workmen. Gavin made what might have been a serious proposal for a date but I wasn't sure how Chris would rate a round of golf for safety and I thought it might score high for boredom. Then I cooked: sauce for spaghetti and chilli con carne. And then my time was my own. Dreadfully my own.

I'd got the marking out of the way by ten on Sunday morning. It was pouring with rain and normally I'd have taken myself to my fitness centre, buying the Sundays on the way back. But I'd agreed to eschew my cycle, and the occasional presence of a large white van fifty yards down the road did little to persuade me to break my promise.

So there was nothing for me to do except plough through the computer manuals and photocopies. I yearned to correct the English of the former, and the latter were all afflicted by an irritating blot in exactly the same place. Chris was right, of course. There was no substitute for hands-on experience. On Monday I would ask Philomena to let me into the Computer Suite—later I'd cajole a key from Richard—and I'd try to get into WordStar or WordPerfect on one of the Amstrads. If the Office Technology kids could master them, so could I.

'Well, Sophie, how you going on?' asked Philomena after I'd been tapping away, much more slowly than the students she'd let in too, for perhaps an hour. She parked her vac, one with a face painted on it, and peered at my screen.

'Fine, thanks.'

'So why you been using all those rude words, girl? If I was your mum, I make you wash your mouth out.'

'Sorry, Phil. I didn't realise anyone could hear.'

'The good Lord, He can hear. Well, you got yourself a document. Now what you going to do with it?'

'Print it. And save it. And all it does is bleep at me.'

'I don't blame it, all that language.'

I never knew quite how serious Phil was when she went into gospel-talk, and I preferred not to risk offending her. So I kept mum.

'An' I think—' I could feel her smile before it broke—'if you want to save, F10 might help you. There.'

There was an eager buzzing. A light pulsed in what I now knew was the disk drive.

'And now you want to get your printer on line.'

She stubbed her finger on a touch pad. The printer clattered into action.

'Look,' I cried, clapping my hands like a kid. My document, there in black and white, peeled towards me. 'That's brilliant, Phil.'

'I just started this course, see, Sophie. With the OU. Computer Technology. But don't tell no one, eh—or ol' Philly, she never get no work done.'

The phone rang. Phil looked at it and at me and picked it up. 'Ms Rivers's secretary,' she said, cool and Moira Stuart. 'No, I'm terribly afraid he's not in yet. May I take a message? You're sure? Very well. Good morning.' She replaced the handset. 'They want the Computer Suite Manager. Only an hour too early for him.'

I grinned in appreciation. Then an idea occurred to me. 'You said Wajid used the phone a lot?'

'Like he owned the place.'

'Did he bring anything in when he came? A little box?'

'Not what you'd call a box. More a little flat packet, this big.' Her hands suggested a cigarette packet. 'First time I saw it, I say to him, "You know you not supposed to smoke in here, young man," and he give me a lot of lip, and say it to do with the computer and ol' Philomena an ignorant ol' woman. But next week he buy two whole books of raffle tickets from me for the Sickle Cell Fund, so I forgive and forget. I don't tell no one about his modem.'

'Modem!' My blush started in the region of my navel.

'I tell you he use the phone,' she said, sardonically. 'Why else he use the phone? I think you better do this course, Sophie.'

I spent the intervals between the morning's classes trying to cajole one of my colleagues into swapping evening classes with me. No one was very keen, but at last Sean, the head of English, agreed that he really ought to be home for his daughter's third birthday party and that he would indeed allow me to get my hands on his evening A-level group.

A three-hour class for a two-hour one—but as a beggar I could scarcely choose. All I had to do now was nip down to his room to collect copies of the texts I would be teaching—Hardy and Chaucer.

The lifts or the stairs with their ninety-degree bends? I hesitated at the staff room door. I was frightened. After all this time at college I didn't want to leave the security of the staff room. I listened. The place was unnaturally quiet. None of the phones was ringing. All my colleagues were teaching or closeted away in meetings. For once there were no students demanding help. The corridor was so quiet I could hear the pings of the lifts. At the far end a class laughed, politely, obediently. In a room nearby someone was playing a French video.

And I had to make my way to the tenth floor.

I did, of course. Used the stairs, too. Found the books and legged it back again. Up the stairs.

The staff room door was unlocked. Surely I'd locked it?

I flung it open. And woke Shahida, who had her head down on her desk.

She blinked up at me. 'You seen a ghost? Sophie?'

'I'm fine. Honestly. And you? Shas, don't make a martyr of yourself. If you feel rough, why not go home?'

'Just tired. But I've got something for you. I suppose I could have passed it on to Chris Groom myself, but he'd rather have it from you.'

'Me?'

'You must have noticed—he really fancies you. And now Kenji's gone home—'

'I'm happily living on my own. Very happily. Just because you're besotted with Tanvir you want everyone else to smell of April and May. What have you got, anyway?'

She burrowed in the chaos she called her desk, sifting through piles of marking. At last she turned to the windowsill behind her desk and grabbed a single sheet from another pile of academic detritus.

'There. Tim was going to throw it out. The report from Wajid's work-experience placement.'

'Why chuck it?'

For answer she glanced across the room. Tim's desk was completely clear.

'I didn't like to think...just because he was dead... Here.'

All our students have the chance to go to local firms to learn about Real Life—shops, solicitors' offices, even a bookmaker's. There was a strong rumour that two of our former business students were financing their course at Southampton by running what was by all accounts an extremely profitable brothel.

I looked at the paper she'd passed me, a single A4 sheet. Presumably it was the standard report. It had been completed in a convoluted script. Wajid had worked very hard and come in early if necessary. He had been pleasant and cooperative. He had learned how to input and retrieve information. His appearance had not been up to standard. He had not therefore worked with the public.

I tapped the sheet. 'This bank. International Commercial. Never heard of it.'

'You wouldn't,' she said. 'You'd be a Barclays or a Lloyds woman. But if you had a shop on the Soho Road, you'd bank with International Commercial. My father did.'

'Did?'

'Oh, there were some rumours a few months ago. He moved his account—to Barclays as it happens. But most of his friends stayed put. Too much bother to change your bank, especially when the staff speak Urdu or Punjabi or whatever.'

'What sort of rumours?'

'Perhaps people's money wasn't as safe as they'd thought. But nothing positive.'

'Would Tim have visited Wajid at the bank?'

'He should have done: why?'

'Just a feeling. And I don't even know what sort of feeling, yet.'

Shahida smiled. 'Trust intuitions,' she said. 'Always.'

Apart from his determination to keep paperwork to a minimum, Tim was an old softie. You didn't even have to wheedle him, you just asked. So I asked him if he'd care to take me to visit the International Commercial. No, he didn't have anything particularly urgent on this afternoon except a meeting he'd rather dodge, and taking me on a visit would provide a splendid excuse for dodging it. He didn't even blink when I told him how he was to introduce me.

I'd rather have gone on my own, of course. But I'd worked out a scenario which shouldn't arouse too much suspicion, and Tim was an essential adjunct. Not to mention a useful chauffeur, though it must be confessed I found his whole approach to wheels somewhat casual. It must have been the influence of Chris and Ian. He rejected two possible parking slots as too short, and, when he finally found one to his liking, didn't so much park the car as abandon it.

The International Commercial staff—the deputy manager and someone whose job I never quite established—welcomed us cautiously. Perhaps they were disconcerted that Tim should want to bring me into what seemed a male preserve. I thanked the gods of coincidence that I'd chosen a much longer skirt than usual that morning.

'Miss Rivers is to take over my job when I retire at Easter,' said Tim. 'I want to make sure she's properly trained.'

They nodded in appreciation. I smiled hard. Perhaps they wouldn't see my clenched teeth.

I started by asking simple questions— how long they'd been taking on students, and from which schools and colleges. They answered courteously and in full, even if they were surprised by my apparent naivety.

Then there was a tap at the door. A young woman in *kameez* and *salwar* brought in tea. It was thick, sweet and milky, the sort Shahida had taught me to enjoy. My acceptance of a second cup seemed to earn me Brownie points.

I was able to move the conversation round to the work Wajid had done. It seemed he'd caused a little irritation by insisting on wearing jeans. The designer jeans, no doubt. But he'd made up for it by the work he did with computer records. He'd had such skill and enthusiasm for his inputting that there'd been talk among the management of offering him a holiday job and possibly a full-time post.

An odd little silence followed that. Almost as if someone had spoken out of turn.

He'd learned other skills—answering the phone, filing. He'd shadowed the manager at a couple of meetings. The bank had clearly been conscientious in their approach to training. The men bowed dismissively when I said so.

Then I stepped up the conversation a gear: had Wajid had access to classified information?

'All bank information is confidential,' said the man without a title.

I decided to turn his implied reproof. 'Then you are all the more generous to have trusted him,' I said. 'Do you ever have students who betray this trust, and try and pry into private files?'

'Never.'

'So you have to supervise them all the time?'

'A bank relies on trust. Your college sends only students worthy of that trust. In any case,' he added with almost a grin, any particularly sensitive information would be accessible only by means of a password.'

'So you'd be happy for someone like Wajid to work on his own.'

'Of course.'

His voice suggested that my welcome

might be wearing slightly thin. Never mind. I pressed on.

'What opportunities would be open to someone as hard-working and talented as Wajid if he came to work for you full-time?'

A gesture from the deputy manager implied that the sky itself was hardly a limit. 'We are, after all, a truly international organisation. Wherever large numbers of Asian businesses are to be found, you'll find us. The Indian sub-continent, of course. East Africa.'

'America?'

'Certainly. North and South. And we'll be developing further still.'

I nodded my admiration. Tim caught my eye. It was time to go. We were both teaching in half an hour. We smiled and shook hands and promised more students as good as Wajid and made it back just in time for me to phone the police. Ian took the call and promised to pass on the message. And he'd make sure I had a lift home, he said, almost as an afterthought.

I suppose I had expected Chris to be waiting when I emerged from the college at six. I felt my weekend's reading and my visit that afternoon had given me some pointers he might use. But it was only Ian, looking weary in an elderly Maestro.

'Appearances can be deceptive,' was all

he said when I commented on it. Then he explained that Chris was having his jabs but might be round later.

'Jabs?'

'For India. Didn't he tell you? He's off to Delhi on some exchange scheme. A month or more. And he's being sensible for once—having his jabs against hepatitis and typhoid and everything.'

'Are you going too?' I could scarcely ask if Chris would be kept here in Birmingham until he'd sorted out the murders. Not to mention the murderers.

'Too old, too lowly. Not that I mind, Sophie—don't think that. I never did like the heat. And it's good for Chris's career. He's a good lad. The best. I didn't take kindly to the idea of some whizz kid as boss, I can tell you, and I don't think I'd have stomached anyone except him. There's this DCI in charge over Solihull way and I tell you—you wouldn't have to look for the murderer: it'd be me.'

I let him talk on. I found I was shaken that Chris hadn't chosen to tell me something I'd have been interested to know. Most of the time we seemed to be functioning as friends, after all. I'd ignore Shahida, who was inveterately romantic when it came to me and my sundry relationships. In any case, fancying and keeping quiet about your future seemed pretty incompatible.

I asked Ian to stop off at Safeway: Gavin and his predilection for cheese had quite made me forget a load of things on Saturday, and I felt like an evening in the kitchen. Ian insisted on pushing the trolley for me, dismissing Gavin's tastes in wine and proving an expert on sherry, not, alas, my usual tipple. His wife, he said, used Sainsbury's, and he preferred Tesco's amontillado. As he watched my selection of vegetables, his expression changed. I deduced that his wife's trolley did not normally include chillies, okra or ginger. I winced at the price of fresh coriander, but bought two plastic boxes holding about a quarter of the bunches you could buy on Soho Road and at twice the price. I'd cook a curry. If I couldn't escape to India, it'd still be authentic. The father of Bashurat Ali had celebrated his son's unnaturally good results by feasting all who'd taught him at his restaurant—and by teaching us to cook what we ate.

On Ian's instructions I locked myself in the house. And yes, I would try a glass of sherry before I set to work in the kitchen.

I had got no further than opening the bottle when Chris arrived, greyish and sweating.

'Ian said you thought it was important,'

he said, lurching into the living room. 'No, I'm not infectious. They said I'd get a reaction. Feels like flu and a half.'

I poured water on three aspirins and thought of a different recipe.

The sight of him asleep on my sofa brought another problem sharply to my mind. Amid my preparations for the coming evening with Stobbard I'd forgotten one small but essential item. In today's etiquette, whose job was it to buy the condoms? When the rabbit-loving Kenji left my life, I went off the Pill, and we were, after all, now in the era of AIDS. So prudence dictated I must arm myself, and must organise—it was horrible that even the simplest visit took on the proportions of an expedition—a trip to a pharmacy. Not my local one, either, whatever his expertise in suggesting remedies for teacher's throat. And I needed someone's expertise. Surely someone must have written a Woman's Guide to the things. They come with a wide enough variety of unhelpful names—Arouser, indeed, or Fetherlite. I plainly needed something called Toughasoldboots or Safeashouses. Or, of course, I might need nothing at all. Chris might even insist on a police escort.

'You know, Sophie,' said Chris an hour

later, chasing the last grains of rice round his plate, 'you really are a brilliant cook. But I still can't see what Wajid's work experience had to do with his getting knifed.'

I passed the fruit—I'm not very good at puddings—and waited till he'd chosen his apple.

'Wajid, according to Philomena, used the Computer Suite telephone. He shouldn't have, but he insisted it was for his computing project. When he used the phone he used a modem. I suppose you haven't found one among his things?'

'No, but that doesn't mean anything. He could have borrowed one, or it could have been stolen by whoever killed him. Go on.'

'He couldn't dial long distance. He'd have had to go through the switchboard for that, and—'

'But he might have done. I'll—'

'I've already checked. The Finance Section have computerised records which show the destination of every phone call we make. All they could find for the Computer Suite extension was a regular, very long call to a bank. Does the International Commercial Bank mean anything to you?'

He shook his head, then winced, as if the movement hurt him.

'I think it's got something to do with his work experience there. Look.' I showed him the report Tim had meant to bin. In his present state of health he'd rather not know about my visit.

'Not much different from his college reports—keen, hard-working, prepared to come into work early...' Chris's voice tailed off.

'And which department was he mostly based in?'

'Computer inputting.' He rubbed his hands over his face.

'Exactly!'

'Sophie, just spell it out, will you? I feel so bloody...'

I poured him more water, and then ferreted through the pile of photocopies which had so amused him the night Stobbard had called round. 'Here, read this. All about hacking.'

'Jesus!' Chris looked like a drooping plant shot a particularly potent fertiliser. 'So you think he spent his time at the bank hacking into someone's system—'

'—and needed to get into their international network to continue doing so once he was back at college.'

'Why should he be killed for doing that?'

I dropped another article on the table. 'It could be something like salami fraud—

slicing bits off some organisation's bank account and salting them away in his own. But killing someone seems a bit excessive for something like that. I'd have thought a call to your Fraud Squad more likely. So what I wondered was could he have found more than just money? Chris? Chris!'

And he passed out gracefully on my table.

Chapter Fifteen

'What you been up to, eh, Sophie? All night partying, eh? You got real big bags under your eyes: I bet you have a good time!' Philomena cackled gleefully as she opened the Computer Suite for Josiah and me.

'No such luck.'

'What you been doing then?'

'Looking after a friend who wasn't very well.'

This was, after all, the truth. Once I'd revived Chris with his own smelling salts, I'd had to sleep, since he was too tall for anywhere except my bed, on the sofa. He still occupied my bed, to the best of my knowledge. Ian and I had decided to leave him there while Ian ran me to college. Chris's car, the large executive Peugeot, slept on outside my front door. The wheels were still in place and no one had yet removed the aerial. Only my reputation was not intact: I'd noticed the ripples along a whole bank of lace curtains even as I'd got into Ian's car—a Montego, this particular morning.

In my driving days I'd preferred to cross the Hagley Road at the Ivy Bush junction, but today Brummie accents on Ian's radio told of an RTA and he kept on Harborne Road till we reached the Five Ways island. He was in the inner lane since he wanted the second exit. This is the island I always cycle under. Up above, it's just a matter of time before you become an accident statistic.

Even Ian.

There are peak-hour traffic lights to control the mayhem. Normally they give you a few yards to get on to the island. This morning, of course, they were out. Each set. That meant there was a continuous line of traffic on the island, moving faster than could possibly be safe. If you knew the buses' numbers and routes you knew when you had a chance. The numbers 103 and 10 would pull off in front of the hordes ravening up from Islington Row. A couple of cars from Harborne Road might be able to make it.

Sometimes there were no buses, of course. So there wasn't a gap. You had to make one.

Ian waited patiently.

Then there was an outburst from someone's horn. And someone else's. Then a regular chorus.

I peered round. Some poor motorcyclist had broken down just behind us. He was rapidly acquiring a massive tailback.

Ian was now almost at the head of the queue. I could feel him tensing, ready to urge the car forwards. If he urged too much, of course, he'd find the Rover driver in front had had second thoughts and he'd end up embracing the Rover's boot and losing his no-claims bonus.

The Rover pulled away smoothly.

Ian's turn.

The Lada alongside him was ready for the same gap. We surged out together.

So did the motorbike. Heading straight for the passenger door. My door.

I didn't have time to cry out.

The Montego was no longer in the left-hand lane, but in front of the Lada on the inner lane. Inches, incidentally, from the exhaust of a cement mixer, trundling round the island at a more sedate pace. Another foot—I covered my face with my hands.

'No point in that,' said Ian. 'If I'd hit

him, you'd have lost more than your looks. Lost your head, more like.'

'Literally?'

'Literally.'

He calmly signalled, found a gap, and left the island. There was another tailback opposite the Children's Hospital—people wanting to turn right for cheap Tesco's petrol. He dodged that, neatly changing lanes again.

The last few hundred yards were uneventful. He parked exquisitely.

'Do you think that was—coincidence?' I asked, releasing my seat belt.

'Lot of mad drivers around,' he said.

'You saved my life.'

'Worth keeping your eyes open when you're driving,' he acknowledged.

A horn sounded loud and long.

'Who the hell does he think he is?'

'Just the Principal. But you are parked in his space.'

Philomena enjoyed that bit. But as if to trump me she produced from her overall pocket a creased sheet of paper.

MEMO
To: All Personnel
From: James Worrall, Principal
Re: Enhanced Security
Following the recent lapse in security,

staff are reminded that all rooms must be locked at all times unless under the active supervision of an authorised member of staff.

'So how do I get authorised, I wonder?'
'Don't ask me. I only Philly the cleaning lady. Philly don't know nothing. She jus' know she love to get she hands on Mr Carpenter's memos and correct them first. "Re", indeed!'

I battled on for another half-hour or so, deciding that I might in fact authorise myself. Then a tough BTEC class, in which I digressed from the syllabus to give a few subtle hints on the delights of the apostrophe, and a quick interview with Richard, who chose to see my attempts to make myself computer-literate as an attack on him for not letting me get trained properly. At last I talked him round, and became the proud possessor of a shiny new Computer Suite key.

Ten minutes till the next class. Somehow I had to fit in a coffee.

I ran up to the staff room. Hang the fact I hadn't washed my mug, and the only milk was plastic, it would be a lifesaver.

Maybe literally.

I'd just switched on the kettle when Winston knocked on the door. It was open and anyone else would have sailed in—the seven or eight students in the room had—but Winston stood on the threshold until he caught my eye.

'Hey, Sophie. My mum says to bring this straight up. She says to tell you it must be from your young man. You know my mum.'

'This' was a Jiffy-bag with what looked like a book inside.

He was obviously under orders from Phil to see what I'd been sent, hovering, as much as thirteen stone of muscle can be said to hover, by my desk.

MS SOPHIE RIVERS
COMPUTER SUITE
WILLIAM MURDOCK COLLEGE
BIRMINGHAM

At least there was no postcode this time. One of my colleagues yelled I was wanted on his phone; while I spoke—it was Chris thanking me for my bed—I wondered who could have sent me a present. I rang off and looked at the package again. The label was typed or word-processed. The postmark was indecipherable.

I've never had a cold sweat before.

The fifteenth floor. Eight students in the room. Six staff. A young man who could become either a fine doctor or a test cricketer. A full classroom on the other side of the flimsy wall.

'Winston,' I asked, very quietly, 'have you been told what to do if there's a bomb scare?'

'Clear the area without causing panic and call the emergency services,' he intoned. 'Then run like buggery.'

'How do we do it, then?'

'Do what?'

'Clear the area. I know how to run like buggery.' And I pointed to my unwanted gift.

'If it's any consolation,' said Chris, his voice heavy with irony, 'it wouldn't have done that much damage. Not enough to justify all this.' He looked at fire appliances. Two were just pulling away. Officers were scrambling into the third.

Students were milling around the car park, waiting to be called back in. Manjit was walking away from a group. Aftab happened to be walking towards it.

'Letter bombs rarely do,' he continued. 'And officially, remember, this was a hoax. Ian's dinned that into the Principal. I've told him I want him to moan about irresponsible people smashing fire alarms.'

I nodded, wondering if I might rub my arm yet. I would have the marks of his fingers just above the elbow for days. It would take longer to forget the anger in his eyes even though it hadn't been directed at me.

The Principal fiddled with his loud-hailer. All the senior staff were grouped around him, like guests at a posh wedding awaiting the photographer. A fire drill's about the only time you see so many good suits around here—mostly male, but one or two women in shoulder pads and grey stripes, too.

'So what would it have done?'

He looked away from me. 'Ripped off most of your hands and forearms, probably. Blinded you, possibly. That's your average device. We'll learn more about yours when—what the devil?'

There was a piercing electronic whistle, followed by high-pitched gobbledygook. The students roared derisively. Even one or two of the senior staff permitted themselves a smile.

The Principal was trying to make the loud-hailer work.

The Vice-Principal's secretary brought us coffee and withdrew, not quite shutting the door.

Ian raised his eyebrows as he walked across to close it. 'Who's she keeping obbo for?'

'Just her boss,' I said, trying to stop my

hand shaking as it reached for a chocolate biscuit. He was a redundant Latin teacher forced by circumstances rather than ability to scrabble up the promotional ladder, and he had, not surprisingly, developed paranoia into a high art. He'd been detailed to go and baby-sit my class of secretarial trainees. I wondered if he would emerge virgo intacta.

Winston sat beside me, overlarge in his armchair. Ian and I chose hard chairs, and Chris was almost absorbed by the executive chair so far leading the field in the hierarchy's battle for status furniture. He struggled out of it sufficiently to reach his coffee. His colour had almost returned, but in repose his face was so drawn as to be haggard.

'Just once more,' he said. 'Exactly what happened, young man?'

'My mum was just signing off, sir, in the caretaker's office to the left of the reception area just as you come in. This motorcyclist came in—Mum and I thought he must be a courier. We get special deliveries from time to time, sir, especially now the public can use the Computer Suite, Sir.'

I glanced at Winston swiftly—all these 'sirs' meant someone had angered him.

'The public? You mean firms or just anyone? I could walk in off the street and say I wanted to use a computer?'

'Provided, sir, you registered as a user and paid a fee.'

'Hmm. I suppose you wouldn't know if they check...check—'

'—their bona fides, sir? You'd have to ask the Computer Suite Manager that, Sir. I believe they keep a register. We get to know regular users of the building but unfortunately, since the influx of private security guards, our rotas have been altered and it's hard for us to keep tabs on people.'

Chris opened his eyes a fraction. He was changing his mind about Winston, who'd obviously chosen not to end his charade. He looked swiftly at me. I smiled blandly.

'I'm sorry—I interrupted you. You were talking about the motorcyclist who might have been a courier.' This time the courtesy seemed unforced.

I relaxed a little. I didn't want Winston to get himself into trouble by overacting.

'He dropped the package on my desk, but when I looked for my biro—we have to sign for things, sir—it had fallen to the floor. When I'd picked it up, he'd gone. Then my mother my mum came over, she say not to stand there looking gormless but to take it straight up to Miss Sophie.' Surely he'd overdone it this time! And it got worse: 'D'you know something, sir? I reckon that ol' courier must have pushed it, sir.'

Chris nodded. 'I reckon you're about right, Winston—well done.'

Fifteen all?

Winston got up and almost bobbed a bow. Then he stopped. 'This courier, sir. I think I've seen him before.'

The timing was perfect, of course. He winked with the eye further from Chris. So he had been saving it up. In a second, however, his downcast eyes and hunched shoulders epitomised guilt. 'The Tuesday Sophie found Wajid, sir—I should have told you this before. I told your colleagues I hadn't left the building. And I hadn't. Except for a moment. A man came in and asked if I'd help push his mate's car—he'd parked with his lights on and flattened his battery.'

I could feel Chris willing him to get to the point. I could also feel Winston playing the moment for all it was worth.

'It was parked at the far end of the car park. When I got there the engine was running OK, and the guy said he'd borrowed someone's jump leads. Gave me a fiver for my trouble.'

'I suppose,' said Chris, trying to sound not at all furious, 'you'd get the sack if your employer heard?'

Winston nodded, humble and lying.

'Sit down,' said Chris gently, 'and tell us every single thing you can tell me about the two men, the car and the motorbike.'

'The man who came in that evening was just a man, sir. Got his anorak hood up. About your height. Big shoulders. That was all. And he spoke very politely—a very odd accent.'

My ears pricked at the word 'politely': I thought of my anonymous note. That was polite.

'Accent?' Ian repeated.

'Almost as if he were playing a German in an old war movie. But not—'

'Authentic?' I prompted.

'The other guy, the one who said he'd borrowed the leads, was shorter. Wore a leather jacket, jeans. Voice a bit raspy as if he'd got a bad throat. But the odd thing was his buttocks. Hips, really. More pronounced than you'd expect on a man. Today of course you couldn't really tell. He wore leathers. And a helmet with a dark visor. Never lifted it properly. I never saw his bike.'

'What about the car?'

'Beat-up old Datsun.'

Chris didn't say anything. Ian got to his feet. 'Could be a red herring, gaffer, but I reckon I'll just check out the Computer Suite—you never know.'

Chris nodded. He looked thoughtfully at

Winston. 'You'll have to make a proper statement back at Rose Road, Winston. At the end of your shift, if that's OK? Did I hear something on the grapevine about your playing for Northants? May I wish you good luck?'

'Well, sir, it's like this. I don't reckon I shall be going to Northants. You see, I got another offer. Middlesex. Lord's, sir, the headquarters of cricket. Just think, walking down the Long Room—'

It was time to join in. 'Pity you won't be signing for either, isn't it? Winston got straight As in his A levels last year, Chris, and an A in his GCSE English. He's got an unconditional place at St Mary's to read medicine.'

At this point Ian returned. 'You'll never guess.'

'Yes, I will,' said Chris and I simultaneously. 'They've lost the bloody register,' I finished.

'That's right. But they say they've just introduced a more sophisticated, indeed foolproof system.'

'Computerised?' I suggested.

'How did you guess?'

'That'll be just fine,' said Winston, 'until the computers crash.'

We all laughed; but he was right, of course.

'Nice young man,' Ian remarked as the

door closed behind him.

'Bright, too,' said Chris, staring hard at me.

'Very bright,' I agreed blithely.

'D'you think he'll keep his trap shut?'

I nodded. 'The only person he'll tell, and it'll be as safe as houses with her, is—'

And Phil erupted into the room. For a moment she was so upset she forgot her patois.

'Sophie, love, I'm so sorry. It's my fault. Are you sure you're all right, love?'

Ian had moved swiftly to shut the door. Phil and I hugged each other hard. I found myself sobbing. Then Chris pressed a firm hand on my shoulder, and pushed his smelling salts under my nose.

Phil subsided on to the chair her son had used and resumed her cleaning-lady mode, dabbing her eyes with the corner of her overall.

'Why did you say it was your fault, er, Philomena?' asked Chris.

'My fault I send Winston up. I never dream it might hurt Sophie. I think it from her young man.'

'Which one?' asked Ian softly.

I didn't look at Chris in case he was blushing too. Instead I asked, 'D'you remember, Phil, yesterday morning? We were larking around in the Computer Suite and someone phoned and you put on your Moira Stuart voice—'

' "Ms Rivers's secretary here." '

'Right. D'you remember who he asked for?'

As if responding to the urgency in my voice, she dropped her patois. Again I chose not to look at Chris. 'It was a she, Sophie. Not a he. And she wanted the Computer Suite Manager. But I think I've heard the voice before. Asking for Wajid.'

'What sort of voice?'

'Very deep, a real chesty contralto. And a mid-Atlantic accent like a bad DJ.'

'Why do you want to know, Sophie?' asked Chris.

'Because of the way the letter bomb was addressed,' Phil replied for me. 'Anyone who knew Sophie would know better than to think she had anything to do with the Computer Suite!'

Chapter Sixteen

It would be foolish to say I thought no more of the incident, but there didn't seem to be any point in dwelling on it. I taught my afternoon and evening classes as usual, even if my heart and mind weren't fully engaged. No one was any trouble, no one stayed behind, no one shed any tears. Ian drove me home. I ate chilli con carne, and found I'd been over generous with the chilli.

On Wednesday things were less straight-forward. Tina drove me in, to the accompaniment of Radio One, and I found several notes on my desk. The first was from the union rep. She wanted to see me urgently. So did Richard. And so did the Chief. Since the Chief's idea of urgent was midday, and Richard generally offered a good cup of coffee at this time, I chose Richard first.

He greeted me affably enough, but I detected a note of unease. We talked generally about my classes and then about the pressures I must be under. And the pressures my colleagues must be under, having me around.

'Are you saying you want me out?' I asked. My voice must have betrayed how stricken I felt.

'I didn't say that.'

'Are you saying other people want me out? Because of one attack?'

'It could have been very serious,' he said, staring at his blotter. 'It wouldn't just have hurt you.'

'It could have hurt Winston,' I agreed.

'And if I hadn't been here to open it, it would have hurt anyone who tried. And if someone had thought of popping it into the post for me at home, it might have hurt them or the postman or whoever.'

'Are you saying it might be more risky for us if you weren't here?'

'I don't know. I wish I did. I couldn't have some of that coffee, could I?'

For the first time he smiled and gestured to the percolator. Then he dug in his drawer and produced a box of expensive-looking—and expensive-tasting—chocolate biscuits.

'Do you want to get rid of me, Richard?'

'You always have been more trouble than you were worth,' he said, his smile broadening to take the sting out of what he was saying. 'And oddly enough—though this may not comfort you, Sophie—I wonder if we're safer with you here. A target, true. But at least if you're here the nutter isn't going to hold a class of kids hostage until we reveal your whereabouts.'

'Gee, thanks. And I suppose the said nutter isn't going to know I'm not here—not unless you hire one of those planes with a banner to tell the whole of Brum I've moved out.'

'That's roughly what I shall say to the Chief when I see him this morning. There's no doubt he finds you an embarrassment. I thought you and I might want to sing the same song. But if you want to disappear, I'll say that's the best thing for the college.'

I stared at the coffee as if it might provide some answer. At last I shook my head. 'I wish I knew. I think I'd go off my head sitting around at home. And I'd hate to give up my exam classes now. And there's a student I'm very concerned about—she's important too. But I don't want to harm anyone here. Tell you what,' I said, taking another biscuit, 'why don't we talk to Chris Groom? He mentioned police protection the other day. I turned it down flat at the time. But if it'll enable me to stay here and get on with my job, I could grovel a bit—'

'You grovel? Come off it, Sophie! You'll make it seem as if the man's doing you a favour. How's your word-processing coming on? Did you chose WordStar or WordPerfect?'

I had to postpone my next meeting—the one with the union rep—until after my class, and I was actually on my way to her staff room when I ran into Manjit. Her lip was indisputably split. I said nothing, but stood still, waiting for her to respond to my inquiring look. A second or two later she was crying in my arms.

Break. Kids and staff would be swarming along here any moment. The only safe place I could think of was the staff loo. I unlocked it and pushed her in. No, there was no one in the only cubicle. I locked the outer door. If only there were a chair for her! She turned from me and leaned against the washbasin.

'Manjit?' I prompted at last. Someone might try to come in at any moment.

Her response was barely audible. But it might have been, 'My brother.'

'Your brother did this?'

She nodded. 'Because I wouldn't let him—' And she broke off, sobbing.

'Let him?'

'You know, miss. You know...'

'But that's against the law. And surely, surely, Manjit, it's against your religion?'

She nodded.

'Can't you tell someone? Surely your mother or father'd be appalled?'

'I can't tell them. I can't.'

'But someone at your temple? There must be elders, community leaders, who'd—'

'I can't tell them.'

'The police?'

She shook her head. She shuddered so violently I thought she might be sick.

I was completely out of my depth. Sure, I'd been on counselling courses, sure, I'd had ten years' experience dealing with

215

students' problems. But incest—that was out of my range.

'Is there anyone you can tell, love?'

Another shudder. Then she was back in my arms, crying.

I waited, feeling the thin bones shaking against mine. All I could do was stroke her hair and mutter useless words meant to comfort her. But at last I'd have to do something: I had a classful of students waiting for me, and though everyone would be very pleased I'd been nice to one student, they'd still hold me responsible if anyone in that group put a chair through the window or set fire to a bin. Most of all, I knew I wasn't doing Manjit any good. She needed an expert. And expert I was not.

'Manjit, love, could you tell another woman? If I found you a counsellor, could you talk to her? She might even find somewhere safe—' I'd meant to say, 'somewhere safe to talk'.

'Somewhere safe to go?' She stared at me, her eyes bloodshot with tears and mascara but also at last showing hope.

I found myself nodding. And having a glimmer of an idea.

When we got to it, the Counselling Room was locked, but I let her into it, and locked it behind her as I went in search of Frances, the counsellor. Flu.

She was at home with flu. And one of her team was in Leeds on a course, the other nowhere to be found. There was a kid here being abused, and no one to help. I could have screamed. And suddenly I was afraid, again. I was hurtling around the building as unprotected as if no one had ever tried to blow me up. And someone else's safety was very much in my hands. I found an empty staff room and reached for the phone.

Chris. Chris might have an idea.

Ten minutes later I was greeting a woman about my age in the foyer. As we went up in the lift—*the* lift, now restored to service—I gave her the bones of the situation. She nodded, anonymous, professional. That was it. She'd be in touch via Frances, she said. They'd worked together before. No, of course I didn't know. That was what it was all about wasn't it—confidentiality. I unlocked the door of the Counselling Room, introduced her briefly to Manjit as a friend of a friend, and left them to it. Back to a classroom full of loud kids and paper darts.

I was glad at lunchtime I was still in the dark about Manjit. The meeting with the Chief, remember. The Principal. He was an ex-Navy man who liked to be addressed as Principal Worrall. God knows how he'd ended up at William Murdock.

He'd have been at home, perhaps, in a protocol-ridden public school. Here he might have been merely an anachronism. But he was implementing changes directed by the government with the enthusiasm of one used to obeying and giving orders, whether the lower ranks liked them or not.

His message to me was apparently coded. It had nothing to do with yesterday's bomb. It had to do with community relations. Staff should not take it upon themselves to criticise community customs, he said. And that was all.

I gaped.

'You have to remember that we draw our clients from a wide variety of social, cultural and ethnic backgrounds,' he continued eventually, at last gesturing me to a seat. 'It is important at all times not to be judgemental.'

I nodded.

'I refer, of course, to that potentially serious incident the other day. The college does not need bad publicity, Miss—ah—Miss Rivers.'

I nodded, and got to my feet. 'Message understood,' I said. But I could not bring myself to call him 'sir'.

During the afternoon break there was another meeting in Richard's room. Chris was there, this time. The two men were deep in conversation by the time I arrived, talking about geraniums, some of which grew rather thinly on Richard's windowsill. But we had gathered together to discuss not flowers but me, and it seemed they'd arrived at the same conclusion some minutes ago. I was to stay in college, provided I had protection. The safety of the staff and students was after all paramount.

'OK, yours is quite important too,' said Chris.

'I told the Chief the flu epidemic had left us so short-staffed I didn't see how we could possibly ask you to take leave. And the budget for VTs—part-time staff—' he said to Chris, 'is almost exhausted at this time in the financial year. He did suggest unpaid leave—'

'Did he indeed!'

But the union rep said that was out of the question.'

So there had been other meetings about me. My future was being manipulated without me. It was what we did to the students all the time, of course—talk about them behind their backs but the excuse was that we knew best.

'You didn't want to consult me?' I said, not entirely mildly.

'The rep said she's asked to meet you

219

but you hadn't turned up. And we needed a fast response for the Chief.'

I pulled a face. 'OK. And how will we explain to the kids why I'm being trailed by six foot of cop?'

'I mentioned Tina the other night,' said Chris. 'And Richard thought she'd be ideal. Young. Knows the place. Gets on well with you.'

'I thought we could say she was shadowing you. Work experience or something,' said Richard.

'So it's all decided then,' said Groom.

'Fine,' I said, backing out and shutting the door on my irony.

So I had a shadow, but she was all too solid. Tina, as one of my ex-students, wasn't such a bad choice. She'd been neither better nor worse than the rest of the group of YTS students aspiring to join the force. She'd put her most serious efforts into escaping the mandatory cross-country runs, as I recall, and had had a passionate crush on her Law lecturer, writing his name on every desk she sat at. I didn't know whether she'd joined as a DC, or if that was some sort of promotion. She'd lost a stone or so since her time with us, and her hair was distinctly blonder, but she maintained her Black Country accent and a love of the louder and less tuneful forms of pop music, if the lifts she'd given me were any evidence. How we'd get on when she was living under my roof I'd no idea. As far as my social life was concerned, I was determined to keep her on the margins. She could drive me to the Friday choir rehearsal, and to the Music Centre on Saturday morning, but that was that. I think she was relieved to avoid such unnatural musical activities—so relieved that I managed to talk her into a cycle ride on Saturday afternoon.

'Cycle? You mean, on me bike, like?'

'If you've got one. Nothing competitive. Nice and level. A good meal at the end of it.'

'Real food? None of your fancy muck?'

'How about chicken and chips?'

With that, Tina became amazingly cooperative. She borrowed her sister's machine, and then organised her boyfriend and his van to ferry the cycles to a suitable access point. She never addressed the boyfriend by name, and he had all the social graces of a Trappist monk. I can't say I felt an instant rapport with him.

As he pulled up, with a rather ostentatious tweak of the handbrake, he offered unenthusiastically to wait.

'Not on your bloody life,' said Tina. 'You pick us up from wherever my bum gets tired—right?'

So the boyfriend's van had a phone. No

ordinary boyfriend this, perhaps.

He watched us unload the cycles and carry them down the steps. And then he drove away.

For some reason people refer to the Midlands as the Venice of Britain. I suspect it's because they've never seen the canals except on a map.

I suppose ours have the same unlovely smell as the Venice ones. In fact, Venice on a hot day might have the edge on them. But Venice would probably score more points for views. In Birmingham there might be vistas, but any that we saw ended in sixties flats or the unkempt sides of churches or factories. Mostly factories. The odd brewery, of course. These days efforts were being made to smarten them up, not just round the Music Centre, and exploit the austere beauty of the blue brickwork. What was once a nice, cheap mooring in Gas Street Basin, for instance, was now being developed, much to the dismay of the narrow-boat owners. And the early-nineteenth-century bridges, elegant cast-iron affairs, were being lovingly restored and repainted.

We got on to our particular stretch of towpath on Somerset Road, by way of an awkward set of steps, and I turned towards the city.

'Are you sure this is OK?' Tina demanded. 'I know you managed to talk Chris into letting you out, but are you sure?'

I gestured. We could see any would-be assailant hundreds of yards away, and if anyone wanted to ambush us from a bridge he'd have to know exactly which way we planned to go. And he'd have to have a thorough knowledge of Birmingham and its one-way streets.

'It's not what you'd call pretty,' Tina muttered, and pushed off.

We passed a couple of mattresses and black sack spilling out nappies. And a comprehensively dead fox.

Tina stopped beside a particularly opaque stretch of water and pointed at something lumpy. 'What d'you suppose that is, our Soph?'

'Don't even ask.'

Grotesque odds and ends of wood and metal lodged half in, half out of the water: God help a careless navigator. A friend of mine who's got a narrow boat claimed to spend more time freeing the propeller from sunken detritus than actually sailing. If you ever fell in, he would add, with a ghoulish smile, you had to be rushed to hospital to have your stomach pumped out. And a battery of injections.

'My brother reckons there was this dog,'

said Tina, 'and it went for a swim in the cut down Oldbury. Any road, it got out and shook itself dry. And blowed if it didn't burst into flame—from the phosphorus or summat. My God, Soph, how much further? Me bum's killing me. I've heard of being saddle-sore, but not on a bloomin' bike.'

We'd hardly started!

'Shall we just get as far as Gas Street? Could you manage that? Or, a bit further on they're doing up an old pub. We might just reach that and it'd be nice and quiet.'

'Ooh, I'd murder for half of mild.'

Soon we reached Gas Street Basin, bright and clean and a good omen for the rest of the canal system. I could see Tina was tempted by the big pub dominating it, the James Brindley. But she had to admit it was far too public for us. We pressed on.

We went under Broad Street, the tunnel rumbling with traffic, and on past the Music Centre and the indoor sports complex being built beside it. We took the route to Dudley, and there, after another unappetising stretch, was a low, brick-built pub—the Bolt 'n' Nut.

'Well, I'll go to the foot of our stairs,' said Tina, beaming with relief, 'if it isn't the good old Matthew Boulton. Looks good, mind you. Like Cornwall or summat.'

She was right. A whole yuppie village was growing up with houses and flats mimicking the sort of artistic jumble you expect of a holiday resort. And it worked, probably because everything was brick-built. All the window boxes sprouted bulbs. You could believe it was spring. Particularly as the pub had a sheltered terrace on to which one or two couples had ventured to find sunny corners for private conversations.

In one of them, the one furthest from the towpath, a handsome young man was leaning intimately towards a bulky young woman. The sun glinted on his hair and her muscles. Stobbard and Jools.

At this point Tina's chain came off.

'Even the old bike needs a rest,' she said. 'D'you know how to fix it? 'Cos I'm blowed if I do.'

I let my bike fall beside hers. It was a simple enough job, if messy.

'There—all you need to do now is pull up the gear lever a little. OK?'

'OK. But I reckon your hands aren't. Still, I don't suppose they'll do a nail inspection when they pull us a pint.'

I rubbed hard with a tissue. The last people I wanted to see me this afternoon were Stobbard and Jools. I put out a hand to stop Tina.

'That man there—I'm supposed to have a date with him on Tuesday. And the woman's the bassoon player—'

'The famous Jools? Built like a brick shit-house, isn't she? He's a bit of all right, though. Hey—you're all right: they're having a barney. If that don't beat cock-fighting.'

We watched as Stobbard stood up and pushed away from the table. He slammed his fist on the table, and Jools stood up too. I think she'd have hit him had he not seized her wrist. Then they flung away from each other, and went off in opposite directions. I'd have given my eyeteeth to know what they were arguing about.

We too drank on the terrace. Tina wanted to hear all about Stobbard and the date for Tuesday. The idea of the ballet appalled her, until she reflected on all those young men leaping round the stage. 'All them tights. All them bums. All them big thingies. Should turn you on nicely. You won't want me around, that's for sure.'

'I won't.'

'You'll have to square it with Chris, mind. I couldn't take the evening off without his say-so. And I'd love to see his face when you tell him why.'

'I may have mentioned I was going with a friend to the ballet.'

'That particular friend? Thought not. Well, you'll have to. And fix up about afterwards. I take it there'll be an afterwards. You want to make sure of it, a bloke with a bum like that.' Maybe I could have coped with the eternal music if Tina hadn't insisted on singing it tunelessly under her breath. And she thought it necessary to ask me where I was off to every time I left the room. By nine I could have screamed.

I would retire to the loo. At least she couldn't follow me there.

There were three conversations I'd like to have. One with Jools, another with Stobbard, and a third with Tony. If Stobbard fancied me—and Tony had assured me he did—what was he doing with Jools, whom he pretended to loathe? All I could expect was reassurance, which I could get more easily from Tony. I found my fingers shaking as I dialled his number. I made a mistake and had to start again.

I got his answering machine, of course. No, I did not want to leave a message. Then I realised: Saturday night. A gig. Worcester, as I recalled, in the Cathedral. Where Tony was, Stobbard and Jools would be too.

So I dialled Tony again. Would he save my life and phone me as soon as he could?

Chapter Seventeen

With rain like this, there was no point in trying to persuade Tina to cycle to the shops with me to buy the Sunday papers. But I had to devise some scheme to escape the incessant noise, and the relentless investigations into what I was marking and the marks I was giving. As before, I retired to the loo to think.

The modem. That was worth pursuing. The most important thing, come to think of it. And it had to be with Aftab. Aftab, whose friend Manjit hadn't been seen in college since I'd introduced her to the Community Liaison Police Officer on Thursday.

'Tina,' I said authoritatively when I returned to the living room, 'I want to go and get the papers. Wouldn't be Sunday without the papers. And the father of one of my students has opened a new shop just down Smethwick High Street.'

'Hell, there's newsagents bloody everywhere. Why bloody Smethwick, and on a day like today, too?'

'Because I want to talk to the student, too. And I want to buy some fresh

coriander and it's cheaper down Smethwick.' My own Black Country roots were
showing.

'I don't like it. What's Chris going
to say?'

'No idea. I'm not going to ask him.'

'But—'

'If you don't want to take me, I'll call
a taxi.'

Having coerced Tina into taking me, I
then had to make sure she didn't follow
me into the shop. It was going to be hard
enough to work on Aftab without having
an official audience. I contemplated taking
a knife to slash one of her tyres, but I
couldn't quite work out the logistics.

'Two minutes,' she said, parking a couple
of yards from the shop.

'I'll come out when I've finished.
Anything I can get you, by the way?'

She snorted sullenly.

The shop was blessedly empty. Aftab
greeted me with a shy smile. He was on
the cash desk. His head was supported by
a padded surgical collar. I made round,
impressed eyes.

'Done it lifting, miss. What can I do
for you?'

I decided to risk the truth. 'Someone
tried to kill me the other day. A letter
bomb, at college. They think I know more
about Wajid's murder than I do. I don't

know anything at all, in reality. But I'd
like to. And you knew about his money.
What else do you know about?'

'Honest—they tried to kill you?'

I nodded.

'And you don't know anything?'

'The clue you gave me about his clothes
and everything's all I've got to go on.'
Hang the melodrama. 'But I think you
know something else. I think you're looking
after something.'

He stared at me for a second and
disappeared through the stockroom door.
I couldn't believe it was going to be as
easy as this. But he returned in a couple of
minutes with a large envelope. I'd expected
a modem but I got a wad of scribbled notes
as well.

I thrust a fiver at him. 'Photocopy the
lot, will you? Fast.'

He did as I asked, and I gathered a fistful
of respectable Sundays for camouflage.
He came back to the cash desk. The
photocopies were still warm, collated and
stapled. My fiver lay on top.

I pushed it back.

'No. Don't want you to pay. OK. But
just for the papers.'

'Thanks.'

'Miss...' he dropped his voice to a whis-
per. 'Any news of Manjit? She was coming
to see you, and I haven't seen her since.'

'I'm sure she's all right. But that's all I know. But—' I was going to add that I'd keep him posted when I noticed a brown Datsun just across the street. I'd no idea how long it had been there. The rain was so heavy I couldn't see who was driving it, and I found my stock of bravery was suddenly exhausted.

'Aftab, does your brother still drive his mini-cab?'

'Sure.'

'Would he take me home? Right now?'

He nodded.

'Is there a back way?'

'Follow me.'

He led the way through the stock rooms. Garlic, aubergines, adverts for Asian films, soft-porn magazines and sophisticated-looking watches, all rubbing shoulders with photocopy paper and Kit-Kats. A kind-looking woman averted her face as I passed. A man, tired-faced and with a nasty cough, shouted upstairs to his son, with a gesture apologising for the tardiness of all sons. At last Imran, gentle and bespectacled with a degree in accounting he couldn't find a job to use, ran downstairs. I scribbled Tina's name and her car-registration number.

'She's in the red Escort just outside, Aftab. Tell her I've had to go home, and that I'll explain why. Tell her I'm very sorry. It's to do with someone outside.'

The whole family whispered, concern on every face. They wanted to help me.

And I might have led a killer straight to their door.

I grovelled to Tina, very thoroughly. I promised I'd explain to Chris and take responsibility and his bollocking. I promised too to hand over the modem and the notes—I'd planned to anyway. Since she didn't know about the photocopies, I reasoned there was no need for him to worry about them and I filed them among my marking. The worst part, from her point of view, was that I hadn't mentioned the Datsun. She'd taken no special interest in it, and couldn't even be sure whether it had followed her back. Now, however, was hardly the time to lecture her on the use of the rear-view mirror.

Chris turned up just as I was getting lunch, presenting me with the problem of stretching chicken meant for two to serve three. Tina watched me slice the breasts, chop onion and mushrooms, find tomato puree, and rescue the cream from a couple of bottles of milk. I think it was the mace and nutmeg that finally drove her to asking Chris if she could take the rest of the afternoon off and go and find a pub steak with her boyfriend. Chris agreed, with an odd expression on his face.

The envelope wiped it off, fast.

'What the hell?' He was on his feet already.

'Calm down. Only papers. Aftab having a belated attack of conscience.'

'Why?'

'Because I told him about the letter bomb.'

'For Christ's sake, I thought we'd agreed—'

'He didn't reveal anything all those hours you people were talking to him. He told me only when he was convinced it was a matter of life and death.'

Chris burrowed in the envelope. 'Wajid's modem. Well, well, well. And what's this lot?'

'Notes for his computing project. I can't make head or tail of them, of course. But I thought one or two of your colleagues might.' I smiled seraphically.

'I suppose you haven't a freezer bag handy? Big enough to hold all this? And one for the modem. I didn't expect evidence with my Sunday lunch. What was it anyway? And Sophie—you couldn't give me the recipe? I've got a foodie coming to supper next week.'

'You've heard of boeuf Stroganoff? Well,

that was chicken Stroganoff. Or chicken Sophie. Any news,' I asked over my shoulder as I went for the bags and a jotter pad and pencil for the recipe, 'from that bank?'

'They make your friend Tony Rossiter look a positive mine of information. Damn it, I'm only trying to see if their telephone system could have been involved with a murder. You'd think they'd be pleased if we located any weaknesses in their security. So far there's no joy at all.'

'Nothing? What about George's bassoon case? Any more on that?'

'Only to demonstrate beyond reasonable doubt that the mud came from the Music Centre site.'

'What about the US connection? One bassoonist dies and his case is done over. What about the other bassoonists? Are they at risk?'

He looked awkward.

'Or is Jools too busy trying to implicate Tony?' I rushed in. 'I'm sure she told you what she overheard.'

'So, to do him justice, did Rossiter.'

Thank God for that.

'The trouble is,' he continued, 'that while the members of the orchestra can largely alibi each other—'

'Are you sure you can use "alibi" as a verb?'

234

'—can provide alibis for each other, he's been travelling by car. I'll have to talk to him again.'

'Do you have to do it publicly? Could you be reasonably low-key? We've been friends a long time, he and I.'

He shrugged a guarded agreement. I couldn't understand the expression on his face.

'While we're on the subject of your friends,' he said, 'I ought to tell you we might want to talk to the other bassoonists. Not necessarily as possible victims. I'm sorry.'

I saw it quite clearly, Jools's new case, standing in the corner of that expensive room. But then I saw the expression on her face that night in the pub: she was afraid, then, not guilty.

'Have you seen her at the fitness centre yet?' I asked, feeling like Judas.

'Been too groggy. But I suppose we could go down there this afternoon. I've got my gear in the car. God knows we've enough cholesterol to burn off.'

I'd hoped to wallow in it a bit longer. But then I thought of another reason to go to the centre. I'd give in very gracefully if he pressed me. Even if I still drew the line at a leotard.

It seemed something of a contradiction to drive to a fitness centre, but clearly he was still revelling in his new car, so I played along. Until he said, rather too casually, 'I gather you saw Mayou yesterday.'

'Twice, actually,' I said, truthfully but with the intention, of course, of confusing him. And then I relented. 'At rehearsal, of course, and then in the afternoon. I'm sure Tina's told you. He and Jools were having a row, but I was far too far away to lip-read.'

'Can you really lip-read?'

'A little. George taught me. Musicians aren't supposed to talk on stage, of course, but sometimes they need to communicate with each other. And it might come in useful in my old age.'

'If you have one. Pity, you weren't closer. I'd give my pension to know what they were quarrelling about.' Then he brightened. 'But I'm sure you'll be able to find out on Tuesday.'

One poster at the fitness centre always dominates my thoughts.

DID YOU KNOW THERE ARE 620
MUSCLES IN YOUR BODY?
YOU WILL AFTER USING OUR
EXERCISE PROGRAMME!

I pointed it out to Chris while I waited to introduce him to Dean, the instructor.

Dean was happy to let him have a trial session, and was convinced by his expensive but battered trainers that he wouldn't do himself any harm. Chris made no effort to make our visit a social affair. He started off at the far end of the gym and worked steadily and privately on the rowing machine and the cycle. I needed to work on the parts of my body that needed most attention—the bits from the waist to the knee. There were a couple of birthing chairs—one for pushing your legs out against weights, another for pushing them in. The effect in both was rather like swimming on your back in thick custard. While I worked, I watched Chris. In general I subscribed to the theory that a slim body looks better than a fat one, and Chris was certainly slim. But he was so slender as to be scrawny, as if a layer of subcutaneous fat had been stripped off, for the benefit of anatomy students, to show all the cords and sinews. In other words, his was the sort of body that looked better clothed.

Dean's body, on the other hand, showed how seriously he took his job of building bodies. I'd never seen muscles in places where he had them. Except on Jools, of course. Despite his immense shoulders and fearsome dreadlocks, Dean was uniformly gentle, even with the most awkward clients. Other young men, clearly aspiring to Dean's physique, clustered round the Multi-Gym, Lycra lads exchanging heavy belts and leather mittens and selecting the heaviest possible weights without necessarily using them. Elsewhere, a couple of middle-aged women rowed hard for the receding shore of youth.

At the rear of the gym was a pleasant area where you could buy drinks, have a sauna and a shower, and generally return your body to normal. There was quiet music—the Bee Gees' greatest hits, this particular day—and some easy chairs with newspapers to hand. Of course, to sit down after a gruelling session was to run the risk of never becoming vertical again.

I waited for Dean to leave the gym floor and come and rebuke me for not coming as often as I should. It was a ritual. What I wanted to do was ask how often Jools came. And then get the subject round to her body building. But I had to be reasonably tactful—Dean had heard me express myself pretty forcibly about the subject when he'd tried to get me to build mine, too.

He exchanged a few words with Chris, now on the ski machine, and patted his shoulder lightly before jogging over to me. I accepted his rebuke with good grace, as he expected, talked about West Bromwich Albion for a few minutes, and then, not very subtly, asked about Jools.

'What about her?' he asked.

'Just that I wonder if she's overdoing it a bit.'

'Overdoing what?'

That wasn't the reply I expected. I looked at him, eyebrows raised.

'Come off it, Sophie. You know as well as I do she's taking stuff. Keep telling her she shouldn't. Bet you have too. Told her, I mean.'

I nodded. 'She says it's just vitamins and mineral supplements, but it's got to be steroids, hasn't it?'

'Bloody stupid cow. She doesn't get them from here, Sophie, so don't go putting that into the pig's head. What're you doing, going round with the filth, Soph?'

'Friend. Nothing more. Or less.' I owed Chris that, and Dean would have to put up with it.

'OK by me. So long as he doesn't go sniffing round.'

'It's me that's doing that, Dean. You heard about that accident at the Music Centre?'

He nodded.

'Well, I reckon it wasn't an accident. And I'm wondering about Jools and her drugs and—well, I'm just wondering.'

'If Jools—? Bloody hell, Soph!'

'No. Not that. She's a friend of mine, Dean! But I just thought: if she could get access to that sort of drug, if she could be getting hold of something else. And maybe—oh, I don't know.'

He looked at me, holding my gaze longer than was comfortable. At last he smiled, crookedly, reluctantly. 'You want me to find out where she's getting it. I don't like it, Soph, but I suppose I owe you one. Or two. Give us your phone number, and I'll see what I can do.'

I'd been wondering how to get rid of Chris, who was lingering unconscionably over his third mug of tea. We weren't saying all that much, but if I looked up I'd find him eyeing me. Perhaps he was wondering if he could ask me what Dean and I had been talking about. I hoped he wouldn't.

Then Tina reappeared. She switched on the radio as soon as she stepped into the kitchen. Chris reached across to flick it off. 'Get yourself a bloody Walkman, for God's sake,' he said. He pulled in his arm a good deal more cautiously. 'Hell,

I'm stiffening up already. Fitness centre,' he added.

She peered in the pot and poured in more water. 'Which one?'

'Down Bearwood.'

'Not the one with dishy Dean? He's gorgeous! How d'you get to know all these sexy young men, Soph?'

'Mostly I teach them,' I said. 'And I feel old enough to be their mother.'

'Did you teach Dean?' Chris pounced.

'Not only taught him,' said Tina, helpfully, 'she got him out of some stink at the college.'

I wished Tina would shut up.

'No point in looking like that,' said Tina. 'Might as well tell him, Soph.'

'Past history,' I said.

'No. This teacher kept on picking on Dean, see, and Soph helped sort him out. Racial harassment.'

'I do wish you'd pronounce it correctly, Tina. That's the American way. The English pronunciation has the stress on the first syllable. Doesn't it, Chris?'

I caught his eye and held it: the message was to let it all drop. He nodded. Message understood. But I knew he'd want me to tell him about it one day. In the meantime, since I certainly didn't need two police escorts, he smiled, drained the last of his tea, and let himself out.

Chapter Eighteen

My too, too solid shadow refused to melt away. Of course, she was only doing her job, and doing it conscientiously. But she developed an irritating habit of putting her head round my bedroom door and wishing me 'Night-night', and offering to turn off a light I've only ever turned off myself, apart from the Kenji episode. And on Monday morning she surprised me in the middle of my Canadian Air Force sit-ups with a cup of distressingly milky tea. In other words, she was a totally nice person doing kind and indeed motherly things, and to the grit of my irritation was added a thick layer of guilt. She drove competently to work, parked immaculately, and insisted we both use the lift. *The* lift, as it happened. Apart from that she accompanied me, of course, even to the loo, and I was regaled, on my return to our staff room, by a psychology teacher with a long story about a man who couldn't pee if he thought anyone might hear him. My sessions in the class room involved Tina sitting at the back and asking questions that amused the students, if not me. She had a very poorly developed sense of discretion, and wanted to be in every conversation. I knew she smoked, and hoped she'd be unprofessional enough to join the little group puffing away illicitly outside the staff room—there was only one door, after all, and she'd have been able to intercept any stray visitor. But since I wouldn't let her smoke in my house, she saw it as an opportunity to give up what she inevitably called the 'filthy weed'.

Shahida came over to my desk at break to make sure I was all right and, she claimed, to make sure I hadn't cancelled the dress she'd helped me choose. And she stood over me while I phoned my hairdresser for a quick appointment between classes. When I suggested the much cheaper Beauty Two group she reminded me of the last woman lecturer who'd trusted herself to their ministrations and had walked down the aisle with her face covered in hives. Stobbard was not to be embarrassed by a pink and lumpy face.

So on Tuesday, with Tina persuaded to sit not at the next basin but in the small waiting area, I was given the treatment. I even allowed Roy to ask the beautician who operated from an upstairs room at his salon to make something of my nails. She made neat, short, pink shells, which might never have done anything more strenuous than tap a word-processor. And as I looked at them I saw them rooting among the rocks in George's garden, and I winced so hard the woman asked if she'd hurt me. But at last we all beamed at each other with pleasure at a job well done. I smudged one of my nails writing a cheque, and Sarah made me wait while she did it again. And I had to promise to return with the outfit I was hiring.

I'd rather it had been Shahida exclaiming over it, the narrow black dress and its heavily beaded bolero top, but it was nice to have Roy and Sarah enjoying it. That's one thing I missed in my newly solitary life—someone to share those moments of excitement. That's why I couldn't at bottom understand my dislike of Tina—she was happy to share, and very vocally too, when I waited for Stobbard to collect me. I'd spent a least five minutes making up my face, so I was a little disappointed to hear the faint note of surprise in Stobbard's voice when he at last arrived—too late for a drink: 'Hey, Sophie, you look really good.'

I looked as good as I was ever likely to: I suppose my ego would have liked a little effusiveness.

Stobbard, of course, looked entirely delectable. His dinner jacket had presumably been tailored for him, and even his shirt didn't seem to have come from the ranks at Marks. He was wearing some of the cologne that had so attracted me after the inquest on George.

I would be too embarrassed to give a blow-by-blow account of the evening. There I was, sitting next to the most desirable man in the whole auditorium, and all I could do was desire him. I did try to follow the rather dotty plot, and I should have admired the grace and athleticism of the dancers. But I was disconcerted by the noise they made. I'd only ever seen the odd *Nutcracker* on Christmas TV, when I was too gorged to switch channels. TV ballet has mikes to catch the music but none to pick up heavy landings. It stands to reason that even a ten-stone man leaping magnificently across the stage will make some noise, but I was illogically disappointed.

And Stobbard was there, close enough for me to feel the warmth of his arm on the rest between us. Instead of resenting his claim on it, I left my hands demurely in my lap. But I was willing Stobbard to reach across to take one.

If I looked down and to the right I could see the length of his thigh; if he crossed his ankles the other way, inevitably his foot would find mine, just waiting to be found. I don't think he shifted position for the whole of the first half.

At the interval, he took my elbow in a terribly impersonal way and guided me to the bar. I was so subdued I didn't even carp at the notice: INVITED GUESTS ONLY.

Chris would probably have given me a provocative nudge just to set me off in my condemnations of a tautology I particularly loathed. Stobbard, however, was more concerned with acquiring our champagne and smiling very public smiles. I smiled too. He was, after all, on behalf of what he would no doubt call the Midshires Symphony, an ambassador, out to cultivate the captains of Birmingham's little remaining industry whose sleekness threatened to overpower his. None of them seemed to have anything discriminating to say about the performance, either, though presumably their lack of concentration stemmed from another cause than mine. They were in no hurry to return to their places, and would no doubt expect to be waited for. George had once fulminated about an out-of-town gig when the sponsors had not thought it necessary to enter the auditorium until the orchestra, the leader, the conductor and the soloist were all on stage.

Another hour of the ballet to look forward to: people being bored, people leaping around the stage, people feeling randy. OK, me feeling randy. I still had no encouragement from Stobbard. I assumed it must be professional interest that was keeping him going, but a covert glance at his face suggested he might be asleep. And there was no George to tell.

Suddenly, in the midst of all the braying voices and champagne, he turned to me. 'Jesus, who are all these goddamn people?' he demanded, taking my arm in quite a different way. I'd been flirting with a man old enough to be my father and rich enough to buy the college a minivan if I'd worked just a little bit harder. I'd been describing the antics involved in getting football and hockey teams across to other colleges on buses that demanded the correct change. The Principal, I was saying, seemed to think we should use Barclaycard.

'But,' said my elderly flirt slowly, 'buses don't accept Barclaycard.'

'Perhaps we should try American Express.'

At this point Stobbard appropriated me, the young stag defeating the old without even a clash of antlers. Now every time he took a step he contrived to brush my breast. My nipples stood to attention; my vagina was salivating so much I could hardly walk. He slung my coat across my shoulders: no doubt he considered the chic rather than the practicalities of keeping warm on a frosty March night. 'Come on, let's get the hell out of here. I could use some jazz.'

'Jazz?'

'C'mon, there must be somewhere in this city where you can hear jazz?'

I tried not to dither, tried not to notice that someone had taken our cab.

'Ronnie Scott's?' Nice and close to the Mondiale, after all.

'Something real, that's what I want.'

A real curry sprang to my mind. Too much champagne and too few nibbles to mop it up. But if the man wanted jazz, the man wanted jazz. 'The Cannonball,' I suggested at last. 'Down Digbeth.'

'Digbeth?'

'We could walk. Just.'

Foolish Sophie. In this wind? At this time of night? The pace he set might have warmed me, if only I'd been able to keep up in my silly evening pumps. We cut through the Chinese quarter to St Martin's. At last we started down Digbeth High Street. Bugger real jazz. If only he'd been charming and gracious it might have been quite romantic. But he was neither.

At last he must have noticed the wind, which was blinding me with tears.

'OK. Let's skip the jazz. Say, don't they have cabs in this goddamn dump?'

Taxis in Birmingham generally wait in ranks for you to go to them. Or you phone and they come. They don't, like London cabs, cruise round helpfully looking for you, and in any case Digbeth at this time of night is not the safest place for taxis. Or people, for that matter.

'Know the number?'

As it happened, I did. But what was the use of a number without a phone? Any public telephone round here was bound to have been vandalised. I had reckoned without his tiny mobile phone. And at last, at long last, he discovered an excellent way of getting me warm.

At first the warmth of the Mondiale was blissful. His suite, however, was baking. While I waited for him to use the bathroom, I hunted for a radiator control. But he emerged before I could find it. I wished he'd waited till I'd got up from my hands and knees.

He looked at me oddly, as indeed he might, and poured the champagne that had arrived almost as we had, together with some minuscule canapés.

'I like the view from here,' he said.

I preened. Perhaps he was a man for small breasts. But he was looking out of the window. He'd meant it all too literally.

'Come and look,' he said, gesturing with his glass.

I stood a foot behind him.

'Aw, c'mon, Sophie.' He reached for the window catch. 'Champagne on the balcony.'

Suddenly I was shivering again.

'You can see right across the city. The lights remind me of back home.'

'Sorry. It's vertigo. I can't.'

'But don't you work in some tower block?'

'I never look out of the window. Sorry, Stobbard. I truly can't.'

If I hoped he'd kiss and caress my fears from me, I was to be disappointed. He merely turned and rang irritably for more champagne.

The arrival of a waiter bringing a fresh supply of ice and two more bottles of champagne made me feel, despite my expensive outfit, cheap. Whenever I'd slept with a man before, it had always been private. We'd both known—or at least hoped—what would take place, but no one else had. Kenji and I had bought our rough Italian wine at an off-licence and retired—to his bed, that time—and that was that. But for all his discreet and downcast eyes, I knew that the waiter knew that we did not intend to spend the rest of the evening reviewing the ballet. I retired to the loo to sit and think.

The bathroom certainly provided food for thought—not only a bidet, a handbasin and a shower, but also a bath big enough for two. Perched on the far edge was a particularly phallic loofah.

Virtue and dignity, or sex? My body cast its deciding vote. It told the meeting it wished to clamp itself round Stobbard's at the earliest opportunity.

He had removed his jacket and tie and was coaxing the cork from the second bottle. I watched his hands, with their long, curling thumbs, making easy an operation that other people make a fuss about. When he saw me watching, he smiled, laying down the bottle, still just corked, and he turned to me. He slipped his hands on to my throat, his thumbs pushing up my chin to the right angle.

And then he started to sneeze.

Stripped, Stobbard was as beautiful as I'd hoped he'd be. All those wonderful muscles, and a fine clear skin. He was lying face down on the bed, as if hiding from the brief embarrassment that had made me offer him a massage. My hands explored the knots of tension, kneading them in the hope that this time he would rise to me. Down to his buttocks at last, and any moment now he'd roll over, and

251

everything would be all right.

Everything went to plan. He groaned with pleasure under my hands. He rolled over.

But he didn't have an erection.

'Godamn it, I guess it's those fucking antihistamines,' he muttered, turning away from me.

'Shall I—would you like me to help?' I asked gently, reaching for him.

He winced from my touch as if my hand were barbed wire.

'I tell you—enough!' He sat up on the far side of the bed, and reached for my pretty dress, his right hand bunching it so he could throw it across to me. 'Just get the hell out of here!'

I wouldn't let him see me cry. I picked it up as it slithered to the floor and carried it to the bathroom.

When I emerged he was wearing a tracksuit.

'Would you mind if I called a cab?' I asked, relieved that my voice didn't shake.

He passed me the phone and poured another glass of champagne.

I called the minicab service we'd used an hour ago.

While I waited I stared at a framed notice advertising the hotel's secretarial service for its guests. Didn't see it. Didn't take it in. It was just something to focus on to stop the tears. But there was something familiar about it.

There'd be a cab outside the foyer in five minutes.

The net curtains washed and billowed over the carpet. He stood by the open window, breathing deeply. Timidly I moved closer. He gave me something approaching a smile and moved his arm, as if inviting me to snuggle up to him. I wanted to. God, I wanted to.

The phone rang. My cab was waiting.

He insisted on escorting me down. Although we had the lift to ourselves, he made no effort to get close. We chattered superficially about his concert with the MSO in Cheltenham the following evening. If only he would ask me to go along—but in any case, I was teaching Sean's class. It was a beautiful programme, if rather long: an early Haydn symphony, Schubert's Eighth (which sometimes appears in print as the *Unfurnished),* and Beethoven's Third Symphony. I would not remind him of another popular misprint—the *Erotica.* Instead, and not much more tactfully, I asked him who was playing the important bassoon part in the Haydn, one of George's favourites.

'Don't ask. Some goddamn extra. Not Jools. Don't even think of it, I told Rossiter. Over my dead body.'

'Isn't he trying to get rid of her? As she's so incompetent?' I added, as he seemed to need some explanation.

He stared at me hard, then said, sounding ineffably bored, 'Musicians' Union. Assholes.'

By this time the pain in my chest was unbearable. My mouth might have been talking but it still wanted the pressure of his. Any moment I was going to cry. I felt so bloody rejected. So bloody all over. Not because I couldn't arouse him. Everyone gets their flat spots and he must have been suffering much more than I. But if a relationship was to develop we should have talked, comforted each other. And he hadn't cared enough.

When Kenji had gone back to his sumo wrestlers, I was so angry I hardly had time to be hurt. But this time my heart hurt, hurt as much as my lips, and still I could hardly walk for wanting him so much.

Chapter Nineteen

The minicab was waiting, the driver drumming his fingers on the Montego's steering wheel. Stobbard made no attempt to open the rear door for me. Then the driver looked up and grinned.

'Hey, if it isn't Sophie!' he said, getting out.

'Khalid! Stobbard, this is one of my ex-students, Khalid Mushtaq—' I turned to Stobbard, smiling. I hoped he'd shake hands with Khalid, and then—why not?— kiss me good night. But he merely nodded, shoved his hands into his pockets and withdrew into the shadows.

Maybe I could replace some of my misery with honest bad temper: how dared he cut Khalid like that? Khalid, meanwhile, had sensed the slight. And I could scarcely explain that it might have been unintentional, Stobbard still perhaps smarting after what he no doubt saw as a failure.

'You OK, Sophie?'

'Sure. Why don't I sit in front so we can talk? You can start by telling me why you're driving a cab. I thought you got a First? In Computing?'

Khalid Mushtaq had been one of my nicest ever students, and one of the very best. At one point it looked as if TB might stop him sitting his A levels, and I'd taken work round, first to the isolation hospital and then to his home. I'd not been the only one by any means, but I suppose I'd been the most regular. And in the end, all the teamwork paid off—Khalid had passed, triumphantly.

'Yes. LSE. Anyway, I thought I'd better move back up to Brum—my mother's not too good at the moment—and I'm doing my PhD.'

'What in?'

'Come off it, Sophie—if I explained all night you'd be none the wiser, would you?'

'Thanks, Khalid. OK, which uni?'

'Brum. But the grant's—well, I shouldn't moan. So I do a spot of moonlighting. You still beavering away at William Murdock?'

'D'you suppose the place would fall down if I built a big enough lodge?'

'Have to watch it if you're still on the fifteenth.'

'I do indeed,' I began, about to tell him my recent woes.

He put the car into gear and started to pull into Broad Street.

'Hang on! Khalid, you'll think I've flipped, but could you take me a really odd way home? Yes, I'm still in Harborne, still the same place. You see, I'm afraid of being followed.' And I was. Suddenly I felt sick with terror.

'What—are you kidding me?'

'No.'

'You mean now?'

'In general. And maybe now in particular.'

'Ah.' I knew that tone. I knew I could rely on him to trust me without question. 'So we head for the city centre, not Harborne, and then do one or two clever bits. Fill me in as we go. Any idea what sort of a tail we could have?'

'I've met a brown Datsun a couple of times.'

'Well, let's just prove—' his speech slowed as he checked the rear-view mirror —'that no one's behind us now, shall we? Hold tight.' Reaching for the handbrake with his left hand, he shifted his grip with his right until it was to the bottom left of the steering wheel. 'OK?'

Before I really knew what was happening, the car was pointing the other way. He accelerated hard, shooting a set of lights I trust he'd normally have stopped at, and headed not for the underpass but for the island at Five Ways. And went round it twice. Just as I hoped we were going home, he took off down Ladywood Middleway. I suppose he could have dropped me off at college—it would have been the earliest start I'd ever made. As we hurtled downhill, I gave him the barest bones of what had been happening.

'And how,' I asked, as we turned right at the island at the end of the dual carriageway, 'can you disguise something really important in a set of notes on computerising the hire of videos?'

'You sure about that?'

'No. But it's the only theory I've got.'

Up to the College of Food and a left down Great Charles Street. And he was studying the rear-view mirror with far more than casual interest.

'Company?'

'Could be.'

'Don't worry if it's the police—all we'd—'

'I'm not worrying about the police—not unless they drive old Datsuns.'

'Not brown?'

'In one, Sophie. In one.'

He'd accelerated, but carried on talking as if doing forty round an island were an everyday event. The back end wanted to break away—I could feel him fighting for control.

'Bloody diesel on the road,' he said, heading back up Great Charles Street. Then he took us under the first of the Queensway tunnels. 'Funny, Sophie, when I was a kid—twelve, I'd be—they tried it on a bit at school. Asked me why all Pakis drove Datsuns. I didn't know what a Paki was, let alone a Datsun. But it's true, you know. Ninety per cent of the cars in our street are bloody Datsuns. Mostly brown Datsuns. But I don't reckon that one's one of my neighbours'.'

We were through the last of the underpasses now, heading briskly down Bristol Street. So was the Datsun.

We crossed the lights at the big McDonald's just as they changed to red. We could hear the squeal of tyres as the Datsun wove under the wheels of a lorry with right of way.

Priory Road lights, next. If he turned left there was Edgbaston cricket ground and Moseley. But he was surely turning right—and then, slewing from one lane to the other, he finally took us straight on: after a short narrower section, a long dual carriageway which led towards Selly Oak.

'Look, I'm going to try to loop round the central reservation—another of those handbrake turns. But at this speed...'

I couldn't even see the gap he was heading for. All I could see was trees, lining the road and dotted along the grassed reservation. They were flashing past with terrifying speed.

Suddenly we were going the other way.

Something moved on the road. It must have caught Khalid's eye. His offside wheels caught a kerbstone and we flashed towards iron railings. But he heaved and tugged the car straight—'There!' And he started to laugh.

I twisted round. 'Khalid, he's still there—No! He's—oh, my God!'

As Khalid slowed, I watched the Datsun spin into the air, bouncing on to its roof and rolling.

Khalid slewed across the road and stopped. His hand was shaking as he reached for his phone.

'Ambulance,' he said. 'And police. And—my God—better make it fire brigade, too. Bristol Road. Those playing fields by King Edward's School. Just by the gates.' He replaced the handset and turned to me. 'Why didn't I think of that before—actually calling the Bill? Might have saved a few miles' worth of tyres. Come on, better see if we can help that guy.'

Another, less humane impulse struck me. 'No! There's a killer out there. And he's after us. Let's—'

He flattened me in my seat, pushing the door open as he did. 'He's got a fucking gun! Get out!'

The windscreen and the window in his door shattered. I couldn't separate sound from light.

I crawled across the pavement, hunting for cover. Khalid was beside me, his hand pushing my head down. The gates! But they were firmly locked, and the racket hadn't yet roused whoever lived in the lodge within.

Then Khalid reeled from my side. I flung myself on top of him. There was nothing to clamp to the gash in his arm except my hand. The blood welled between my fingers.

'It's just a scratch,' I whispered. For my benefit, not his. He was unconscious.

Bristol Road is one of the main arteries into the city. You'd think there'd be someone driving along nosy enough to stop and investigate. But the road was deserted.

Apart from the Datsun driver.

There was another quick burst of gunfire. Not at us. At the car. The tank.

Then there was the sound of a motor-bike. The vomit of fear rose in my throat. One we might escape. Not two. But the Datsun driver stopped firing. I could see the figure recede. The motorbike was almost at a halt.

Both cars exploded into flame.

Suddenly there came another noise: the pon-pon of an emergency vehicle. And another. The bike roared off. And at long last the sodium lighting was slashed by the blessed blue lights I'd been praying for.

I couldn't bear the heat any longer. I was screaming for help. But I couldn't leave Khalid. And then he and I were both lifted clear by strong hands that came with Brummie voices. I took in the yellow Day-Glo jackets but didn't care what the words on the backs were. Some must be ambulance men. I was soon hunched away from Khalid.

I crouched near the gates and threw up all the champagne. I could hardly wipe my mouth, I was dithering so much. Someone—a teenager whose jacket insisted he was in the police but whose voice kept cracking with panic—called me miss and tried to get me to stand up.

At long last my brain seemed to clear. If he was panicking, someone had to do something. I invigorated him with Chris's name, agreed to sit in his panda and sent him to find a blanket.

What about Khalid? A couple of figures left the little knot surrounding him. At last I could see—yes, they'd set up a drip. I could see him try to lift his head. But they came with a stretcher. I was torn: should I go with him or wait for Chris?

I had to speak to him anyway. Gathering my blanket, I set off, only to find the heel coming off my shoe. I gave it a final wrench and slung it at the wrought-iron gates, still implacably shut. It clanged back towards me.

'Can I speak to him?' I yelled, hopping inadequately.

'He says he won't go till he's spoken to you,' the driver said, dryly.

Stepping into the ambulance was like

262

reaching the stage after the darkness of the pit. Khalid, the star, was far from recumbent. He reached for my hand and shook it gently from side to side.

'You mix with some bad types, Sophie,' he said eventually.

'Just these Datsuns don't hold the road like your Montego. How are you, Khalid?'

'Even they say there's not all that much wrong. Can't help passing out if I see blood. Specially my own. Tell you what, they say I won't be driving for a couple of days. You get all that computer stuff—right? Might as well have a go at it while I've got the time.'

'Could lead you into more danger.'

'Who are you going to tell? Don't be daft! Besides, I'd like to fix the bugger that did that to my poor old Monty.'

One of the ambulance people checked his drip rather ostentatiously.

'They want to be off, love. Shall I tell your mum? Still in Victoria Avenue?'

'Number 10. Sophie, I don't want the Bill scaring her.'

'I'll go myself. Promise.' I kissed his cheek lightly.

I staggered as I stepped down, which prompted the medic to invite me to go along. I insisted I had to wait for the police.

'But they'll find you easy as wink up

at the Acci, love. And you've got some burns need looking at. No? Not got the sense you were born with?'

Maybe I hadn't. I hadn't. What was I doing here, amid all this mess, among all these people? What had been going on? I wanted to sit in the gutter and cry.

Then I saw another car, a big Peugeot, nosing its way purposefully through the cluster of emergency vehicles.

I lurched towards Chris as he got out. I'd rather not have landed in his outstretched arms. I couldn't bear it if he started being nice to me. But he grinned, ironically, and said, 'My word, you have been having an eventful evening, haven't you?'

'You've no idea how exciting the ballet can be,' I agreed, steadying myself and stepping back.

'Oh, I have. I've just been watching you. Who was it,' he continued, dropping his voice, 'who hopped forty paces in a public street?'

I had to get rid of that tender note. 'Someone who'd easily pass for forty-three in the dusk with the light behind her!' I said, surprised I could remember Gilbert and Sullivan at that time of night. 'And I don't suppose she was swathed in a National Health blanket at the time. No wonder it's short of money.'

'Why didn't you do the sensible thing

and go off to Casualty?'

I didn't know. I stood on one foot looking for a reason.

'I wanted to remember what happened,' I said at last. 'And in what order it happened. Because there was something odd.'

'Odd?'

'The way things happened. There was a definite order. And it happened surprisingly slowly.' I put up a hand to stop him interrupting. I focused on Khalid's burnt-out Montego first. Then on the Datsun. The Datsun driver had fired, then stopped, then the Datsun had caught fire, then the Montego when he'd fired again. It didn't make sense. Nothing was making sense.

The top of my head lifted clear of my brains.

'Put those bloody things away,' I said, fending off another attack from his smelling salts. 'Let me just think.'

'Think on the way home. Your teeth are chattering again.'

He held open the car door, and I allowed myself to collapse on the front seat. He let himself in the other side.

'One thing about being in charge of this lot,' he said over his shoulder as he reversed whence he had come, 'is that you don't have to spend your entire night on your hands and knees searching for—'

'For clues? Do say clues! I've never heard you use the word yet!'

'Clues,' he said, obligingly.

Chapter Twenty

It wasn't quite light as Chris turned into Balden Road but there was a very strong sense that it was going to be, at any moment. Certainly there were joggers already popping out of double-glazed porches, and my milkman was awake enough to wave to some of them. Out loud I promised myself a long, hot bath, and wondered if Chris might turn his hand to toast. And then I panicked at the thought of the day's teaching: there was preparation left undone, and God knew how I was to keep my eyes open anyway. But I ceased to be tired as soon as I opened my front door.

'How many people,' Chris asked, surveying the mess, 'knew you were planning a night on the tiles?'

I could scarcely take it all in. Whoever had broken in had certainly wanted something very badly. Every one of my books was on the floor, and all my drawers and their contents tipped on top. Two china vases had been smashed, but not a cut-glass bowl. The grate had been pulled from the wall.

Chris spoke with barely controlled venom into his radio. I wondered if I was brave enough to look into the other rooms. I dragged myself back into the hall and towards the stairs.

'Stay where you are,' Chris rapped, still holding his radio.

I stayed.

'It'll be as bad as this everywhere, you know, and there's just a chance there may be something—'

'What sort of something? Not another bomb?'

He smiled grimly: 'I was thinking more along the lines of dust from shoes, a thread from clothing. I have to ask you: do you know what they were looking for?'

'I haven't anything worth nicking. No jewellery or anything.' He waited. 'You don't mean that sort of thing, do you? You mean Wajid's notes? Something like that?'

'Good job they're safe with us,' he said.

And a good job the photocopies I'd made were secreted in the entrails of my college filing cabinet.

Chris took me back to his house, a detached modern one not all that far from

Jools's flat, in one of the more expensive parts of Edgbaston. He reached me a thick towel and promised that when I emerged from the bath I'd find something I could wear. This turned out to be a tracksuit that made me look as if I'd shrunk in the wash. The only shoes I'd been able to retrieve were the ones I cycle in, still in the polythene carrier in my hallway. He made me eat toast as we drove to Khalid's house in Moseley.

It was a semi, from roughly the same era as mine but a little smaller, with an awkward triangular garden at the back. The front garden was looking a little depressed: Mrs Mushtaq's arthritis must have stopped her tidying up over the winter, and it looked as if Fatima was no more a gardener than her brother. It was Fatima who opened the door, sleek in a silk dressing gown. Her mother was behind her, fully dressed. Chris waited behind me. They wouldn't ask what I was doing there until they'd invited me in, I was sure of that. So I said, 'I've got a message from Khalid—he gave me a lift last night, and he wanted me to tell you myself.'

The women exchanged glances, but stood back, smiling politely. As soon as I was over her threshold, Mrs Mushtaq reached for my face, cupping it gently for a moment. When I introduced Chris, she hitched her *dupatta* more firmly over her hair, and shook hands.

She would not sit until we were seated. Then she took a hard chair. I moved as close to her as I could, took her hand and explained. Occasionally she'd fire a question in Punjabi at Fatima, who stood beside her.

'I promise you he's not badly hurt,' I repeated. 'But they may keep him in hospital for a day or two. So he'll want pyjamas and shaving things.'

'And books,' Fatima added, laughing. 'I'll go and sort things out.'

Her mother too excused herself Chris and I were left with the walls and each other to look at. Chris peered closely at the holy pictures and the texts from the Koran. They'd made the Haj, the pilgrimage to Mecca, since I was here first.

'Nice people,' said Chris, eventually.

'They could do without this business,' I agreed.

Fatima reappeared first, with Pakistani tea and some viciously sweet biscuits. I ate from hunger, Chris, to judge from the careful nibbles, from politeness. We talked about Khalid's degree and Fatima's job. She taught Law at Birmingham University, and was sour about the increase in student numbers without corresponding cash injections. I thought darkly a spell at William Murdock might be a salutary experience, but I could hardly say that. And at last Mrs Mushtaq came back, carrying a small sports bag. She gave it to Chris. She gave me a small paper bag. 'Halva, Sophie. Home-made.'

And I had led her son into such danger and proposed to lead him into more. I hoped my guilt didn't show.

Back to Rose Road to make another statement, and to consume another breakfast packed with cholesterol.

And then some shopping.

I'd have thought Chris a bit elevated to accompany me to Marks and Sparks—we were the first through the doors—but he insisted that he wasn't going to let me out of his sight until he could hand me over to Tina, who came on duty at ten. And I had to have clothes, we agreed on that. Even my insurance company conceded that I could spend enough money to render me decent and warm until the police had finished what Chris promised would be a microscopic examination of my house. I consoled myself with the thought that while I might have to spend a long time tidying up, the place would get one hell of a spring-clean and I could enjoy my Easter holiday doing something less killing.

What we didn't agree on was what I would do in my new clothes. My theory was that I should go and teach. Chris—and Tina, when we met up at her flat—thought a day off would be more sensible.

'Doing what?' I demanded. 'And more to the point, where?'

'Better kip down on my sofa,' said Tina.

Chris agreed, so quickly and with such an edge to his voice that I wondered what had upset him. But he hadn't had much sleep either. Perhaps that was it. Otherwise I might have suggested I bed down in the more spacious and civilised surroundings of his house, which would be guaranteed pop-free, whatever else. At last, I shook my head firmly. 'Work,' I said.

I got through the morning on automatic pilot, and thought I was doing all right with the afternoon class. But quite suddenly I found myself terribly close to tears, and dared to leave the room and hurry upstairs without warning Tina. She was furious when she caught up with me.

'OK, so I climbed three flights of stairs without you. What could you do, anyway, if anyone set on me?'

I suppose I rather expected her to declare she was the Midlands karate champion ready to kick an assailant downstairs. Instead, she looked at me steadily for a moment. 'Didn't Chris mention this?'

'This' was a handgun small enough to fit into the pocket of the bulky tops she always favoured.

'Ah,' I said.

Since Tina's reign—and the letter bomb, of course—my colleagues had been much more punctilious about keeping students out of the room. If they wanted one of us, they had to wait outside. There were a couple of lads there now, asking, if I would send Shahida out. It was about a bus pass—really urgent.

I let myself in and told Shahida, who looked as if she too had had precious little sleep the night before. She pressed her hand to her stomach as she walked to the door; I felt sick with fear for her.

But when she came back in she was shaking with laughter: in the middle of his desperate plea for financial help her tutee had broken off. Another, more important matter had claimed his attention. On his mobile phone.

We were enjoying a giggle and a cup of tea when Winston arrived. As usual he waited by the door; as usual I waved him in. This time I could see the reason for his reticence. In his left hand, the hand he uses for bowling those devastating inswingers he was clutching a cellophane-wrapped rose.

'This is for you, Sophie,' he said, shoving it forward.

'Winston! How lovely of you!'

'No, Sophie: this came for you.'

So he wasn't holding it gingerly because he was bashful but because he was scared.

'Put that bloody thing down,' Tina snapped.

'Tina—please!' It's not every day I get a rose, after all.

'You stupid bitch, don't you realise—'

I realised all too well. I'd no idea how large a disguise an explosive device might need, but I had seen on TV how much damage a so-called controlled explosion can do. And I didn't reckon there'd be much left of my rose.

'Isn't there some way we could check?' I said. 'To see if it's authentic?'

In the end I managed to persuade her to phone the firm who'd delivered it, its name brightly stamped all over the delivery paper. And yes, they'd delivered a rose. They were terribly concerned: was there anything wrong with it? They assured us they used only the very best floral materials.

Tina cut them short. 'So no one could have touched it except your people?'

'No one except Irene, and ever so particular Irene is, and Wayne, he'd be the one who delivered it—'

'Who placed the order. Did you see who placed it?'

It was an Interflora order. From Cheltenham. There was a message inside, said the florist. Ever so lovely. She'd written it down herself. She could trace it back if we needed—we only had to ask.

'Let's see what the message says first,' I said. I fished it out, and turned so that no one else should see it.

'Sophie: a small token of thanks for your sweet understanding. Til next time. S.'

Kind words. And I was sure the spelling was not his.

I could have sung and danced my way through the rest of the day, evening class included. Chaucer—yes, we had fun with the Wife of Bath, her and her lovely Janekin. Shame the golden-haired, clean-limbed young man turned out to be such a comprehensive louse.

The rose was waiting for me when I took my break.

Sean had set an essay test for the second half of the class. All I had to do was write it on the board and sit down and watch them. 'Explain why Clym Yeobright's marriage to Eustacia was doomed to failure.'

Invigilating has all the charm of watching the stubble grow back on your legs. Any ordinary day I'd have marked, but now I was too sleepy to do justice to it. I could feel myself drifting off. Even I would regard dozing in front of a class as unprofessional and the Principal might well regard it as a sacking offence. So I hauled myself to my feet and prowled round, peering over the students' shoulders to see what they'd written and even, if I felt generous, to dab a finger on more obvious mistakes. Apostrophe errors abounded, and some spelling was so original it verged on the dyslexic. Then there were odd sentences to enjoy. 'Clym wandered about the countryside exposing himself at intervals.' Sean should enjoy that. And then—who says great literature is not applicable to every generation?—'the trouble with Clym is pathetic phallusy'.

Chapter Twenty-One

Tina's young man and his unlikely van took me back to Tina's flat. In fact, the young man himself seemed less and less ordinary: I didn't expect to see Russell's *History of Western Philosophy* tucked into the door pocket. And when he whistled under his breath, it wasn't pop or rock but Bach. Apart from his whistling—he took us straight through the Fourth *Brandenburg*—and my occasional *a capella* contributions, there was silence. I was too tired to speak. Tina might have been too bored. Or too pissed off with me for singing along with her bloke. If he was her bloke. I didn't know.

I longed for a hot bath to ease the bruises and ache and gravel rash and singed hands. A bath, a cup of cocoa and *Persuasion* but *Persuasion* was at home. At this point I believe I might have started to cry. But I didn't. I swore instead. Who should be sitting in the middle of Tina's living room, a particularly severe expression on his face, but Chris Groom?

I'd hardly sat down—circumspectly— before he started asking me questions. When Tina and the whistling philosopher sat down on either side of him, it felt like the start of the Inquisition.

Particularly when the boyfriend took out a notebook.

There was only one way to deal with this: so flippantly I wouldn't cry.

'We have met,' I said to him. 'But we've never been formally introduced, have we?'

He blushed: it was good to know I could still produce a satisfactory twirl of teacher's sarcasm.

'Thought I'd told you,' said Tina.

'No. And since you never address him by name—'

'OK. Seb, this is Sophie: Sophie, this is Seb.'

I held out a social hand. He pulled himself up—only an earthquake would have shifted me from my chair—and offered a reasonably firm grip.

'How do you do?' I pursued. 'And what do you do, Seb?' Joyce Grenfell would have been proud of me.

'Can't we get on with this?' Chris said, roughly.

'With what, Chris? I'm just making Seb's acquaintance—isn't that quite important? All I know about him is that he's interested in philosophy and may have perfect pitch. What I want to know is what a nice young man like him is doing in a place like this.'

'For fuck's sake,' Tina muttered.

'Taylor's in undercover work. Isn't it obvious?' said Chris.

'Isn't the whole point of undercover work that it shouldn't be?' I asked sweetly. But I was too tired to play the game any longer. I started to sag.

Chris must have noticed. He sat up authoritatively. 'There's just a few details I want to go over, Sophie, if you don't mind,' he said.

'I do mind. I thought I'd made that clear.' But I was too stiff to rise with dignity from an armchair as squashy as Tina's.

'I said I needed to talk, Sophie.'

Vertical at last, I was perceptibly swaying. I didn't care.

'I believe,' I said, 'that you are all sitting on what is meant to be my bed.'

'For God's sake, woman.' But he stood up too.

Seb and Tina retreated through an open door.

'I've not slept since yesterday morning. I want to now.'

'Mrs Thatcher says she only needs two hours a night,' he said.

'Look what happened to her.'

'We're investigating—in case it has slipped your memory—two murders. Which are undoubtedly tied up with attacks on you. Don't you think a little cooperation might be useful?'

'Tell you what, we'll have a meeting tomorrow.'

'Nine?'

'No. Teaching at nine. Teaching all day, come to think of it. And a meeting at lunchtime I can't miss.'

With a bit of luck he'd wake me up by exploding.

'What do you suggest, then? Eleven o'clock next Sunday?'

'How about breakfast tomorrow?' I'd had enough of this round, too.

He stepped towards me, half-smiling. 'You mean—'

'Breakfast,' I said.

If the meeting had been minuted, I should think about a page would have covered everything. As it was we went all round the Wrekin, to use the Black Country expression, and got nowhere at all.

Accents: we chewed them over for a while.

Motorbikes: those too.

Computers: a prolonged discussion which would have amused Phil no end. The police were so short of manpower (gusty and ironical sigh from Sophie) they'd not yet come up with anything in the computer project.

Banks: the police team were notably reticent on the matter of ICB, so I threw my threepennyworth of rumour in. Chris was not amused.

Then things got more frightening.

Names of possible suspects:

1) *Iqbal:* the cousin had temporarily interested them, but had been eliminated on two grounds: he was left-handed and the murderer was right-handed, or vice versa, and he'd been helping the police with their enquiries into quite another matter—cheeking the constabulary.

2) *Tony:* unfortunately he'd got an un-shakeable alibi, too, for the time of Wajid's death, but they were glad to say that for

George's death he hadn't—

'I beg your pardon? Did you say glad? Tony's my friend. My oldest, dearest friend.'

But that wouldn't have been minuted.

3) *Jools:* I could vouch for her being in the pub. And—news to me—Stobbard swore he'd watched her leave the building by the front door.

4) *A.N. Other:* my choice. But I couldn't identify him or her. Someone at the bank? The man without a job title? Chris favoured someone from the Asian community—anyone—but hadn't found anyone to pin it on, hard as he'd tried. (That wouldn't be minuted either.)

Motive: ('Ah,' I said. 'Now we're talking. Shouldn't we have done this first for the victims? And treated them separately?'

'We're only brainstorming,' Chris said defensively. 'But maybe you're right.'

'How can we treat them separately?' Seb put in. 'Ms Rivers is involved with both.')

How would that work out if officialese? 'It was pointed out that determining motivation for the murders might be instrumental in discovery of the murderer. So far as was known, Ms Rivers was the only common factor.' Something like that?

a. *Wajid Akhtar:* no known enemies, within the Asian community or outside it. Popular at college. But suspected to be involved with computer fraud.

b. *George Carpenter:* no known enemies. But his knowledge of the members of the orchestra and their affairs might have made him dangerous. There is no question that he might have been blackmailing anyone.

'So why,' asked Seb, 'encourage a man carrying his bassoon case on to a building site and whack him on the head with a scaffolding pole?'

A O B: Ms Rivers's burglary. Police confirmed that the security lights and the burglar alarm had been left inoperative by what appeared to be professional thieves. A neighbour had reported seeing heavily built men getting into a parked Transit. No ID yet.

The meeting was adjourned *sine die*. It was time for college. Tina jiggled her car keys at me, Seb consumed the last of the toast, and Chris stared at his coffee mug as if he'd never seen one before.

'Tell me, Chris,' I said, 'how you propose to guard me tonight. I've got a ticket for the Music Centre—I've had it for months. Brahms, Mozart and more Brahms.'

'Skip it. Listen to it on the radio.'

Tina's eyes widened in horror.

'Tina's hi-fi can only get Radio WM,' I said.

'But—' And then he realised it was a

joke. He blushed very easily for a grown man. 'I'll see what I can do,' he said at last.

'Hi, girl,' said Philomena, 'how your boyfriend, then?'

Tina, a little breathless from the stairs, asked, 'Which boyfriend?'

'Oh, she got plenty, our Sophie.' Philomena laughed. 'The one what sent you roses, Sophie.'

'Rose. Just the one.'

'No. Roses. You want to see your desk.'

'I don't. It's a mess.'

'What's new, eh?'

Even the very best minder needs to go to the loo at one time or another. With Philly beside me I saw no reason to follow Tina. In fact, I had every reason not to. I wanted a little help from Phil, which Tina would be happier not knowing about.

'I'll be up in ten minutes, Sophie,' she assured me a minute later, winking luxuriously. And then, for public consumption, 'You go look at that desk.'

'Sophie,' someone's ill-formed handwriting said, 'have tried endlessly to reach you. All I get is your answering machine. Are you all right? Please contact me to let me know I'm forgiven. S.'

And there were a dozen roses this time, as Phil had said.

I'd already opened the cellophane wrapping when Tina returned. I looked at her ironically.

'Ah,' said Tina. 'Flowers.'

While she went off to fill an old jug we keep just in case a grateful student says it with flowers—and a surprising number do, bless them—I dug swiftly in my files and shoved the photocopies of Wajid's project in an envelope. The scrawl which constituted the address would have done credit to an old-fashioned GP. I'd just had time to slide some stamps on when Tina reappeared. While we arranged the flowers and brewed a celebratory cup of tea, Philomena came in unobtrusively, removed the envelope from the corner of my desk and strolled out. If assorted police computer experts couldn't crack it, we'd see what one whizz kid could do.

When the phone rang in the staff room during our lunch break, Tina was the only one whose mouth was not too full to answer it. She passed it to me, with an ironic lift of the eyebrow. It was Chris, in his far-from-official voice, offering to guard me. Somehow he'd managed to wangle tickets for a pair of seats.

'Is Gorgeous Bum conducting?' Tina demanded when I put down the phone.

'No. An equally lovely Frenchman,' I

said. 'Stobbard's carving in Liverpool—'

'Eh?'

I waved my arms about. 'You know—carving. He was already booked there before he picked up Peter Rollinson's schedule. Don't worry—we're not in for the clash of the Titans.'

'Thought it was the cymbals!'

On impulse, and to stop myself screaming, I offered my original seat to a nearby History lecturer.

'It isn't your usual seat or anything, is it?' he asked.

'No, I sit anywhere I can get tickets. Why?'

'Wouldn't want to get blown up, that's all,' he said cheerfully.

I wasn't surprised when Chris didn't use the underground car park: there would be far too many places for people to lurk. He found a slot in a crowded, brightly lit shoppers' car park and we walked bunching in with other pedestrians as much as we could. Then we had to cross the wide spaces of Centenary Square. In the daytime, the trees offer an oasis of green amid the city grey. Now they were little islands of shadow. It was all I could do not to reach for Chris's arm. Perhaps the events of the last forty-eight hours were catching up with me. And I was still tired:

I hoped to God that I wouldn't fall asleep during the concert. But it was no thanks to the conductor that I didn't.

'Don't glower,' Chris said, as we pushed our way out two hours later.

'I'm entitled to glower. Waste of time and money. God, to think he made Brahms sound boring!'

'That overture always takes me back to when I was a kid. My brother singing it: *"Gaudeamus igitur, Iuvenes dum sumus.* Bombs shall dig our sepulchres—bigger bombs exhume us." D'you reckon Brahms would have approved?'

'Moot point, isn't it? The man admired Bismarck, for God's sake! But I love his music,' I added, inconsequentially and unnecessarily. 'Was your brother part of the protest movement?' I asked. I ought to make some effort to be sociable.

'Yes. Very much so.'

'What does he do now?'

'He's a priest in inner-city Glasgow.'

'Priest? Are you a Catholic too?'

'Yes. But don't worry: I'm one that believes that contraception should be used in every conceivable situation.'

I would not pursue that: flirting is all very well when your heart is disengaged, but the evidence of the past weeks was beginning to suggest that Chris's was not.

'Do you believe in God, and the Trinity

and everything?' I asked instead.

He was silent. We were retracing our way across the square, and our separate sets of footsteps rang out, mine roughly twice to every one of his.

'Well,' he began, diffidently, 'I certainly agree with Hamlet, that there's more in heaven and earth than in Horatio's philosophy.'

And at that point I saw George. Shortish for a man. Heavy-shouldered. A flat-footed walk. I gripped Chris's arm and pointed. I couldn't speak. The figure, carrying not a rectangular bassoon case, but a cylindrical one, moved under a streetlamp. Then it approached the parking rank reserved for motorbikes.

We said it together: 'Jools!'

He wanted to ask me all sorts of sensible questions, of course, but I couldn't form the words, my teeth were chattering so much. As she roared away, I let go of his arm, only to find him taking mine.

'Supposed to be brandy for shock,' he said. 'Only I know a pub where they do a very mean single malt.' He dropped his hand and we walked in companionable silence.

I'd never liked him so much: I could feel his effort not to intrude on a renewal of my grief for George. But that wasn't the only thing I was thinking about, and

I was glad when we reached a pub I'd never ventured into. For all its dirt and the horrified silence when I walked in, there were twelve or thirteen malts behind the bar. I settled with lamentable lack of enterprise on Laphroaig. He followed suit. The silence deepened agreeably as we swished the whisky round to release the peaty fumes.

He raised his head to look me full in the eyes. 'How are you getting on with Mayou?'

'I beg your pardon?'

'Mayou. How are you getting on with him?'

'Tina's told you about the roses,' I said, accusingly.

'Uncommonly romantic.'

'Probably the floral equivalent of "have a nice day",' I countered.

'Or night?'

'You know what time of night I was shot at. Hardly time for Khalid's Montego to turn back into a melon.'

'Are you going to see him again?'

I slammed my glass down on the table. I was up and out of the door, without looking back. Only a couple of hundred yards to Centenary Square and the taxi rank. I'd get home that way.

Only I couldn't go home. I had to go to Tina's, to her incessant music and her Oldbury accent and her whistling boyfriend. Except he probably wasn't a boyfriend. When he stopped whistling there'd be Ian and his cottage-pie-cooking little wife. And Chris.

I was profoundly angry. He never stopped manipulating me. If I'd liked him half an hour ago, I hated and resented him now.

I like teaching my students about bathos. Don't confuse it with pathos, I tell them. It's what you call it when moments of high drama come to a ridiculous conclusion. That's how my evening ended. I'd reached the taxi rank before Chris caught up with me. I'd got in and was leaning forwards to tell the driver to go to Tina's. But I couldn't remember the address—I don't think I ever knew it, to be honest. So I had to wait for him. But at least I went alone. He wasn't leaving the city centre without his new car and I wasn't leaving my taxi.

Chapter Twenty-Two

I had not been at my best on Friday, even for my favourite group. They had reacted to the presence of Tina with some distrust, and refused to contribute with

288

their usual delightful enthusiasm. In fact, the whole session had all the charm of wading through cold porridge. Then there was a lunchtime meeting on some college policy I knew from experience we'd discuss endlessly and never truly implement. This time Tina's presence made the wordy even more verbose, to the point where most of us were yawning, and Tina was quietly but literally asleep. Then there was the usual tussle with my Beauty group. There were only two bright spots in the day—I saw Aftab going into class, still with his surgical collar but at least back on course, and there was a note from Manjit. It was waiting for me on my desk after my attack on the beauticians.

I was confused at first: the writing on the carefully sealed envelope was the counsellor's. I'd know Frances's scrawl anywhere—thick, confident strokes in black, italic felt pen. Stylish but illegible. Inside, however, was another envelope, addressed in small blue-biro letters, with the legend PRIVATE AND CONFIDENTIAL in red. At least the envelope was too thin to be another bomb.

It was from Manjit. She was staying in a refuge on the far side of the city, she said. They were hoping to fix her up at another college, maybe not in Birmingham at all. Would I try to see Aftab and tell him she was all right? If he wanted to write, Frances would pass on a letter. If I wanted to write, she'd pass on a letter for me, too. But she didn't want me to tell anyone where she was. Since there was no address on the note, I could scarcely do that anyway.

Poor kid! Giving up her family, her friends, at sixteen. Goodness knew what she'd been going through at home to drive her to that. I'd write her a chatty letter at the weekend, and try to persuade Tina to take me shopping to buy her a couple of gifts something both nice and practical. And I'd make sure, next time I saw him, I said something positive and private to Aftab.

Choir practice tried poor Tina's patience almost to the limit, and the morning rehearsal, taken by our choirmaster since Stobbard was still swanning round the country doing pre-arranged gigs, drove her still further. Fortunately she turned out to be one of those people who can dissipate bad temper by energetic housework, and she attacked the ravages on my house with a will. I should have been even more grateful had she not compensated for her overindulgence in Orff with a particularly tuneless set of tapes played loudly through my hi-fi. The grate was back in place, thanks to another of Chris's contacts, and by the end of the afternoon our combined efforts had rendered the house more or less back to normal. Except for the gaps where my china had been. I'd spread out the books to try to fill the shelves, and Chris had tried to cheer me up by offering to take me touring antique shops when the insurance money came through, but I was still melancholy at five when the phone rang.

Tony Rossiter.

'I've been gated for the weekend, Tony, and unless someone takes pity on me I've nothing to do but clean my carpets.' I could say that sort of thing to him. 'At least I'm back home, though. Got to be thankful for tiny mercies, I suppose.'

'So you can't go anywhere without protection?' His voice came shrill over the phone.

'Nope. Well, to be honest, I'm not sure that I even want to. I've got to that state of paranoia where I'm convinced whoever's after me is chasing me when he's probably safely tucked up in bed. I'm afraid to open the post, damn it all.'

'I'm not surprised, after that letter-bomb business. Poor old you! Tell you what, if you cook me supper, I'll bring some booze—a lot of booze.'

'But I've got a load of booze. The insurance will pay for all the smashed bottles, and I'm damned if I'm going to claim for plonk. I got Ian Dale—the sergeant who fancies himself as a bit of a wine buff—to go to Majestic, so there's a whole case of Australian and New Zealand in the pantry. Red and white. And some interesting European ones. But, Tony, I've got no proper food.'

'Never heard of a takeaway?'

But a takeaway meant a stranger delivering it to the house. For a moment I couldn't speak.

'Or shall I bring something in with me and we'll cook together? Or—tell you what—we'll order and I'll go and collect it just to make sure no one shoves any arsenic in it. How's that?'

Perhaps, after that bit of intuition, he wouldn't be surprised by the fervour of my voice when I agreed. Thank God for old friends!

Tony arrived clutching a couple of Safeway's carrier bags.

'There,' he said, delving. 'I can't be your taster all the time, Sophie, but you at least see if anyone tampers with these!'

'These' were ready-mixed drinks—gin and tonics, and so on and a huge variety of miniature liqueurs. At the bottom were two large boxes of individually wrapped chocolates. Tony is not usually the most generous of men, but when he splurges, he is unbeatable. Once or twice in the past when I've kissed him he's become embarrassingly amorous but I risked it tonight—who wouldn't kiss an out-of-season Santa Claus? His buss on my cheek was refreshingly fraternal. One complication was out of the way, but there were plenty of others to keep us going.

Tina had tactfully and resolutely declined to eat with us. She really didn't like all this fancy food, she said, even curries. She phoned through our order, however, and waited while Tony whizzed off in his posh-mobile to get it. When he got back, we shoved everything in the oven while we sank an aperitif.

'I propose,' he said, reaching a bottle of Ian's Tio Pepe, 'to get rather drunk.' I raised an eyebrow: he was normally the most abstemious of men.

He responded by picking up a poppadom.

'Tony, I—'

He sighed. 'OK, I know we need to talk. In fact, I need your help. But let's eat first.'

I wasn't sure about that. Is it better to eat with a sword of Damocles over you or in you? We opened lager and the smallest of the aromatic foil containers.

When it came to main courses, we

shared. Chicken tikka masala, golden chicken and a rich vegetable curry. We digested, exhausted, for twenty minutes or more. Then the man demanded pudding. So we ended up, giggling, in the kitchen, concocting a dish in which I tossed bananas in orange juice and caramel and flambéed them in one of his miniature liqueurs, topping the lot with scoops of ice cream. It wasn't until we were finishing our coffee, and a miniature of Amoretti each, that he started to talk. We were both sitting on the floor, but he hunched gnomelike three or four feet from me. I moved into the shadow on the far side of the lamp, trying to merge with the furniture so he could talk freely.

He took me back through our childhood and schooldays. Then his face softened as he talked about playing the violin. Studying music at university, he said, was his first mistake. In the shadow, I nodded. He should have been playing, a practising musician, he continued. But at university his ambition had changed. There was more money, he rapidly saw, in administration. So with his First and an appropriate postgraduate management course, he was off. Regular promotions, stamping on the odd finger as he swarmed up the ladder. Nothing new yet. The job with the Midshires Symphony Orchestra was what he'd always wanted. General manager. Power. Money, too—he gestured ironically in the direction of his car. But...

This was important. It was the first time he'd ever used the word 'but' in connection with his work. So I waited.

'It's so stupid,' he said, 'so bloody stupid. I can't possibly leave.'

'Leave?'

'I don't want to go and I don't want to stay.'

'Go? Go where?' He mustn't hear the anxiety in my voice: he'd always been there, part of my life. Now George had gone, I couldn't bear it if Tony left too. And yet if he needed to leave, maybe I'd have to help push him.

'I'd never even have considered it if it hadn't been for George's death. It was me the police asked, Sophie—I don't know why—to say it was him. Damn it, did they think I'd break down and say I'd killed him? I didn't. I told you the truth. If I say to you, 'I'll bloody kill you,' you don't expect me to. Do you?'

' 'Course not.'

'I cared for—loved—that man, you know. Like you did. A friend. I trusted him. He was right all the time, too. Mostly, anyway. Sometimes he'd feed me snippets I ought to know. Like not to be too hard on someone because his wife was miscarrying, or it was time to mention moving someone up a desk, or sometimes down.'

'Or out altogether?'

He was silent again.

I was desperate for a pee and another drink, in that order. If I got up, would it break his mood?

'Or out altogether,' he said at last. 'Jools. You know she's blackmailing me.' His tone was flat, prosaic.

'No,' I said, quiet, bitter, understanding more at last.

'Last three years, I should think. Not money. Never asked me for money. Apart from—oh, Sophie, I've been a complete shit. When I started, I didn't realise you had to keep work and pleasure apart. Until George told me, of course. By then—it's all so trite, damn it! I mean, we had a few drinks one night, and somehow ended in the sack. You know what a randy bastard I am. She said it didn't matter—damn it, I wanted to go with her to the Family Planning or whatever for the morning-after pill. But she said she'd got a loop and not to worry. Then I didn't see her again—OK, well, maybe a couple of times. But she came to me a few weeks later. One Tuesday evening. I was just about to run the conductor to New Street to catch the London train. And she comes to me and says she's pregnant. Her loop had shifted or something. Did she—didn't she ever tell you?'

I shook my head.

'So at least she kept her part of the bargain. I paid, of course. No problem. Flowers. Counselling afterwards. I did all I could, Sophie.'

Then I asked a question I wasn't specially proud of. 'Did you actually see the hospital bill? Nursing home, or whatever?'

'No. Why do you ask?'

'Just interested.' I thought of the flat off Augustus Road, with its expensive furniture, and the David Cox on its beautifully lit wall. 'But you mentioned blackmail. Blackmail but not money?'

'Well, she kept her job, didn't she? And don't tell me there aren't thirty or forty bassoonists who could do it a damned sight better than she does.'

'Did George know about this?'

'You were his dearest friend and he didn't tell even you. Of course he knew. He used to spend hours helping her, you know. And people said he used to do all the out-of-town gigs where you might have expected her to sit up because he was too selfish to let her get the experience. He did them because he couldn't trust her to do a halfway decent job, and he cared about the bloody orchestra so much. And the music, of course.'

'Tony—forgive me, I have to ask this:

why didn't you just confront her? Get rid of her?' After all, we are in the twentieth century. Even if the story of the pregnancy were true, men and women do sleep together, and loops do slip. Presumably. It would scarcely have caused a tremor in the orchestra, where the pressures of the job, the touring, the weird hours do cause such liaisons.

'Because it didn't just involve me. At least I've always assumed not. I mean, her flat...'

'I'm sorry?'

'I thought she might—other people...'

I should have picked him up and shaken him. Anyone else I would have. I'd have pointed out that if he'd confronted her, better still gone to the police, all her power over other people would have been weakened. There was something I had to pursue, though, and yelling at him wouldn't help me. 'George—did she have anything on him? Because I don't think George...I'm sorry...'

'Would have lain down under it? I don't think so. But I don't know. You see, he did say he'd got to talk to her. That there was something very serious he had to say. We were joking, that Friday morning, Sophie. I haven't said anything before because I thought it might upset you. I'd just been with him to the solicitor's, you see, to witness his will. And he said, "Glad that's all over. I wanted it all tied up. Now I can confront our friend" '.

'Could it have been any other friend?'

'Not a man for rows, George, was he? He was in this ongoing battle with Mayou, of course. They were rehearsing *Le Matin* and they couldn't decide on the tempo for the slow movement. And George reckoned that bit in *The Firebird* could do with slowing down.'

'But you don't kill people because they dislike your tempi. I thought George and Stobbard got on with each other quite well. That's one reason I—' I stopped. Then I got going again. 'And Jools couldn't have killed him because Mayou saw her going out through the front door. He told the police.'

'Front door? I thought he'd have swaggered through the admiring crowds outside the stage door!'

'I thought you liked him.'

'So did I. He's offered me a job, you know. As his personal manager.'

'Gofer. Oh, Tony.'

'Sounded better than that when he said it. More—much more money than I get here.'

'How does he propose to pay you? Private oil well or something? Damn it, conductors aren't pop stars.'

'Must have money in the family, I suppose. Certainly spends it like water. And I know how much he's getting from the MSO, and it isn't enough to pay what he's offering. More than a policeman, though, Sophie. You could do a lot worse. He's very concerned you've not been in touch, by the way. I explained about your problems, though. But you must contact him.'

By this time I needed the loo so badly I could think of very little else. But it was Tony who got up first, and headed for the stairs. I looked at my watch: two-thirty. What I'd give for Mrs T's capacity for work without sleep. As soon as he came back, I headed loo-wards. I ought to tell him off for assuming I wanted anyone, policeman or conductor, in my life. But that would divert me from what I needed to say.

'You realise,' I said, as stern as if he were one of my students, 'you have to tell the police all this.'

'I'll go first thing Monday morning. Before we set off for Bedworth.'

'You ought to go now.'

'Too pissed.'

'Tomorrow.'

'Going to—let's think—Bristol. Colston Hall. Afternoon concert. We leave at nine. Rehearse at eleven.'

'Tonight. You ought. The fuzz'll drive you, and I'll guard your car with my life.'

'I want a solicitor with me and you'll be too busy looking after your life to lay it down for a car.'

I found a sleeping bag and covered him with it. Slipped off his shoes, shifted the cushion so he wouldn't get a crick in his neck.

I stood watching him. I ought to rouse Tina, or even phone Chris. But Tony had to do it himself—prove something or other, no doubt. I didn't think I'd sleep, but I must have done. Certainly I never heard him or his car leave. Bristol, was it? No one could accuse him of not being a conscientious boss at least.

Chapter Twenty-Three

One thing was certain. If I told Chris any or all of what Tony had said, he'd be hauled in, for the simple reason it would justify Chris grilling someone. Chris wouldn't see the big snag I saw: hating Jools was no reason for killing George. Jools had a motive for killing George, but she had not struck me as a woman who had killed someone the night she came into the pub. The emotion I associated with her was fear. Even the memory of George's death had made her blanch. I had to talk to her again. Of course, she'd be well on her way to Bristol now. I left a message for her to call me urgently. My voice may have sounded rather grim. I left another message too. Couldn't think why I hadn't done so before. Thirteen roses deserved acknowledgement, and it was sheer bad manners to ignore his messages. And it might have seemed to him that I blamed him for being impotent, that night. Crass and ugly, that was how I felt now. Bloody hell, it should have been me sending him flowers with messages telling him not to worry and inviting him to a return match at my home. In private. Except it couldn't be. Sounds of Madonna percolating down the stairs reminded me that Tina was irrepressibly here, and any moment now I'd be subjected to a barrage of heavy witticisms about my sex life. Should I leave the sleeping bag lying apologetically where Tony had left it, or should I remove it and smooth the hollow from the cushion? Which would irritate Chris more?

The living room was pristine when she crawled down.

But I used the telephone extension

upstairs to phone the Mondiale. There must be an art in dictating loving messages to complete strangers. What did I want to say? That I'd been too knackered and knocked about to think about him? I tried—amazing how useful it can be—the simple truth.

'Tell Mr Mayou,' I said to a genteel-voiced clerk, 'that I was in a bad car crash, and that burglars wrecked my house. I had to spend a couple of nights away. But I'm back home now and would very much welcome a call.'

The call I actually got was from Dean. I didn't recognise his voice at first. And he was slurring his consonants as if he were drunk. But that is a state I'd never associate with Dean. He said he'd got the information I'd wanted. But—

'I'm not a woman for buts.'

'But I don't know whether I ought to tell you.' Then I thought he said; 'Safer if you didn't know.'

'I beg your pardon?' Hell, I didn't mean to sound like a schoolmarm.

'Safer. For you, Sophie. Because if you don't know you won't get done over, see.'

'Done over?' My voice shot up an octave. 'What the hell—?'

'Found a place. Two places. Sophie: isn't safe, you know.'

'Not safe? Dean, love, you sound all funny and what you're saying doesn't sound like you either.'

'Not surprising. Lost a tooth, got two black eyes, a few bruised ribs.'

'Bloody hell! What can I say? I never meant—'

'No, it's OK.'

'We need to talk. The police—'

'Don't want no filth.'

'But, Dean, it's—'

'I said no filth. Got a record, Soph. Remember? GBH. Wouldn't believe me.'

I bit back all the things I wanted to say. Who was I to argue? In any case, I might be able to work something, face to face.

'And I don't know I ought to see you,' he said. 'I might lead them to you.'

'I've got a police minder at the moment, I'm in so deep.' I gave him a brief résumé of my recent activities. 'But perhaps you shouldn't be seen coming here. Couldn't I just casually drop by at the Fitness Centre? Nothing odd in that.'

'Could talk in the sauna, maybe.'

'Only if you turn the thermostat right down!'

'Come on, Sophie. If you can't stand the heat, get out of the sauna!'

They decided it should be Seb who'd accompany me, much to my surprise. I'd laid down some ground rules, first. My informant and I would talk in private. I would not be party to any of Seb's neat little transmitters. I'd do my utmost to persuade my informant to talk to them, or even let me pass on the information. In return I had to promise not to organise a one-woman raiding party on the premises he fingered. I wasn't quite convinced they'd keep their part of the bargain.

Seb, as a potential new member, insisted on looking everywhere, including the sauna, before he paid. He might well have planted a bug. And when we cycled side by side—I wanted to keep the muscles ticking over—he wore a Walkman. So did half the people working out, actually: it's probably only the younger ones who enjoy the canned pop music. Maybe it's there to stimulate us to greater efforts, maybe to drown the grunts of the Multi-Gym males. But after Tina and her Radio Whatever, I would have done much to have had a Walkman tinkling out some particular jolly Telemann.

At last, having cycled and rowed and birthing-chaired with such dedication as must have convinced any casual bystander that I was a genuine fitness freak, I left for the changing area, emerging with a towel wrapped sarong-wise around me. Dean was already there. As I entered, he passed me a notice to hang outside: SORRY OUT OF ORDER.

Dean's skin, normally a rich purple-brown, had faded to a patchy grey. His face was swollen, but not as badly as I'd feared. His usually elegant movements were cramped. He'd done what I should have done: used the phone. His contacts had come up with a couple of names, but recommended extreme caution.

'Where?' I prompted.

His answer stunned me. But on reflection it shouldn't have done. Not sleazy back-street gyms, where poor black kids were encouraged to make money damaging other kids' brains, but an extremely couth city-centre Health and Beauty Club used by anyone who was anyone, a video shop and, of all things, a health-food shop. Then he'd had a brilliant idea. He'd follow Jools. I thought that must have been a long shot, to say the least, but he'd had some luck, he said. She said she'd got to cut short her session because she'd got to do some shopping. And something in the way she said it made him think it was something she shouldn't be buying. Normally he finished every conversation telling her not to be an idiot. This time he tailed her. To the video shop. She left with a carrier bag. Just an ordinary carrier bag, as if she'd been borrowing *Rambo* or whatever. He went in and asked—this was where he made the mistake, he said—for what they'd just lent to Jools.

And they'd offered him cocaine.

'Gobsmacked, I was, Soph. Bloody gobsmacked. So I said, no, I wanted the steroids, see. And they sold me them. Easy-peasy. But just as I was about to pick up my bus home, these two heavies invited me to have a conversation with them. Told them I don't talk to no strangers. When they tried it on—' he touched his face—'and I grounded them both, blow me if this third chap didn't come up and slosh me. Sock full of sand, I reckon. Went out like a bloody light.'

'I know it's a daft question, but if there were three of them and you were unconscious, how come you got away with...with your life, Dean?'

'Bit of luck. There was this woman at the bus stop when I came round. Said a funny-looking woman had stopped them. Just like that. And they'd all scarpered. Just like that. Christ, Soph, I'm bloody scared. And so should you be.'

'Got to be the fuzz, Dean. Got to be.'

'You promised—you said you wouldn't fucking call them!'

'You don't call this lot. You ask permission to go out. I can't go to the bloody bog without them knowing.

307

And I'm not bugged. Wouldn't let them, because I'd promised you, right. But I want you to tell them. One of them. He'll believe you if I do.'

'That stringy chap you came with the other day? Thought you looked kind of good together.'

'Gee, thanks. As a person—well, sometimes he's OK, others he's a total pain in the arse. But I think he's a decent cop, honest enough.'

Dean evidently thought that was an oxymoron, even if he didn't know the term.

'I don't know. I really don't, Soph.'

'But—'

'I mean—Christ, there may be no one to stop them next time. Never been so fucking scared.'

'Police protection?' Not that I could recommend it with wholehearted enthusiasm. But at least Dean liked pop music.

'How long for? Even when they're in the nick, these guys can still get at you. Have you thought of that?'

I hadn't. I ought to have done. I'd have that to live with, wouldn't I?

He took my hand. 'Sorry. Didn't mean to upset you, Soph. But it's right, isn't it?'

I nodded. 'But we've both got a marginally better chance with them on our side. No one'll notice a couple of unrelated deaths unless someone knows who the corpses are. At least we might get avenged.' I can't say that reassured him.

'Tell you what: I'll sleep on it. I've got me mate to pick me up tonight. I'll shake down on his floor. And I'll call you, let you know what I decide. Right?'

'Right. But—but if you need help, or if anything happens—to you or to me—promise me you'll call Chris Groom.' I'd memorised the number. Now Dean did the same.

What I wanted to do was tell Chris and Seb everything, but I owed it to Dean to keep quiet. At least while Dean made up his mind. The silence in the car was uncomfortable, even hostile. When I got home, I couldn't stop shaking. Tina had to peel the potatoes. At last I realised what a mess I'd got myself into. Me, and Dean, and possibly Aftab, and possibly even Khalid's family. I'd had regular progress reports from Chris so I knew he'd left hospital yesterday evening. I should have phoned. I could phone now. But I was suddenly afraid—how illogical can you get?—that even a simple telephone call might draw danger to his door. I pushed the phone away. One of Tony's gin and tonics called me, loudly. But all it did was make me weepy.

Tina had obviously not heard the phone above the sound of her sewing. At my suggestion she had installed an electric machine and yards of material and lining in my spare bedroom, and was hoping to produce curtains for the whole of her new flat—it seemed preferable to her going out of her mind with boredom, now Seb had gone to pursue other callings. The rest of Sunday promised to be very boring. Or very lonely and frightening.

I'd long since finished *Persuasion*. Everything else on my shelves seemed to have been soiled by the activities of my intruder. Needless to say I had no new library books.

Radio Three was into thirteenth-century religious music. It didn't take me long to discover that I was not. I'd decided that this was the moment when I really ought to write to my more distant relatives who didn't justify an expensive phone call, and was digging in my bureau to find paper, when I found George's holiday snaps. The phone rang. I dropped the photos and snatched up the handset. Maybe it would be someone I could gossip to, even someone solidly reliable like Chris. But it was not Chris.

'Hi,' this lovely American voice said softly. 'I hope I'm not disturbing you?'

'Stobbard! No, anything but—'

'Tony tells me things haven't been so good with you. And your telephone message: I'm very concerned.'

'Nothing life-threatening—not for a while. But I seem to have lost my nerve. When I was really in danger I was quite cool. Now I'm just a gibbering mass of potential hysteria.'

'Are you—the police aren't stopping your visitors?'

'They don't let me open the door. And Tina did say she ought to search Tony.'

'That's awful! A total violation of—'

'I was joking. She rather liked the look of him. Any groping would have been strictly friendly.'

'Oh.' He did not sound amused. 'Does she have to check everything? Your mail? Things like that?'

'I suppose so.' She'd been too entertained by Tony's carriers to do more than shake them hopefully. 'She did try to stop me handling those lovely roses, Stobbard, but—'

'You liked them?'

'Loved them. Really.'

'I was wondering if I might see you.'

'Were you? Oh, that'd be wonderful. Shall I—would you like a meal?'

'I guess it might be late. I'm still stuck in Devon or some goddamn place. Where did you say it was, Tony?'

There was a muffled murmur.

'Guess it'll be an hour or more, Sophie. See you then.'

Tina was not altogether sure that she ought to leave me while she bought champagne at the off-licence down the road, but I wanted something less pragmatic than ready-mixed gin and tonic to offer him. In any case, she was back in time to let him in, much to my embarrassment. We might have been two spotty adolescents for all the poise we exhibited for the first few minutes. He sat as awkwardly as if my room were a dentist's waiting room. I talked too much. Eventually he consented to drink coffee, if it was not too much trouble, but did not follow me into the kitchen. I spilt grounds everywhere, chipped a mug, and could find only stale biscuits.

But suddenly it didn't matter; from my living room came the sound of Cole Porter. He was playing my piano.

'There's only one problem, Sophie.' He laughed. 'I can't play and dance at the same time. So I bought you these.'

CDs. Two of them. Not the entire Mayou oeuvre, but, as he said, 'Guess we could dance to these. Always liked

Gershwin and Cole Porter—even though they did insist the singers should be opera stars, not show singers. Can't stand the big vibrato these operatic people are trained to use. Just doesn't sound right with these intimate little numbers.'

I nodded and demonstrated, making my voice wobble ludicrously.

He laughed.

But still we did not kiss. He accepted the little social peck I gave him as thanks. It was a pity I did not have a CD player.

'Tell me,' he said, putting his hands to the small of his back and easing his shoulders. Evidently the piano stool was the wrong height for him. 'Why do they keep you in the back row? That's some little voice you've got there.'

I leaned against the piano and smiled. 'But it is little. Wouldn't fill the Music Centre now, would it? And in any case, I'm not reliable. Because of my job, I can't get to all the concerts. Every year I miss all the ones I really want to do: Barbican, Festival Hall, the Maltings. But the Chorus Master puts up with me since I can usually manage Birmingham gigs.'

He closed the volume of Schubert songs and riffled through Brahms and Schumann. I slipped out, returning with glasses and the Moët. I wanted to celebrate the musicmaking apart from anything else—can you imagine the joy of singing your favourite lieder with a world-class musician as accompanist? Although he demurred that he was no pianist, he could still play better than any of my friends, his hands, with their elegant long fingers and strong palms, easily spanning a couple more notes than the eight notes of a scale, and stretching further if necessary. The first bottle took us through some Debussy, which I couldn't manage, to some Weill I could.

Suddenly, he pushed away from the piano. 'Come on! Guess we can dance anyway!'

So, to the accompaniment of our own voices, we waltzed around and around my living room. At first it was strictly ballroom stuff, not at all erotic. But as we sang more and more softly, and the pace slowed, I grew more aware of him—and by the feel of him against me, he was beginning to want me as much as I wanted him. We slowed almost to a stop, our hands exploring in a way that would have had us instantly debarred from *Come Dancing*. It was then he discovered that my T-shirt separated quite easily from my jeans. Shame it was only a Marks and Sparks bra. I'd have liked something more seductive. But I found it didn't matter. Forget about dancing. Forget about everything but his lips against my skin. And it seemed that he was, after all, a man for small breasts.

'You're so beautiful: God, I just want to fuck the ass off you,' he whispered. 'But not here. Not with her up there. I'll call a cab. Come back with me. Now.' His tongue did wonderful things to my left nipple. His hand was busy elsewhere.

The phone rang.

'Can't that officer take it?' he murmured, dabbing little kisses on my stomach between words.

'No. She only answers doors.'

'Do you have to take it?'

With great strength of mind, I eased myself away. It took me a couple of seconds to reorientate myself and work out who was speaking.

'Khalid?'

Not that it was anything like his normal tones: he was shouting into his end so much it hurt at mine.

'I said, I've bloody cracked it!' he yelled.

'Cracked it?' For a moment I could only think he meant his injured arm. Then I realised: 'Khalid! Really? The computer stuff? But they've only just let you out of hospital.'

He wouldn't tell me, he said; he'd show me. He was well enough to get into the Computer Department at the university now, he insisted; he'd spent the afternoon there, in fact.

'But it's Sunday.' And Stobbard was exploring my pubic hair.

'Is it? Oh. Doesn't matter. I've got my own key, and the security guards all know me. So come on round. Now.'

'But it's after midnight!'

'Shit! Security will have locked up the main doors. And there's some outside course on tomorrow morning: they won't let us in till twelve-thirty.'

'But if it's so important—'

'Don't suppose a couple of hours'll make any difference. In any case, I'm due at Outpatients at nine going on twelve.'

'What about Chris?'

'Chris?'

'The Chief Inspector who said you must be crazy to have anything to do with me.'

'OK, bring him. And any of his boffins who want a lesson in logic. Come straight to the room I'm working in.' I wrote it down carefully on my pad. It was recycled paper, rather thick and garishly coloured. The sheet was vermilion. So was the sheet underneath, but I would soon be moving on to an altogether more restful green.

On impulse, I took it up to Tina. It might do her career some good if she were the one who told Chris. It meant fastening my bra and reorganising my pants and jeans as I went up the stairs.

She was sitting cross-legged on the floor, hand-finishing her curtains. She looked at me quizzically. 'God, I've heard some weird ways of making love, but caterwauling at each other takes the bleeding biscuit.'

'Oh, you know what Shakespeare said—"If music be the food of love..." '

'Planning a bit of a banquet, were you?'

I blushed. Then I thrust the note at her. She winked, and pretended to stuff it down her bra. She could use the extension in my bedroom.

When I got downstairs Stobbard had the telephone directory open and was looking up taxi firms.

'Guess it's late,' he said, with no insinuation in his voice. 'Nine-thirty rehearsal tomorrow. Can't understand you Britishers. They say they'd rather have a free afternoon. Back home we sleep in the morning, rehearse in the afternoon, then everyone's ready for the evening show.'

I could think of nothing to say, except to apologise when he picked up the handset to dial and found he couldn't because Tina was already talking. I expected him to fling it down in temper, but he replaced it slowly and thoughtfully. Turning from me, he drained his glass of champagne, but gestured a refusal when I lifted the bottle to offer him a refill. At last the phone pinged. Tina had done her job.

I watched while he dialled, regretting that those long fingers were engaged in nothing more than poking telephone digits. It appeared that the person answering was not cooperative; but then I could hear her laugh as she lapped up his suggestions: 'Don't just try—try hard.'

There wasn't much to say after that. Nor much time, actually. At least, as we heard the diesel chug of the taxi, he turned and kissed me, with the sort of expertise I'd hoped he'd show in other areas. He managed, in a very short space of time, to thrust his tongue into my mouth in a particularly erotic way, to nip little kisses in my lip, and to run his mouth over my eyes, down my neck and on to what in my case passes for a cleavage. As he got into the taxi, he blew another kiss. 'I'll be in touch,' he called softly.

'And what the fuck d'you think you're doing?' asked Tina. 'Christ, don't you know better than to stand nicely framed and outlined with a light behind you? All anyone's got to do is aim for the middle of your silhouette!'

I shut the door, quickly. She snapped off the hall light. 'And I suppose you think a piece of plate glass is bulletproof.'

I sat on the stairs, my head in my hands.

'Chris says he'll collect you at eight tomorrow morning,' she said, more mildly. 'There's no way he'll wait till the afternoon. And he's arranged for this boy wonder of yours to do his stuff on a police computer.'

'Can you do that? Hack from another computer?'

Tina sighed. 'Don't you know anything at all? Even my kid brother knows more than you!'

'He's the right generation,' I said. 'Did Chris say anything else?'

'One or two rude words when I told him how you were spending your evening.'

'But he can't be afraid—surely he knows I'm safe with Stobbard?'

'Depends which way you mean safe.' She giggled. 'Oh, and he said you were right about that Datsun blowing up well after the crash. Seems some clever bugger fixed some sort of remote-control device, probably in the petrol tank.'

'How on earth did they work that out?'

She sighed. 'You've seen the television news, where they have these pictures of policemen crawling inch by inch over some bit of a field or summat? Right. They don't do it for their health: they do it because they're looking for—'

'Clues?'

'All right. Clues. Bits and pieces that mean summat to the lads in Forensic.'

I didn't bother to correct her. 'So these bits were fragments of something electronic that the bod triggered as he ran away,' I said.

'Right. And tell you summat else: you know you were hiding from someone on a motorbike? Well, the geezer was just some innocent passer-by who didn't reckon cars should be left burning on a public road and went to the trouble of going to the nearest police station to complain about it.'

'Bona fide?'

'Eh? Well, he was the bishop's chaplain, so he ought to be bona.'

I'd better go and tidy up. The remaining champagne was warmish and flat. I poured it down the sink. I washed the glasses and dried them carefully. I reached a fresh loaf from the freezer, wrote a note to myself to take milk for our coffee into work—it was my turn. My carrier bag already bulged with my marking. I stood staring at nothing.

'Come on,' said Tina kindly, padding in behind me, winding her alarm clock, 'it's time for bed. Everyone feels like that after too much booze.'

'Why don't you get a neat little electronic alarm clock like everyone else?' I asked, as I followed her and her ticking burden upstairs.

'Never trusted them: batteries always fail just when you need them most. In any case, this old thing helps me go to sleep.'

I could hear it through her closed door and mine. It did not help me sleep.

There was someone in my living room. In that twilight between waking and sleep I heard him: then I heard my door catch, and Tina breathing, rather than whispering, 'Sophie? You awake? I'm going down. Stay there.'

'OK. Be—be careful.'

I could see her gun, outlined against the lighter patch of the open door. Whether she was abnormally silent on her feet, or whether I was deafened by the blood rushing in my ears, I heard nothing of her descent. Then came her voice—strong, authoritative. Then silence. I strained for the sound of a struggle.

Silence.

I don't know how long it took her to come back upstairs.

'I thought I told you to stay put,' she snapped.

'I had to know—'

'Nothing to know. Unless you've got a bloody ghost. I heard him; you heard him.

Nothing there. Fucking hell!'

We stood petrified on the landing. Perhaps he was still trying to dig his way in.

She dropped her voice again. 'Bit difficult to tell where the sound's coming from when you're three-quarters asleep.'

I nodded.

'How quietly do your windows open?'

'The double-glazed ones at the front are OK.' The frames at the back were the original wood, to be replaced when I had my next pay rise.

'Right.' She padded into the little boxroom and reached for the window catch. I followed. She glared, then shrugged.

'Hold this, then,' she said, passing me her gun, so that she could brace her hands against both frames, opening a fraction of an inch at a time. Then she leaned out. She pulled her head back. 'God almighty, Sophie! Look at this little lot.'

Together, we watched the foxes circle. One broke from the group, running hard towards the house. For twenty or thirty seconds he scraped at the wall. Then he dropped back. Another came, scratching at the brickwork, then another, and another.

'Go away!' I shouted at last, unable to bear it any longer. 'Just clear off! Leave me alone.'

Their posture, the expression on their

faces, said quite clearly, 'Who's going to make us, then?'

They dropped back perhaps fifteen yards, in a semicircle in the road. And waited.

Chapter Twenty-Four

'So why does your front garden smell of curry powder?' asked Chris, with distaste.

Tina told him about the foxes.

'But curry powder?'

'Well, Chief Inspector, sir,' she said pertly, 'I couldn't get the garden centre to sell me any of them pellets you're supposed to use, not at three in the morning.'

'In any case,' I added, 'It's not curry powder. I wouldn't give the stuff house room. What you can smell is *hing*, otherwise known as asafoetida. You put a pinch in vegetable curries. It's supposed to reduce—er, flatulence. Aftab put me on to it.'

At the mention of Aftab, Chris looked at me coldly: I was obviously in disgrace for failing to mention the photocopy of Wajid's file. But then inquisitiveness took over, and he asked, too casually, 'What were the foxes after, anyway?'

'No idea. All I know is they were trying

to get into my living room.'

'Stay here,' he said, and went outside. Tina and I exchanged a look: this morning we would not risk following. My pulse was uncomfortably fast already. But he was soon back, throwing a word over his shoulder to an officer whose silhouette we could see through the front door. 'How long,' he asked me, shutting the door behind him, 'have you had a loose airbrick?' He wiped his muddied trousers, ineffectually, with his handkerchief.

'Didn't know I had,' I said, passing a box of tissues. 'Well, the whole place needs repointing, so I suppose—'

'Surely it's the sort of thing your average householder would notice?'

I looked at him. I wished anxiety wouldn't make him sound so much like an irritated academic.

'It's usually hidden by flowers, and to be honest I haven't had much chance to tidy the garden and examine the fabric of my little castle, have I? You wouldn't let me start pruning in the back garden, even, so I didn't dare start out at the front.' And my anxiety made me sound defensive and uncooperative.

He glared at me, and spoke into his radio. I waited until he had finished—such was our relationship this nasty Monday morning—before asking, in as quiet a voice as I could muster, 'What was that you were telling your colleague about getting up my floor? I've only just finished putting everything back after last week's visitors—'

'Do you or do you not want to find out if some enterprising soul has managed to insert a listening device under your floor? Or maybe a time-delayed bomb?'

'How many floorboards do you want to get up?' I asked, drearily.

It was the sort of weather that would have driven me to public transport: rain that was not particularly heavy but falling with the sort of determination that convinces you it will never to stop. This morning, of course, I would be late going in to work. Nothing would have kept me from Khalid's tricks with the police computers, and it was obviously pointless asking Chris to defer the experiment.

I would probably have been late for work anyway. The main roads were completely snarled up with traffic—one person per car as usual—and Ian took to the highways and byways, not to elude a possible tail, but simply to get there at all. When Chris spoke, it was to remark on the number of big Volvos and Peugeots cluttering up the roads outside schools, parking regardless of yellow lines so that the

325

rain wouldn't touch their delicate little burdens. A more enterprising Mercedes enlivened the proceedings by reversing on to the far lane of a main road.

At last we reached Lloyd House, police headquarters: for some reason they'd chosen to hack from there, not Rose Road. More aspiring boffins, perhaps. They kitted me out with a visitor's label, found us all coffee, and sat on desks to await the arrival of Khalid.

'Where the bloody hell is the man? Didn't anyone send a car for him?' Chris paced up and down the open-plan computer room like an expectant father. I fiddled with my ID. Tina came into the room. 'He's on his way all right. Robbo's collected him. But Bristol Road's solid. And all the roads that have to cross it. They think some tanker's been leaking diesel, and there are no end of minor crunches.'

'All we bloody need. Any ETA?'

'Robbo says should they winch him up into the chopper they've got on traffic surveillance?'

'Why not? It might as well do something useful. Let's have a bit of drama. And invent some story to feed to the press. On the other hand, where could we drop him? Better wait.'

Suddenly he caught my eye and grinned.

But neither of us seemed to have anything worth saying.

'What did the Principal say when you said you needed me?' I asked, not specially because I wanted to know. I hoped he'd be furious and demand my instant return, so Chris could enjoy himself denying it.

'He said it was a good job someone did,' said Chris.

No one else laughed.

When the phone rang, it was more pounced on than answered. A minion passed the handset in Chris's direction—'Sir!'

We all watched him, but his face gave little away. And all we heard were little grunts to prompt the caller. Finally he yelled, 'Take him into custody, of course,' and slammed down the phone.

But he wasn't angry. The crow's feet round his eyes refused to go away, and his mouth wouldn't take itself seriously. Did I dare catch his eye?

'You'll no doubt be relieved to learn, Miss Rivers, that we have completed our investigation of your foundations. No listening or explosive devices. All clear.' He was willing me to ask about the arrest.

Just to humour him, and to fill in time because it was still raining incessantly, I said, 'But you said something about custody. Have you found—?' And I allowed a touch of hysteria to creep into my voice.

'My officers found,' he said, impressively, 'and have duly apprehended, a small male hamster. We believe it may answer to the name of Eric, since one of that name was reported missing last week.'

'Not my neighbour's little girl? She's got a hamster.'

'That's right.' His face started to relax. 'Any idea why it's called Eric? I'd have expected Hamlet or Henry or something.'

I gave the answer I'd been given. 'Because he's a hamster,' I said.

And then there was a stir—Khalid had arrived. He was greeted with what might have been slightly derisory cheers, and I could see that he didn't make an impressive figure amid all these tall, broad-shouldered people. He'd always been slight, and his TB had left him slightly hollow-chested. But there was something about the way he sat down at a computer that silenced them, the way Alfred Brendel draws everyone's attention when he walks to his piano.

I wish that watching Khalid at work had given me an object lesson in hacking. I suppose if I'd known enough to follow it would have. All I could do was watch, fascinated but confused.

I suppose asking how he could do

it without a modem wasn't particularly sensible. Clearly everyone thought I should have known that this sort of computer had one built in.

'What he's doing now,' whispered Tina, 'is getting into Dialing Directory.'

'So I see. Why does it have only one "I"?'

She didn't bother to reply. Whatever Khalid was doing, the computer was producing odd little noises. First a dialling tone, like on a telephone. Then one ring. Just one.

'What's that whistling?'

'The modem taking over.'

'Oh.'

'See—the call's connected.'

Khalid typed very rapidly.

'That's the user name and password.'

'Where'd he get that from?'

'Wajid's notes, of course.'

Each of my questions had been greeted with ironic sighs from the knot round the screen. Khalid alone spared time to grin up at me at last. 'Still in the dark ages, aren't you? Never mind, I'll take you through it slowly another day.'

'No, you bloody won't,' said Chris. 'What you're doing is illegal.'

'Oh, I'll find somewhere else to hack into. I often use other universities' systems. Ah.'

There were occasional bips like those from a computer toy. Figures moved—or were moved—across the screen.

'Ah,' Khalid said again. 'Ah-ha!'

The gasps from the police computer experts were like those of a Wimbledon crowd watching a crucial point being disputed by two champions.

'This is where it gets a bit trickier,' said Khalid.

The others nodded, leaning closer to him, pointing, murmuring.

'There's this time trap, see. You have to do it at exactly the right speed, or it closes down on you. I used a metronome eventually. If you could just count out the seconds?'

'One-two-three—'

I think all of us were counting under our breath in time with Tina, who had clearly elected herself his assistant. The screen emptied.

'Shit,' someone said aloud.

'No. Wait. It seems like for ever, but just wait.'

A phone rang. A constable answered it, and gestured to Chris.

'Later!' he snapped. And he turned, as we all did, to the screen.

Contact, from Birmingham, with somewhere in Bogotá. And lists of all sorts for us to stare at, the little white cursor summoning us on deeper and deeper into some very private files.

'There! *Narco traficantes,*' I crowed.'

'What's that?' It was Tina's turn to expose her ignorance this time.

I translated. 'And there we are: *Inglaterra.*'

People were cheering and hugging each other. Chris put a swift arm around my shoulder but remembered and took it away as if it burnt him. One name stood out. Harding, Julia. Birmingham. And her address.

'Chris! What about Dean?' I was gripping his arm. Chris stared at my hand, and then at me. At first there was that painful, vulnerable expression; but he soon replaced it with tart irritation. The irritation turned to anger when I stammered out my fears. 'Was that him on the phone?'

'Later. You don't know it was Dean, but I'll get someone to phone him, on the off chance. Come on: first things first.'

'He promised to call me. He promised.' Jools. She might have saved him once because it suited her to, but you couldn't rely on her generosity. But Chris was relieved to be doing something, and to be doing it well. 'Ian, we'll go and get Harding. Oh, unlawful killing, I should think. Or illegal substances. OK? And you

331

get out a general call—her motorbike or her car.'

They didn't have to ask for addresses or registration numbers.

'Killing whom?' I asked.

Perhaps he hadn't heard. Khalid's new fans were escorting him noisily to the canteen.

'Killing whom?' I repeated, more loudly.

Chris turned and stared at me as if I were an idiot. 'George and Wajid, of course.'

I shook my head. 'And what about Dean? And what—'

'We'll get him afterwards.'

'And what about me? Do you propose to leave me on the loose among all these computers, or are you going to return me to William Murdock?'

'You'll be easier to keep an eye on at home. Tina, do the honours, would you? Oh, book a mobile out, of course.'

'But, Chris—' Tina bleated.

Poor Tina—to be denied a piece of the action.

Then I saw an aspect of him I'd never seen before, though I suppose I must have known it would be there. He didn't speak: just looked at her.

From Lloyd House one of the quickest ways to Harborne is, oddly enough, an indirect one. You go through the Queensway underpasses on to Bristol Street, the route Khalid had taken the other night. Then you turn right at the big McDonald's and explore the leafier parts of Edgbaston. It was not such a good choice this morning because the traffic was still messy, and Tina flicked the radio in irritation to the police wavelength. I hardly listened. I'd found the tunnels claustrophobic.

'Vincent Drive?' she said. 'Here, Sophie, isn't Vincent Drive near you?'

'Not specially. It runs between the university and the medical school.'

'How far from you?'

'A mile or so. Why?'

'Sounds like there's summat up. Shall we take a look?' And she swung the car around with an ease that Tony or Chris would have approved and put her foot down. Hard. The nearest cars could get was Somerset Road; but when Tina spoke to the constable redirecting the traffic he waved us on into Pritchatts Road. It was where Farquhar Road crosses Pritchatts Road and becomes Vincent Drive that the accident must have happened. She threw the car half on to the verge, behind a couple of patrol cars and a fire appliance.

'Stay there, Soph,' she said over her shoulder, as she slammed the door.

But I'd heard the ID over the radio too, and I couldn't. Chris found me as I was retching up nothing in the gutter. I'd got rid of everything in the previous bout of vomiting.

'Serves you right,' he said. 'I left orders you weren't to come anywhere near.'

'No one told me,' I said, groping for a tissue.

He helped me to my feet and steadied me. Just for once I didn't shake him off.

'Will the bus driver be all right?'

'Should be. Eventually.'

We looked again at what remained of his cab. The impact that had torn his arm so badly had sheered the metal back. But it was hard to see details because, like the rest of his bus, it was charred and twisted. There was a grotesque mess Chris said was a motorcycle. Then they started to erect screens.

'Funny,' he said. 'I came to pick her up—and they've had to scrape her up.'

I looked at him sharply. But his face told me he was only trying to cope with it his way.

'She was my friend,' I said quietly.

'How would she have survived all those years in gaol?'

'Oh, Chris.' I thought of the flat; her money; her love of music, however limited compared with George's. 'All the same.'

'Very, very quick. Quicker even than George's or Wajid's.'

'What was that they were saying about an explosion?' I asked.

He gestured: there would be, wouldn't there?

'But I heard someone say—I know I did—the poor driver insisted there was an explosion. Impact, explosion, more destruction.'

He looked at me and was about to speak when a colleague summoned him. He was to talk to the press. Tina was on the other side of the road, looking pale. Perhaps Chris had already found time to tell her what he thought of bringing me here. If he hadn't, now was perhaps time for a judicious retreat. In any case, I wanted to bounce ideas off someone. I caught her eye and we went back to the car.

'If the bus driver was right,' I said, fastening my seat belt, 'why would there have been an explosion?'

'Fuel,' she said promptly. 'Look, Sophie, I know she was a friend of yours and all but she wasn't a nice lady. I've seen what drugs do to kids. Slow death. Not a nice quick one. And their families and all.'

I nodded: I'd lost precious students that way. 'But why should she choose to explode on a road leading to the university?'

'Why not? Good place—awkward road junction, they're always having accidents there. And diesel, perhaps, on a wet road. Visibility poor. Textbook, our Soph.'

'But why here? Not in Erdington or Moseley, but here. On a road leading to the university where Khalid was supposed to do his hacking.'

'Bloody hell, don't be so-so...'

'Paranoid? But just because you're paranoid it doesn't mean they're not out to get you.'

'Soph, for pity's sake. She was a bad woman. Killed your mate and that kid. She got what was coming to her. Period. Here—you teach English: what d'you call it when you get what's coming to you?'

'Nemesis.'

'No. Summat to do with hoisting. That's it. When you try to blow up someone's castle and the bomb goes off too soon?'

'Hoist with your own petard.' I laughed, but not with amusement. 'I rest my case, m'lud. Still, I'm sure your colleagues will turn up something interesting, like they did on Bristol Road.' And then I said, 'Take me to the fitness centre. Now. Fast.' It was the tone I use when I don't want any argument. I didn't get any.

'Funny thing that,' said Elaine, one of the

other instructors, 'you're the second person to ask after Dean.'

'Where is he?'

'Like I told him, this man, we don't normally disclose that sort of information.'

'I know he's not at home. He wants to see me. It's a matter of life and death.'

She walked slowly over to her desk. 'H'm. Funny, must be his day. That bloke, he said he'd got to pay him some money, or something.'

I felt colder than ever. 'Settle a debt or something' would be more like it. 'Now,' she said slowly, dithering with little heaps of paper, 'where'd I put it? Can't think, for the life of me.'

I'd never done this before; I thought it was only done on TV. But I fished a crisp new twenty-pound note from my purse and rustled it. In a second it had gone, to be replaced by a scrap torn from a paper bag. An address in Handsworth.

Even as Tina turned the car I knew we wouldn't get there in time. I used my teaching voice again. In a second, Tina was summoning support. When someone at the other end balked, she added, with a voice like mine, 'On DCI Groom's authority. Now.'

On the whole I was glad I hadn't had to say that.

There is no quick route to Handsworth.

There are canals and railway lines to cross, for one thing, and that means bridges, old and narrow bridges. So the maximum of traffic is funnelled on to the Outer Ring Road. Which is where we were sitting now. The traffic lights changed and changed again. If we couldn't get through, how would anyone else?

'Motorbikes and blue lights,' said Tina tersely. 'But,' she added, catching my fear, 'getting an ambulance through might be trickier. Why the bloody hell they can't afford that sky ambulance is beyond me. Dave, he's my other brother, he's on the ambulances, top end of the M5, he says—'

But we were moving again. And Tina put all her concentration into forcing her way to Dean.

We were too late, of course. But a motorbike paramedic patrol had got to him, and there was hope, they said. The only question was whether to take him to the nearby Dudley Road Hospital or to the Accident Hospital, further away but with a specialist major-injuries unit. They chose the latter. Six motorcycles accompanied his ambulance to close roads so he could pass. Renal damage. Ruptured spleen. A fractured skull. The sort of damage boots can do. And it was all Chris's responsibility. At least that was what he said. He should have taken that phone call, should have taken time to listen.

'I shouldn't have got him involved in the first place,' I said.

'Why did you?'

'I just had this hunch about Jools. One I was afraid of voicing. In case...in case I was right.'

'You never told us who he fingered. Sophie, why can't you trust me?'

'It's not that I don't, it's just—Chris, it's loyalty, isn't it?'

'Sometimes misplaced. Come on. I have to know what Dean found so we can nail the bastards that—'

'—that may have killed him. OK.' I told him all I knew.

'Did you say video shop? Address?'

'I never knew, not all the details. Chris, I didn't want it to be Iqbal's.'

'You didn't want it to be Iqbal's. Jesus, Sophie, we've had Iqbal's little place under surveillance for months. Why d'you think we let him go to Amsterdam? Not for his health! What can you get in Amsterdam?'

I turned away—I didn't want him to see the shame on my face.

We stood there together, in the mean street, letting the rain soak us. I hoped it would never stop. Suddenly I thought of another family.

'Chris—Khalid's family! What about them? What if anyone's found out? They must know his registration number—what if they trace him?'

At last Chris turned to me, his face softening into the grimmest amusement. 'No need to worry about them, Sophie. As soon as I heard about—about this, I sent a patrol round. Armed, before you ask. Sophie, they're safe. Safe, I tell you.'

But at this point the world folded in on me, and not even Chris's smelling salts could bring me round.

Chapter Twenty-Five

I came to in time to stop Chris dashing me to hospital. Food and a drink were what I needed, I insisted. But not necessarily in that order. Somewhere warm. Despite Chris's jacket round my shoulders I was still shaking, and words I should have been able to say disappeared in a chatter of teeth.

I wanted company, too. There would be no escaping yet another statement, so I couldn't just bunk off and seek comfort with Shahida or—if I thought about my friends, I would cry. I mustn't cry. I wanted George to hold me while I sobbed out the truth about Jools.

'Sophie. Sophie?'

I turned blindly: Chris was shaking my arm gently.

I made a great effort. All his colleagues who weren't cordoning off the street—rather belatedly, surely?—were enjoying a ringside view of their boss making a spectacle of himself. I found I cared too much for him to become a laughing stock: I'd have to find enough energy to make an effort. I managed to grin.

'Food,' I repeated. 'Have you got time to have a bite with me? There must be some pub round here.'

The one we found must have been the worst in the Midlands. Quite blatantly the other drinkers tried to work out my price. The tables were dirty, the mats, pretentious with hunting scenes, filthy. We ought to have got up and walked out. But we stayed there, and chose—waitress service!—from a greasy menu. I found I couldn't face meat. But they microwaved my chicken-and-Stilton pie so long it was empty by the time it reached me. Chris ordered another, and pushed around chunks of his steak while we waited.

Clearly a little conversation was called for, if only to disguise the culinary inadequacies. And I'd have to talk about

341

Jools some time.

'I can accept that Jools killed Wajid—and I suppose you lot have broken her alibi?' I demanded, forgetting that Chris wouldn't have followed my thought processes.

He blinked hard, made an obvious effort to catch up, and repeated, 'Alibi?'

'That Tuesday. When the orchestra were playing at Lichfield and Wajid was killed.'

'She went on the coach to Lichfield but was late on to the platform.'

'So the assumption must be that she had left her motorbike somewhere in Lichfield, came back in their tea break, met Stobbard, killed Wajid and hurtled back to Lichfield.'

'Not all that much of a hurtle on a motorbike. Not too much traffic at that time of night. But she was late on stage.'

'Why didn't you tell me all this?'

'Because I didn't see why we should worry you until we'd got absolute proof. And we haven't yet. But we will.'

I nodded. I hoped they would. But one thing still bothered me: 'So why should Jools alter the signs in the Music Centre?'

He was ready to bluster.

'I just can't see why she should have changed the signs,' I insisted. 'Can you?'

'Of course. To lure George out into the open so she could commit the perfect murder.'

'But we have a witness to say she left by the front door.'

'There isn't any reason why she shouldn't have killed him first and then left by the front door. And then joined you at the pub. You said she was late.'

'But not muddy. If she'd been out in all that mud, it would have stuck to her clothes. And her shoes.'

'You keep a spare pair: she might. If not in a disgusting carrier bag.'

I wished he'd stop smiling at me like that. Every muscle of his face betrayed him, and embarrassed me for him. I glowered at my plate. 'I told you: something scared her that night. Scared her.'

'In your judgement.'

'OK. In my judgement. Let's ask another question. Why kill George?'

'Because he'd found out what she was up to.'

'George wouldn't have found out.'

'Surely if someone had given him the wrong case—'

'He wouldn't even have opened it. He'd have known his own in the dark! His own instrument, anyway.'

'OK. So it was dark and he opened it. And he found out it wasn't his, but as he fastened it to return it to its owner, he discovered a substance which made him tackle her.'

'I suspect,' I said slowly, 'that if he thought there was any drug involvement he might have called you people straight away. Even if Jools were a colleague.'

'Are you sure you should use the subjunctive that way? Shouldn't it be "was" a colleague?' asked Chris.

I shrugged, unamused.

'All right. Perhaps she knew he was going to call us.'

'How?'

'Or perhaps George hadn't even noticed but she thought he must have done, and decided not to risk it.'

'There are an awful lot of perhapses, Chris.' I gave up on the second pie, and pushed it and the cold chips away. What I'd really like was a nice, comforting, sticky pudding: sago made with extra cream and golden syrup instead of sugar, or Bakewell pudding, or treacle tart with custard. 'The other thing is, Tony does know one or two things about her. He told me he was going to tell you everything today.'

'Bloody decent of him! Well, he hasn't. I'll have him called in. Ruffle his dignity a bit.'

'He may have been trying to get in touch too,' I said quietly. 'He promised me he would.'

'I doubt it. He's a devious bastard, your Tony. Deserves a bit of a shake-up.'

'He might be a foolish man but he's not a bad one.' I wanted to tell him that there was no point in treating Tony as if he were a rival to be bullied. Perhaps I could make a joke about it. 'Your car's nicer than his,' I said.

He didn't reply. The waitress had slopped over, told us to have ice cream and slopped away with the still-full plates.

'I'm sorry,' he said. But he might have been referring to the meal as much as his crassness.

The ice cream was covered in shaving-foam cream.

'So what about Wajid?'

'You never let go, do you?'

I shook my head.

'But that's one of the more obvious answers, anyway. If Wajid got into that file he'd have seen her name. And he probably tried to blackmail her. Perhaps didn't get anywhere: after all, we never found any trace of large sums of money. Though that bank he worked at—ICB—it's going bust, they reckon. The Bank of England's expected to stop it trading any moment now. The sad thing is a lot of ethnic-minority traders used it—there'll be heartache in many Asian homes when the news breaks. But that's strictly between you and me and my friend in the Fraud Squad.'

'OK.' Then I thought again. 'But people like Aftab—his family are so nice, Chris—shouldn't we warn—'

He shook his head sadly. 'How can we? Without starting panics and runs on the bank?'

'There'll be those anyway.'

'No. No, Sophie, Please!'

'And you'd be found out, and the force'd have to make you a scapegoat and sacrifice one of its best ever detectives,' I said, with a little irony.

'You flatter me. Look, it's time we were off. You've got a statement to make. And I've still got some ends to tie up. All those loose ends you've picked up on—don't think the DPP won't find them too. What are you doing for the rest of the day?'

Damn: I'd hoped he wouldn't ask me. I didn't want to rebuff him. I wanted him to realise that it was no go for him without my having to spell it out.

'There won't be all that much left. But I thought I might stroll into Harborne when your lot have finished with me. Window-shop. And there's a concert at the Music Centre tonight. Tony's got me a free ticket. Not the MSO. A modern-music ensemble. They couldn't sell many tickets, so they're papering the house with comps.'

'Comps?'

'Complimentary tickets.'

'Anything I know?'

'Never heard of any of it myself. But I know a couple of the players...' And Stobbard was carving. After last night I thought he would expect me to be there, and to go round to the Artistes' Room afterwards. I'd just have time to wash my hair and change into something attractive.

'Er?'

Poor Chris. But I wished he wouldn't make me do it.

'I'll probably be going out with some of them afterwards—old friends.' I'd intended to discourage, not snub, but Chris looked hurt.

'Come on,' I said, probably sounding quite horribly bracing. 'There's work to be done.'

He smiled wanly. 'Of course. And I see the sun's trying to come out.'

The sun was shining by the end of the afternoon. There was just time to slip into Harborne. I would celebrate my return to the world with a new suit even the Music Centre clientele wouldn't sneeze at. In the event, I bought two matching blouses, too, and put the lot on my Barclaycard. I'd have a huge bill next month, but sufficient unto the day was the evil thereof.

Chapter Twenty-Six

When it came to it, I didn't want to go to the concert, new suit or no. But I couldn't think of anything else to do. I certainly didn't want to be on my own. I was afraid of what my head would find to fill the silence. I sat on my bed, my hair still wet from the shower, hugging my old teddy bear for comfort. Tony would be with the MSO wherever they were, and he hadn't George's gift for making phone calls when I needed them. Tomorrow he'd have to talk to Chris. But surely he'd be in the clear. He had to be.

In the end, I knew I had to go. It was fine enough to walk down to the bus stop, and, in the absence of Tina, that ought to have been a pleasure in itself. But I saw shapes in the shadows. I hadn't wanted to contradict Chris when he said I didn't need a minder, but I had a nasty fear, at a level I didn't care to explore, that he might have been premature.

I was early. I had a drink, and ordered another for the interval, in case there was a rush for the bar. But when I reached the auditorium I knew there wouldn't be.

My lovely new clothes were all wrong. This was not the sort of music yuppies would go for. It was Serious and Modern and attracted students who looked like latter-day hippies. There was a proliferation of corduroy among the older element, and a tendency among the women to aggressively flat shoes and overlong skirts. You'd have thought them more at home at Dartington. In my Marella suit, a rich petunia pink, I stuck out like a sore thumb. Apart, that is, from a group in the centre block of the most expensive seats. From their general gloss and excess of teeth, I deduced—correctly, as it transpired—that they were American. The music was—but I don't want to prove that I am as much a philistine as people who denigrated Beethoven as a tuneless impostor. No, there was no obvious melody, but I wasn't so naive as to expect that. But I couldn't detect rhythm or form either. George had no time for music you couldn't sing in the bath. He wouldn't have enjoyed this. We'd started with a minute's silence for Jools. Then they played the Barber *Adagio for Strings* in memory of her. I pretended it was for George.

I'm not sure how seriously Stobbard took the rest of the concert. I wondered if there was something exaggerated about his beat, something rather studied in the way he brought in players. I was too far back to be sure, but I thought he ghosted a smile at me. Maybe he even winked after a piece which we were assured by the programme note sounded exactly the same backwards as forwards. The noise levels were phenomenal. All in all it was a pretty taxing evening, and I wished I'd been to an honest pop concert, or at home with my radio and my teddy bear. But then, of course, I wouldn't have been able to spend any time with Stobbard. My interval wine—I knew better than to bother him before the end of the concert—made me feel sick. And the tam-tam chorus of the last piece—so loud it made my breastbone resonate—brought on the sort of headache you get when you've marked all your end-of-year exams.

Or watched them take what was left of a friend to the morgue. On impulse I found a phone. Dean: how was he? The hospital was reticent: 'critical but stable'. I tried Ian Dale. He was more detailed—Dean was on a life-support system, he said, in intensive care. But the brain scan had been what they called encouraging. And, he said, a big healthy lad like Dean would surely have more of a fighting chance than most. It was the 'surely' that worried me.

If I'd had any sense, I'd have crawled off home there and then. As it was, I pushed my way through the earnest young men telling an exhausted-looking bunch of musicians how meaningful the evening had been, and headed for the Artistes' Room. Since it wasn't a Midshires Symphony Orchestra gig there was no Tony to admit me when I knocked. In fact, the raised voices inside might well have meant no one heard anyway. For a moment, I felt so dismal I wanted merely to turn tail and escape. But then I thought of Stobbard and, deciding that a good bonk was as good a way as any of pushing my misery to the back of my mind, edged my way in.

He was hugging and kissing his way round the sleek group I'd noticed in the auditorium. I thought he hesitated marginally when he saw me—perhaps he was so knackered by the day's work (don't forget he'd spent the afternoon rehearsing the ensemble) that he could scarcely place me, particularly as I was nearly as well-dressed as the other women. But he broke away and thrust his way to me, scooping me into his arms and kissing me, rather hard, on the mouth.

'Now, folks, this is the young lady I've been telling you all about: she's the one who's made life bearable in this goddamned hole.' Stobbard kept his arm possessively around my shoulder. He nuzzled my hair. I was glad it was clean and smelt nice.

He didn't, to be honest. He was wet with sweat, and smelt as if he'd run a marathon.

As if he could read my mind, he pushed me away from him, towards his friends. 'God, I shouldn't be anywhere near you civilised people. Guess I smell like the men's restroom. Give me just five minutes, will you?'

He disappeared into the inner room. Suddenly he dodged back out again, and picked up his baton. He disappeared again. Luckily it didn't fall to me to remark on it. A lovely middle-aged lady, with the scars of a face-lift just visible under her hairline, screamed with laughter. 'Did you ever see the like? Fancy taking your baton to the goddamn john!'

'Perhaps he's superstitious about losing it,' I said mildly. 'Some conductors are, aren't they?'

Someone took up the theme: a Japanese conductor who insisted on having his favourite baton in the room when he meditated, an English oboist rumoured to take his instrument to bed with him (in its case, of course), a pianist who carted his own Bechstein around the world with him. We were quite old friends by the time we had worked out all the variations. The face-lift lady was delighted he'd met with a nice English girl: she wanted to hear all about my connection with music, the orchestra, the choir, my work. She introduced some of the entourage, and I found myself apologising to a man of about my own age, with a fine-boned, intelligent face, for not understanding the evening's fare.

'I'm not a musician, you see,' I said, expecting him to play—oh, a melancholy profile like that ought to play the viola. But when I looked at the fingers of his left hand, the nails were long, and there were none of the blackened grooves in the tips you expect on a string player.

'Oh, me neither. No, I just came over to see Stob with this bunch of alumni. We've been friends ever since our freshman year.'

'So what—' I groped for the term—'did you major in?'

'Math.'

That didn't surprise me. Our university orchestra had been packed out with medics and mathematicians: the latter reckoned they had an affinity with music stretching back to the Greeks. 'Stob was always top of our group,' the young man continued. 'And it seemed to come so easy, too. His music. His drama. He played Hamlet, you know. Had all the girls weeping over him. Before Mel Gibson's time, that'd be! Stob—he's one of those disgusting people,' he said laughing, 'who are good at everything they touch.'

'Renaissance man,' I agreed, my head pounding so hard I was afraid someone would notice.

'Right! He can fix anything the experts can't touch. The electronics on my car, my hi-fi: anything like that. Always asks, when he comes to visit with me, 'Anything to repair, Lew?' That's Stob for you.'

'So what do you do?' I asked, at last remembering party etiquette.

'Bit of this, bit of that.' He laughed again. 'I like to be on the move. Upwards, preferably!'

'He's so modest,' said Face-lift.

I looked as alert as I could: any moment now I'd literally have to hold my eyes open.

'He's just become the youngest president they've ever had at—'

'Now, Mrs Mayou—'

She was his mother!

'You all right, honey?' She was peering at me anxiously.

'Bit of a headache,' I said.

She laughed. 'You English folk and your understatement. Migraine?'

I nodded; wished I hadn't.

'Stobbard must run you home, sweetheart.'

'No. No, please. I'll get a taxi.'

'But—'

'I don't want to spoil the party. Please. Just explain. And tell him I'm sorry.'

She put her hands lightly on my arms. 'Sure. And I'm sure we'll be seeing a lot of each other real soon. Fancy Stobbard finding a real little English rose. Don't worry, Sophie: I'll send him your love. Hey! Sophie! Did anyone ever tell you you look just like—? Lew, who's she like?'

But the door slipped shut behind me, and I was able to ignore her.

One of the Centre's security staff called me a cab, and let me sit down at his desk till it arrived. He was a sufferer, he said, and his wife and daughter. He'd tried everything the doctor could throw at him and acupuncture and homoeopathy and damned if he wasn't going to try a faith healer he'd heard of. He'd let me know if it worked. Nice man. Took my arm to help me through the door. Wouldn't take the fiver I tried to push at him. Told the driver I was a friend of the Chief Inspector. Perhaps he wasn't a security guard.

It wasn't a bad migraine. Not the sort that lays you out for days. In any case, unlike my fellow sufferer, I did have some very effective tablets, and I could still see enough, when I got home, to tear a couple out of their foil jackets and drop them in a tumbler of water. I overfilled it: drops

355

spattered out on the working surface. I ought to mop up. But I left them. All I could manage now was to crawl up to bed.

Chapter Twenty-Seven

I didn't feel too bad in the morning. I'd already showered and was thinking about breakfast when the phone rang. It was Sean, the head of English, to ask me if I'd mind taking an extra class in the afternoon. Shahida: it looked as if she might lose her baby. But she'd cared enough about her class to ring him from hospital. Crying for her wouldn't do any good. Taking her class and sparing her worry might.

I picked up my phone pad to write down the details. The top sheet was green. I had to press quite hard to get the biro to work. I tore it off, and went into the kitchen. I put the paper on the working surface while I filled the kettle. It was green. It should have been the last vermilion one.

It didn't make sense.

I made a mug of weak tea, and thought about toast. Next to the bread bin, on the working surface, were little specks of powder. They seemed terribly familiar.

Migraine often leaves you fuzzy, but not usually mad. How could I see grains of powder on someone else's table? I wished the migraine would come back. I didn't want to think what I was afraid I would have to think.

I reached for the telephone. Tina had sufficient common sense to talk me out of my panic. Her answering machine told me she would phone back. Chris: I'd really wanted to speak to him, so God knows why I hadn't tried him first. He was with the Chief Constable, said a bored voice; I could leave a message. I did. Ian. He'd do at a pinch. His wife said he was on the way to the dentist's. He'd broken his dentures. By the time I'd made all those phone calls, I was too late to go by bus.

It would have to be my bike. I quite enjoyed it, actually, bowling along past all those stationary cars. The sun was shining, birds were announcing it was spring: all I had to fear was death. I tried to persuade myself that I would be safe as long as I was in class; at least I could ask Winston to make sure he kept out anyone likely to harm me. When I mentioned the name, he shrugged, but he thought he dimly recognised the face in the photograph I showed him. He taped it to the porters' desk, so that the people replacing him would know.

'Won't you be here all day then?'

'Nope: only the early shift. I'll be out in this sun. Going for a jog.'

Out of courtesy and a desire to catch my breath, I popped in to see Richard and apologise for missing all of yesterday. He waved the coffee percolator at me, produced those wonderful biscuits and thanked me for agreeing to take Shahida's class. His daughter had been through this often enough: how many times had I seen him grey and sweating, wondering if this time she'd be all right?

'They say it's nature's way,' he said. 'But nature can be so bloody cruel.'

I nodded.

'You're sure you're OK?' he asked. 'You've been through quite a bit yourself.'

I nodded again.

'Meanwhile,' he said, as if sensing that I couldn't handle it if he were kind, 'have you seen Brenda's new eyes? You know she was going to have contact lenses? She's only been and bought bright turquoise. Quite arresting they look, in an Afro-Caribbean face! Another biscuit?'

If I'd protected myself as much as I reasonably could, why did I then expose myself and a number of other people to a quite crazy risk?

Before lunch, I had some free time.

We're supposed to spend it in college doing something useful. Counselling, attending meetings, answering the phone: that sort of useful. One or two people try to do their marking, but with the staff room always full of people and three phones constantly ringing, this takes powers of concentration I can only envy, like those of people who can do crosswords on commuter trains. I sat staring at a pile of marking. Then I moved it. I found a blank sheet of paper—no mean feat since our budget had run out six weeks ago and the stock cupboard was as bare as Mother Hubbard's. A red biro that still worked. And I started work on a set of structured notes that I'd have awarded an A. Problem. Motive. Evidence. Some of the sections were probably incomplete. But my jottings pointed inescapably to the fact that when Jools had died, justice had not been done. Not completely, though I did rather think that at least Wajid had been avenged. It would be easier to do nothing for a bit. Chris would phone as soon as he got a chance. Or Tina. Or Ian Dale. I could have tried Seb, I suppose, or even just walked down to Ladywood nick and asked for the duty inspector. I embarked on a long, elaborate doodle. The biro expired.

On impulse, I phoned the Accident Hospital again. Without comment they put me through to Intensive Care. I found myself gabbling that it was my fault he'd been killed.

'Your fault it may be,' said a cool voice rather like Philomena's, 'but he's not dead yet. His condition is stabilising satisfactorily.'

'What's the prognosis?'

'I'm not a doctor.' Then her voice softened. 'But I've seen worse cases than this survive and return to a normal life.'

When the phone rang on my desk there was no reason for me to jump as if I'd been kicked. Nor for my hand and voice to be shaking when I answered it.

It was Winston, from the security desk. One of the security guards had intercepted some visitors for me. Did I want to see them?

I said cautiously that it rather depended who they were.

Aftab and his parents, came the reply.

There was only a classroom to put them in, of course, and if they wanted tea I'd have to wash some cups. But I was intrigued. Our students' parents tended to regard their offspring as independent, so they didn't come into contact with us all that often. And why me? I wasn't Aftab's tutor or anything.

I was scarcely reassured by the solemn expressions on their faces. But they smiled when I did, and sat down, looking at Aftab to explain.

'It's about my cousin, miss. Iqbal.'

I nodded.

'The police have picked him up. Drugs, miss: he was handling drugs.'

His father cleared his throat and spoke. 'He has been a very wicked man. He has corrupted our young not only with drugs but with filthy films.'

'Porno videos, miss,' said Aftab. 'Really bad. And I wanted you to know that was why I went to Bradford.'

'Bradford?'

'Because he said if I didn't make myself scarce he'd tell my parents about Manjit.'

'You and Manjit?'

He reddened, then flashed a quick smile at his parents. In a moment we were all smiling.

'I told them myself, miss. And about Manjit's brother. Making her—oh, miss, making her—'

'I did not want my son to love a Sikh girl,' said Mr Hussain. 'But it seems to me enough wrong has been done. My family—my nephew a purveyor of filth, another nephew killed.'

'We still don't know why he was killed,' I said.

He smiled grimly. 'Young men who keep good company and behave themselves don't get murdered. Not very often.'

His wife said something. He nodded to her, and turned back to me. 'Young Manjit has left home. Aftab tells me her brother has been lewd, and Manjit has been trying to protect her purity.'

I nodded. 'It seems that way to me. She must have had a very good reason to leave home. Manjit was always a good student. She wouldn't risk damaging her education if she didn't have to.'

'Miss Rivers, my son says he loves Manjit, and he says she loves him. He says you can get a message to her. I want you to tell her that if she and my son... You understand, I don't want this. But I am a fair man.'

'Yes, you are,' I said. 'And I think a kind one.'

He was nearly in tears. His wife was, openly, and she touched her son's hand.

'Dad says if we still love each other when we're eighteen he'll let us marry,' said Aftab.

'If she takes our faith. If she embraces Islam,' Mr Hussain added.

'I'll pass the message on,' I said. 'Gladly.'

The phone on my desk rang again a few minutes later. Not for me, this time. For Jim Ryan, lecturer in Business Studies.

He'd got the job, the voice said. I'd been so preoccupied recently I didn't even know he was job-hunting. This offer came hard on the heels of his gaining his PhD, so I rather assumed he'd be off to some university or other. But he'd escaped from education altogether. He'd just got a job with a bookmaker. We were to go to a pub to celebrate: yes, me too, since everyone assumed I was safe. We cut through the housing estate opposite the college and headed for Broad Street. Jim rather fancied the Glassworks, right down by Gas Street Basin, but a couple of people vetoed that—they had classes to teach in half an hour. My first afternoon class had been cancelled because the students were all on work experience—though not, presumably, at ICB. I could settle down with a pleasant half-pint. Yet I chose mineral water. If I was going to do what I thought I was going to do, I'd need the clearest of heads. But I might not do it. Finding the payphone next to the loo seemed an omen. I dialled and was put through. Yes, he'd be delighted to meet me. This afternoon? But he had a rehearsal at two-thirty.

'Just ten minutes,' I urged. 'Please, Stobbard.'

'Guess you want to see me real bad?'

Why had I never noticed how complacent his voice could sound?

'Yes. We—I'd like to talk.'

'I'd like to do something more than talk, honey. Maybe we can fix it then.' Stob'll fix anything. Stob and his drama—had all the girls weeping over him.

We agreed to meet at the back of the Music Centre, and I put the phone down. This time I wasn't surprised I was shaking. I refused to allow myself to vomit. I needed all the strength I'd got for what I had to do.

I was only twenty yards from the Mondiale when I realised how stupid it would be to encounter him there, although there were plenty of people around. Men, mostly, the double-breasted suit variety. Some conference, no doubt: they all sported little labels and carried blue and silver Mondiale folders. One bloated-looking man let his slip. Sophie, ever the Girl Guide, to the rescue! Although he was positively effusive with his thanks, I didn't listen. I was concerned with something more interesting. I knew it would be there. I'd known it would be there ever since my evening with Stobbard. A little zigzag mark on each photocopied page.

I don't remember crossing the road. I must have done. I was lurking as close as I could to the walls of the office blocks and shops. When I tried a more confident stride I suddenly had an absurd

364

vision of myself as a diminutive John Wayne. Laughing helped. I stopped by another phone and left a precise and urgent message for Chris. He'd be furious if he didn't get it, I said. 'I don't care whether he's with the Home Secretary,' I insisted. 'Tell him. Now.'

Past Maples and Lee Longlands: they'd lost a good customer when Jools died. From the window of Lee Longlands a particularly appealing teddy bear beamed at me. I might just need you, I said. I hoped it was under my breath. Soon I would cross the road and take the steps down to the half finished piazza that lay between the canal and the Music Centre. It was already paved in attractive patterns of blue and red brick, and at this side there were futuristic but surprisingly comfortable benches. The far side was cordoned off, with a mass of scaffolding still scaling the rear section of the Music Centre. Since George's death they'd looped barbed wire round the high wire fence. There were also gates, but though I could see the padlock and chain which normally secured them, they were propped open to allow a dumper truck to chug in and out. I had to face him as he approached. If I didn't I'd risk a quick squeeze on the throat and a slide into the oily polluted waters of the cut. He'd tried often enough before to get rid of me. I was now convinced the would-be Harborne rapist was him. It was all too neat to be anyone else. The Datsun, the stage make-up, maybe—thanks, Richard—maybe even tinted contact lenses: and of course he never once spoke. And there had been no reports of remotely similar attacks on other people. If only I'd thought to ask Chris to check the time of his flight to Munich. Then there was the letter bomb. If Jools had delivered it, then I'm sure it was Stobbard who'd fixed it. OK, I exaggerate. That wasn't an attempt on my life. Just my hands and face. But what about Jools's last mission? Quite a powerful explosion, that. The ballet. Or, more particularly, his hotel afterwards. I suppose it would be difficult to get an erection if you were planning to push your partner off your balcony. Or, of course, if you're snorting coke so hard you have chronic rhinitis. That was something I had to ask him about. The car chase: no, I really couldn't have identified the driver. Maybe under hypnosis. The burglary. The mark on any photocopying done on the Mondiale's machine. The attack on Dean.

I'd stationed myself not in the bright sun, but in shadow. I was shivering already. I'd still got a few minutes to wait. And then I saw him walking towards me. The sun glossed features I could have loved dearly.

My eyes travelled down—I wanted one last look at the broad shoulders, the hips made neater still by the cut of his trousers. But he'd pulled his jacket well down. I noticed a bulge. Somehow I did not think it was because he was pleased to see me.

Then I thought for one crazy moment that he was. When he saw me, his face broke into a charming, delighted smile. He opened his arms wide, palms out, inviting me. I retreated to the far side of my bench.

'You'll be glad to know Dean might live,' I began.

'I'm sorry?'

I could have sworn the bewilderment was genuine.

'Dean. The young man you had beaten up.'

'Sophie, what the hell are you talking about?'

I explained, very tersely. And mentioned Jools's part. At that point his face changed.

'Jools. You know she was handling drugs, Sophie? I'm sorry, I know you were a friend of hers. But she was a bad lady.'

'Drugs and blackmail—a pretty lethal combination,' I agreed.

At the word 'blackmail' his face did change. For a second. Then he had it under control. If not his voice.

'Blackmail?' His lips seemed stiff.

'She blackmailed Tony. What about that pianist who tried to fly? Or was that badly cut drugs? Have those she sold you been all right? Pure enough?'

'Nothing wrong with coke for personal use.'

I agreed. 'Until someone tries to blackmail you. And the pressure grows until you try to kill her. You lure her into the open—just there, see!—by changing the notices on the doors. Only it's George, isn't it? George who gets—' My voice had started to shake. I took a deep breath and waited. His face was so still I could guess the effort he was making not to react. 'And Jools. A very messy death. I suppose it was convenient.'

'I didn't mean—'

At last!

'You didn't mean to kill Jools then. Quite lucky for you she was carrying a pretty unstable burden to the university. Where was she to take it to? The room where Khalid was to do his hacking? And why try to stop us hacking? You weren't implicated. There wasn't a list of Jools's customers.'

His mouth moved slightly.

'Do you know what I think you ought to do now?' I asked conversationally. 'I think you ought to have a nice long talk with Chris Groom. I'm sure you get a shorter sentence if you confess before they get round to asking you. And they say, don't they, that confession is good for the soul.'

We stood staring at each other. Neither of us moved. My hands were clamped on the bench-back. His stayed as fists in his pockets. I didn't dare look round for Chris. I held him where he was as long as our eyes were locked. This time I wouldn't panic. I wouldn't run. There was nowhere to run, anyhow. If I took off down the canal towpath he'd be able to pick me off like a rabbit. Because that was what he was going to do. Use that gun. There was a faint click. Metallic. From his right pocket.

I ran.

I ducked and wove my way through the last of the lunchtime loiterers. Surely he wouldn't risk hitting someone perfectly innocent.

I had run. And got myself cornered. Remembered all those muscles of his: he was going to catch me any moment. No darkness. No tricky footpaths. And a wonderful story for him to tell the coroner. I was so disturbed by the deaths of my friends I was going to jump from the Music Centre. He'd tried to talk me out of it, tried to catch me as I ran. But he'd been too late. A quick push, then. Much better than a gun. I cursed my week's inactivity. I was tiring already. But I was past the dumper truck. All I needed was a way into the Music Centre. Whatever level. The lower the better. Or a workman. British workmen wouldn't take kindly to people settling their differences on their site, not when they were so far behind schedule. I could hear someone yelling at me already. And another.

I risked looking back. A man trying to intercept Stobbard fell frontwards on to a pile of concrete. Stobbard was shoving his gun back into his pocket. I prayed he'd just used the butt to sock him below the line of his hard hat. There was a lot of yelling now. And Stobbard was yards nearer. I threw down my shoulder bag and started up the nearest ladder. As I clambered I had a wistful vision of myself swinging the bag at him and knocking him backwards into that cement. But it was too late. At least I had both hands free. Another level up, or risk this catwalk?

My hands and feet took me up. Someone was trying to grab my ankle. I kicked hard, and swung on to the uneven planks of the catwalk. I started to run. There was so much noise from my heart and ears I couldn't hear anything else.

Except someone yelling, 'No! You'll have to stop. *No!*'

And I saw why. At the end of the planks was nothing. I exaggerate. There was nothing for five feet.

Nothing below, of course, for about—no, I didn't want to know how many feet. Death by an awkward fall or death at Stobbard's hands? A very public death.

And then I decided I didn't want any sort of death. Not yet. I was young and I could jump. Even five feet. Suddenly my brain clicked up a gear.

To clear the gap I'd have to take it at a run. If I hesitated—no, I wouldn't hesitate. He nearly had me in his grasp.

I ran. I jumped.

There was wood beneath my feet. I fell on to the planks, clutching at the boards, netting and metal poles, and waited. There was no more I could do. He'd clear it far more easily that I had.

I pulled myself to my elbow to look back.

He was running now, gathering himself He sprang. And then as he flew, an avenging angel, between the pieces of wood, he stopped and doubled in mid-flight. And dropped from my sight.

The scream stopped abruptly.

But it rang on in my ears, on and on, until I realised the scream came from me.

371

Chapter Twenty-Eight

'Loves me, loves me not,' the nurse was saying, laying a little log trail of splinters on a piece of kitchen towel.

In the next cubicle, I could hear them trying to reason with a hysterical Winston. Rationally he could understand that he'd saved me: emotionally he couldn't cope with the knowledge that it was his well-aimed stone that had brought about Stobbard Mayou's death.

I wasn't sure that I could deal with my part in his death, either.

By the time I'd come down, they'd taken away his body. They'd had plenty of time.

Vertigo.

I suffer from vertigo.

Why the hell I'd gone shooting up those bloody ladders and leaping around on rocking planks, I'd no idea. How the hell I'd get down I'd less idea. I'd sat like a garden gnome and contemplated. Chris, white-faced, urged me from the far side of the gap. A couple of scaffolders watched him with considerable irritation. They wanted to fill the gap. I couldn't have walked across it if they'd filled it with the Severn Bridge. At last, I found I could look about me a little, provided I held on with both hands and stayed put. I knew I'd fall if I stood up. Below they'd acquired television cameras, several fire appliances, and a bearded man yelling at me he could teach me to abseil.

A fire appliance won. Or at least the fireman who shinned up this enormous ladder as easily as I run up stairs and offered to carry me down.

'Fireman's lift, see,' he said encouragingly. 'You could close your eyes.'

I stood up, drew myself to my full five foot one inch, and reached for the ladder.

'If you'd be so kind as to hold my skirt,' I said with dignity, 'I'll bring myself down.'

Jaunty. Chirpy. A good performance. The people at the bottom had applauded. And I was buggered if I was going to cry my eyes out in front of the cameras.

Without a doubt it was the splinters under the fingernails that hurt the most. By the time the nurse had finished those, Philomena had come to sort out Winston, had remonstrated with the doctor over her choice of drugs, and had taken him home to sleep everything off. Someone would be coming for me, too. I hoped to God it wouldn't be Chris.

Oddly enough it was Richard. And he took me to his home where Sheila ladled home-made soup and exchanged recipes and told me that Shahida had lost her baby.

'There,' Chris says, raising his voice a little: the Tannoy's just announcing a flight. 'All checked in.'

'Good.' I shuffle the magazines I've bought him for the flight.

'Quite convenient, really. Everything being neatly tied up before I left. Not that—not if—you do believe me—I wouldn't have agreed—'

'No. Thank you. I'm glad you were there to see it through.'

I don't know why I agreed to see him off. I don't like airports very much. Apart from their inherent nastiness, they remind me how little I've travelled. I've always dreamt of India, and here is Chris actually on his way.

'Sophie, tell me something.'

As if I haven't been over it three or four times, not just with him but with people from the Fraud Squad and from the Drugs Squad, not to mention a quick dalliance with Customs and Excise.

The men who attacked Dean—well-known heavies—have been identified by the woman at the bus stop. Dean can't corroborate. They say his coma is much less deep, that he'll be moved into an ordinary ward soon. But it'll take him maybe a year to learn to walk and talk again.

'Sophie?'

'I'm sorry, Chris, I was just thinking.' As if I've done anything else. Round and round in unproductive circles, I've been going. Phil says what I need is a good cry. I've had flowers and chocolates and a nasty crop of offers from the gutter press to tell my story—'My lover tried to kill me'—and a request to coach someone through his GCSE. What I haven't had is a good cry. I'm weighed down with a constant dull ache and I get angry very quickly, but I can't cry.

'When did you first suspect him? Stobbard. The first moment?'

I can tell from the way the words rush out that this was not what Chris wanted to ask, but I will reply as if it were. I talk about the evening when Stobbard took his baton to the loo, leaving that dusting of white grains behind. I remind Chris that he came round when I'd got photocopies all over the floor, that Stobbard took the sheet under the one I'd written down the details of Khalid's university room. They never did establish exactly where he was the night Wajid was killed. I reckon he was in Birmingham with a car that he told Winston wouldn't start. Certainly his flight to Munich had been at 6.00 a.m. on the Sunday after I'd been attacked. But they never found make-up or contact lenses in his effects.

Jools: perhaps I can talk about her instead. A blackmailer. Not the nicest thing to believe of a friend. But then, I think she killed Wajid. She'd be strong enough. And maybe she'd learned about anatomy for her body building. She'd have reached Lichfield on her bike in time for the concert. The orchestra were so used to her bad timekeeping they wouldn't have turned a hair if she was only slightly late.

Why should she handle drugs? Power, I suppose. Or money. The David Cox wasn't the only painting in her flat. What I'd always thought was a very fine print turned out to be a genuine Bonnard. Starting to take steroids—they found plenty when they did the postmortem—made her less stable, I suppose. All that temper waiting to flare up. And goodness knows how much she was trying to screw out of Stobbard. Or maybe she kept upping the price for his fixes. Enough to make him want to kill her.

'And Wajid,' I conclude. 'Need his family know? They all looked up to him so much. And after Iqbal's disgrace—'

'Well, they'll never find anything he stashed in ICB. They got there before the Fraud Squad did. Practically all the computer records wiped. And literally bonfires of paper records all over the country: must have been like the coming of the Armada.'

'So his family needn't—?'

'Well, the DPP have got other things to worry about.'

'And isn't there some fund for the victims of crime? They're not very well off, remember.'

'I don't know. He wasn't exactly—'

'A victim of poverty. A victim of a racist system that stopped his dad doing the well-paid job you do.'

'For Christ's sake, you sound like a fucking sociologist.'

That's better. The last thing I want to hear is him tenderly breathing 'Sophie' at me. But I am surprised by the force of the adjective. Perhaps he's found his time at William Murdock more stressful than I realised. Maybe nearly as stressful as teaching there.

'Hi! Chris! Chris! Over here!'

I've never welcomed the sight of Tina as much as now. She and Ian Dale bustle over, she with a duplicate pile of magazines, he with a Boots carrier bag.

'Brought you some tummy pills. And a spot of the old kaolin and morph. Foreign food.'

'Poor Ian,' I say, tucking my hand into the crook of his arm. 'Your face on the supermarket run. When I made you buy okra and chillies.'

'Come on, they're making the last call,' says Tina. 'Stir your bloody stumps. Anyone'd think you'd rather not go.'

'Sophie—' he's trying again, in a desperate undervoice.

I find it easier to ignore it. I think he wants to know if I loved Stobbard Mayou. And maybe he wants to know if I'll see him when he gets back.

And I don't know. I just don't know.

This Large Print Book for the Partially sighted, who cannot read normal print, is published under the auspices of

THE ULVERSCROFT FOUNDATION

THE ULVERSCROFT FOUNDATION

. . . we hope that you have enjoyed this Large Print Book. Please think for a moment about those people who have worse eyesight problems than you . . . and are unable to even read or enjoy Large Print, without great difficulty.

You can help them by sending a donation, large or small to:

**The Ulverscroft Foundation,
1, The Green, Bradgate Road,
Anstey, Leicestershire, LE7 7FU,
England.**
or request a copy of our brochure for more details.

The Foundation will use all your help to assist those people who are handicapped by various sight problems and need special attention.

Thank you very much for your help.

Other MAGNA Mystery Titles In Large Print